C000298018

THE HELPDESK

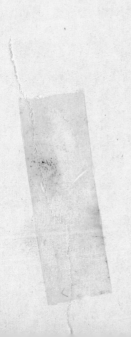

Shane Dunphy (who also writes as S.A. Dunphy) is the author of the David Dunnigan series, which begins with *After She Vanished*, and the Boyle and Keneally series, which begins with *Bring Her Home*. He has also written several non-fiction books.

The Helpdesk

SHANE DUNPHY

HACHETTE
BOOKS
IRELAND

Copyright © 2023 Shane Dunphy

The right of Shane Dunphy to be identified as the Author of
the Work has been asserted by him in accordance with the
Copyright, Designs and Patents Act 1988.

First published in Ireland in 2023 by
HACHETTE BOOKS IRELAND

First published in paperback in 2023

1

All rights reserved. No part of this publication may be reproduced,
stored in a retrieval system, or transmitted, in any form or by any
means without the prior written permission of the publisher, nor be otherwise
circulated in any form of binding or cover other than that
in which it is published and without a similar condition being
imposed on the subsequent purchaser.

All characters in this publication are fictitious and any resemblance
to real persons, living or dead, is purely coincidental.

Cataloguing in Publication Data is available from the British Library

ISBN 9781529371109

Typeset in GaramondPro by Bookends Publishing Services, Dublin
Printed and bound in Great Britain by Clays Ltd, Elcograf S.p.A.

Hachette Books Ireland policy is to use papers that are natural, renewable
and recyclable products and made from wood grown in sustainable forests.
The logging and manufacturing processes are expected to conform to the
environmental regulations of the country of origin.

Hachette Books Ireland
8 Castlecourt Centre
Castleknock
Dublin 15, Ireland

A division of Hachette UK Ltd
Carmelite House, 50 Victoria Embankment, London EC4Y 0DZ

www.hachettebooksireland.ie

For Kristina. More than anything.

PART I

PART 1

Taken from 'Controlled Rage: Mapping the physical and psychological effects of the suppression of aggression responses in professional men and women, and an analysis of socially sanctioned dominance behaviours in the corporate world', PhD thesis by Bella Murphy Fitzpatrick, City, University of London, 2010.

In the last year of his life, Sigmund Freud was asked by a student what he believed drove the human psyche, and his response was terse and immediate. He informed her that there are two unconscious drives that affect us equally, from which all other responses are derived: sex and aggression. They propel all behaviours forward, and it is from these that our personalities are forged.

You can't get more definitive than that.

Such a declaration presents us with some problems, though.

We all know what sex is; aggression is more difficult to define.

Many class it as a feeling, but that is not entirely true. In actuality, aggression is the *physical expression* of a collection of feelings: anger, anxiousness, antipathy, panic, jealousy – all the negative emotions human beings encounter with shocking regularity every day. Aggression is what we do with these feelings if we do not suppress them, which, most likely, we will. Social norms encourage the suppression of aggressive acts.

We are instructed to find diplomatic solutions to conflict. As children, teachers tell us to 'use our words' when we are experiencing distress, to develop a vocabulary that enables us to enumerate and codify the challenging emotions that assail us every day.

If we can name these dark companions, perhaps we can control them.

The question I am asking in this thesis is twofold: *can* we control what Freud believed was one of our most powerful driving forces, and *should* we?

Because the energy this drive generates has to go somewhere. And when it seeps out, the events can be catastrophic.

Chapter 1

James

It's funny how everything can be going just perfectly and then, out of the blue, completely out of left field, comes a gut punch you really weren't expecting, and everything is knocked arse over tit.

Okay, when I say things were going perfectly, that's probably an exaggeration. I mean, I'd been working flat out for weeks, and was bloody exhausted.

I was barely sleeping, grabbing two or three hours at home before rushing back to the offices of London law firm Astley, Clifford and Kenworthy, where I was a senior associate on the Corporate and Mergers and Acquisitions team, to continue working. I'd creep in to our apartment in the small hours of the morning, anxious not to wake Bella, crash in the spare bedroom, with a 7 a.m. taxi pre-booked to take me back to the office before whatever meeting was due to begin.

Don't get me wrong, this is not the ideal way to work, and it's even less ideal for a marriage, but sometimes – like when you're driving yourself hard in a bid to make partner – it's *necessary*.

Partnership is so close I can smell it.

You can function pretty well on virtually no sleep for a day or so, but by the time you're hitting the second night you're more likely to make mistakes. This isn't a physical job we lawyers do, so the issue with lack of sleep isn't that you're going to accidentally cut off a finger or drop something onto your toe or take a misstep and break your ankle. For a corporate lawyer, the problem is very much a mental one.

After a couple of nights with little to no sleep, your mind begins to get foggy. Information you can usually access instantaneously, brought to mind without thinking, seems to be a long way away, or, worst-case scenario, you can't remember it at all. In a job where the ability to communicate is your most essential tool, you start to trip over words, and your speech can become slurred. When a person is *really* fucking exhausted, it can sound as if they're drunk. And that's not a good look for a lawyer.

I'd tried to get as much sleep as I could during the early days of the Fahlberg/Copping merger. But it all caught up on me.

In more ways than one.

I'd been there three nights in a row before the 'incident' occurred.

I don't think my wife Bella even noticed I was gone, to be

honest. It wouldn't be the first time I'd headed off to work and only been back for a few hours here and there. But it was the first time I'd done so and not called to let her know. Interestingly, she hadn't messaged me to find out where I was, either. Which says a lot, I think.

Bella and I used to be so tight, so together. In the early days, when she was a shit-hot doctoral student – a rising star in the field of psychology – and I was an up-and-coming lawyer, tipped to shake up the City, we'd make it our business to create time for one another. We would get together for lunch a few times a week, arrange date nights and book weekends away where we barely got out of bed.

It hasn't been like that for a while. My career went stratospheric, and hers … well, her thesis research didn't come to what she'd hoped, and she made the jump into teaching. So while she's finished teaching the rich teenage students of Ashton Wood and at home by 5 p.m., I'm usually still at the office. It got harder and harder to find a free weekend, and I'm lucky if I even get to eat lunch at my desk these days.

I had to prioritise. Making partner would benefit us both, even if it meant we didn't get to see one another as much as we'd like to.

I did get the impression Bella was losing patience with the whole thing, though. There had been a coldness there, a distance for a while now. I tried to tell myself it was that we were both tired – I mean, teaching teenagers can't be easy, can it?

But I knew it was more than that.

I had been pulling a series of all-nighters on the Fahlberg/ Copping merger, and it was on night four when I hit a serious bump in the road. This merger was the most significant – I would go so far as to say – the most *historic* deal my firm has ever handled.

And this bump threatened to derail all the work we'd done.

Let me explain.

Fahlberg Financials, a banking and investment company, and Copping International Insurance (which does exactly as their name suggests) were both large and extremely successful multinational companies who had, in a bid to widen their profit margins, decided to come together.

My firm was acting for Fahlberg Financials, which brought more headaches with it than you could imagine. While on the face of it Fahlberg was simply your standard massive banking corporation, those of us privy to the behind-the-scenes antics were aware there was a shady side to their dealings. We also had to contend with the fact that the CEO of their parent company had a rather colourful reputation – one that left a bad taste in my mouth, if I stopped to think about it.

But all of that comes with the job. Lawyers are trained to push aside their personal scruples and just do what they're paid to do, within the confines of the law. So that is exactly what I did. I didn't like the guy. But I didn't have to have much to do with him.

I, and several other grey-faced associates from various other practice groups around the firm, had spent long days, and even longer nights, trawling through documentation in a data room as part of an intense due diligence process. We had to carefully examine and inspect every single aspect of Copping's affairs – from its assets, liabilities, intellectual property right down to shareholder information and employment contracts. We had to ensure Fahlberg knew exactly what they were taking on, and also, and most importantly, to determine the price to be paid.

I had been given the responsibility of collating all the information and drafting the due diligence report. This was a big deal for me, and I had been grateful when Kenworthy had barged into my office a few weeks ago to bestow this honour upon me. I knew partnership was within my grasp and I couldn't fuck this up. This report was critical as to whether the merger would go ahead or not. Everything could literally fall apart on the basis of this report and, if this deal didn't go ahead, my bid to make partner would stall.

And finally, at one in the morning, after weeks of arduous work, I finished the report. It was ready to be sent to Fahlberg's senior management. Once this document was read and accepted, a meeting would be called in which Fahlberg would formally initiate their side of the merger, and ideally things could move to the next stage.

I had uploaded the document to a secure folder in the company cloud and attached a link to the email. Everything now in order, I was about to click 'send', when, just to be sure, I decided to check the link to be certain it would bring me to the correct file.

And the link didn't work.

I hit the left-side button on the mouse three times, each with increasing levels of annoyance and panic, and then right-clicked instead. The first option in the drop-down window this produced was: 'Open link in new tab.'

With some relief I clicked on this, but rather than revealing the folder containing the report I had spent the day writing, to my horror the screen froze momentarily before showing a message window:

Error executing script _import_not found

Swearing, I forced myself to remain calm. I had uploaded everything to the system, so it had to be there, and even if it wasn't, I still had the original file, so could go right back to square one, which would be really fucking annoying, but if I had to …

Taking a deep breath, I held the on/off button on my laptop for ten seconds, causing it to power down. I left it for a bit, getting up and pacing my small office for a couple of minutes, then switched it back on again.

'Right, James, let's not get over excited,' I said to myself, and opened my email account, going directly to the Drafts folder.

The text of the email was there, but without the attached link.

Staving off panic, I logged onto the OneDrive that was the company's little corner of the cloud.

There was no sign of the file there, either.

I'd like to say I dealt with the issue with stoic good humour, but that would be a lie. I was, in fact, beginning to freak out. This was a perfect fucking example of how working yourself into a state of exhaustion is a really bad idea. Slowly and deliberately, I went to the flash drive I use, a 30GB affair that is only for transferring large files from one computer to another. It's purely a transport device, and as soon as I'm finished with it, I delete what's on there.

I plugged it into the USB port, and then clicked on the respective icon that emerged on my laptop's toolbar.

It, too, was empty. I must have, unconsciously, as a matter of routine, deleted everything as soon as the file uploaded.

This was not good.

I had somehow lost the due diligence report, which contained commercially sensitive and highly privileged information, somewhere in Astley, Clifford and Kenworthy's company cloud.

I knew I had uploaded the files. So they were definitely there. But where exactly? That was my problem. Where? And what the fuck even is the cloud anyway? I always imagine some kind of ethereal filing cabinet floating about somewhere in space, but I have no idea if this is accurate. I'm not a tech head and won't apologise for it.

That's if it even was still in our cloud, of course. It might not be.

And now, the report on which the whole deal rested was lost. It would take me days to redraft it, which would make both me and the firm look hugely incompetent. We could lose not only the client, and the huge fees that were set to run into the millions, but I would lose any chance of partnership.

I was in trouble. Serious trouble.

And I knew it.

Chapter 2

For a few seconds, I just sat at my desk, gazing blankly at the screen. I didn't know what to do.

My mind froze. It just locked.

I got up, paced the few steps it took to traverse the length of my office, and then back again, but that didn't seem to bring any fresh solutions to mind, so I opened the door and half-ran/half-walked the long corridor outside, trying to just shake myself back into some semblance of calm. I thought the exercise might burn off some adrenaline and permit me to think.

It half worked.

I'd done maybe three laps of the space when my knees came unhinged and I sank into a heap on the floor, panting heavily. For what felt like an eternity I just lay there, gazing at the ceiling through the darkness, wondering if I was having a stroke. When enough time had passed and I could still feel both sides of my face and had full use of all my limbs, I realised I was, in fact, having a panic attack, and slowly dragged myself upright.

I took long, deep breaths and told myself that, yes, I was deeply in the shit, but I was also a smart guy, and I'd been up to my neck in it before and survived. I would this time too.

I just needed to work out what to do.

I stiffly made my way back to the office and sat down, gazing at the screen of my laptop, which seemed to be peering back at me with an accusing eye. I pulled over a legal pad and began to compile a list of options:

1. *Turn my computer off and on again – which seems to be the panacea for all computer ills.*
   I'd already tried this, though, and it hadn't worked. It struck me that trying a second time was unlikely to end in a different result.

2. *Put the file names into the 'Search' facility on my computer menu. Maybe they were on my hard drive somewhere.*
   I did, but to no effect. Wherever they were, they weren't on my computer.

3. *Search my email folders. Maybe I had somehow, without realising it, attached the link to another email, or sent it to myself rather than the client.*
   I gave this a go and drew another blank.

4. *Admit I know nothing about fucking computers, and ask someone who does.*

I wrote that sentence on the pad, and stopped for a moment, looking at it.

The reality is that I do know very, very little about the inner workings of a computer or how the internet does what it does or what the cloud is or any of that. I have a Facebook page and an Instagram account, neither of which I really use, and Twitter scares me – why would anyone want to spend their leisure time on something so toxic?

As far as I'm concerned, computers are tools for my work, and I don't have a lot to do with them other than that.

I was out of my depth, and I knew it.

But who could I ask?

There's an associate on our team called William Sullivan who has a reputation for knowing a thing or two about computers, and I wondered if he might be working late. But that seemed a dim hope, and would I want to admit to a lowly junior associate that I had screwed up to this level?

I got up again and stretched, walked around my desk and leaned in the open doorway, feeling the coolness of the almost empty building. I could go and see who else was working late, I supposed. See if there was a friendly face among them. Someone might take pity on me.

I dismissed that idea almost immediately. Would I have taken pity on someone in a similar circumstance? I had to admit there was no fucking way I would. I'd see it for the opportunity it was and bide my time before feeding the poor unfortunate to the wolves, hoping I'd step into whichever part of the gap they left that benefitted me the most.

What I needed was technical support, but I had no idea

which firm our company was using, and I didn't know anyone I trusted enough to ask.

I was about to give in to despair when my eyes fell on my laptop. My gaze fixed on something stuck to the back of the screen. There, right in the middle of the laptop cover, was a sticker with red lettering on it, and below the lettering what looked to be a number, in black digits. I walked over quickly, and saw this:

For 24hr assistance, call the Tech Helpdesk at:
020 4366 7811

Could this number solve my plight, or just confirm that I had royally screwed up? I decided there was no harm in dialling it just to see who answered and if they could help. The assistance the firm offered might be only to fix hardware malfunctions, for instance, and therefore be of little benefit in my current dire straits. And who knew, with the rapid turnover of staff in phone support, there may be no one on the other end when I called anyway.

I picked up the office line and dialled. It rang once. Twice. And then a very clear, confident 'Hello?'

'Hello,' I said, all business, 'is this Tech Helpdesk?'

'Yes, this is Tech Helpdesk,' the voice said, and I could hear it was a young woman. And one who spoke English with a mild London accent. 'Can you please provide me with the name of your company?'

'I'm with Astley, Clifford and Kenworthy.'

'Thank you. And your name is?'

'James Fitzpatrick.'

'Hold on, Mr Fitzpatrick. I'm Charlotte, and I'll be on your system in just a second. Once I'm in, I'll be able to help you.'

'Okay.'

I could hear computer keys rattling, and her gentle breathing.

'So what can I do for you this morning, Mr Fitzpatrick?'

'I've lost a file.'

'Could you clarify what you mean by lost?'

'I uploaded it to the cloud, tried to attach a link to an email, and when I went to check the link was operational, it all seemed to disappear.'

'So, you accidentally deleted it?'

'I have no idea,' I said, probably with more annoyance in my tone than she deserved. 'All I know is that the folder disappeared.'

'I understand. Could you tell me the name of the folder?'

'FahlCoppInt,' I said, spelling it for her.

'Thank you,' she said, keys clattering the whole time. 'Now. Let me walk you through this, and let's see if we can get your folder back.'

'Can you?' I asked.

'Oh, I think so,' she said soothingly, and in that moment I think I felt a rush of love for Charlotte on the Helpdesk.

It's irrational, I know. But I think I did.

I would remember that, later.

'Your company is using an IaaS system.'

'I don't know that that means.'

'Astley, Clifford and Kenworthy rents the server and the storage. You're using something called OpenStack, which is very common. Lots of companies utilise it and it has very thorough and reliable backup systems.'

'That sounds positive,' I said.

'It is. I can see your firm uses something called Triliovault.'

'Which is?'

She laughed.

'It's a mechanism for backing up everything that goes on to the cloud. You can think of it as a series of safety nets, one hung below the others, so even if something slips through the first, or even the second, it'll get caught on the third. It's virtually foolproof.'

'How do I access the backed-up files?'

'Okay, are you on your OneDrive?'

She talked me through it, step-by-step. Her commands were always clear and precise, and even when I fluffed things occasionally, she was patient and went right back to the point where I'd gotten confused and did it all over again, never losing her cool.

It took us two and a half hours to retrieve the folder that contained my file. The backup system involved a sequence of tiers, each of which had countless directories into which different types of data were stored. It was hugely confusing, and I realised quite quickly that I would never excel in the field of IT, but Charlotte patiently went through the process of retrieving the file, and by 4 a.m. I had located the missing file and it was ready to be uploaded again.

By this stage, Charlotte and I were chatting away as if we'd known one another for years. It's funny – as soon as I realised she was confident in what she was doing, I relaxed. I knew I was in safe hands.

And she was funny in a nerdy kind of way. Not uproariously so, but, yeah funny, and she was clever.

At one stage, for instance, we were painstakingly scrolling through a User file, looking for the file name.

'It feels like I'm on a cop show,' I said to her. I was talking because I felt a bit helpless. I was there, but she was doing all the work, and that bothered me. I hated it, being so useless.

'Hunting for clues,' she agreed.

'Yeah,' I went on. 'Except it's not one of those glamorous shows. It's one where the detectives have to put on surgical gloves and climb into a dumpster to look for DNA the killer might have left on a scrap of tissue paper. They have to pick through every gross piece of garbage to get what they need. This feels like the digital equivalent of picking our way through rubbish. I mean, what even is all this stuff?'

She laughed.

'This isn't the bin we're in. It's the inner workings of the drive system. We are inside the machine, looking at all the things that make it tick. Have you ever seen the movie *Fantastic Voyage*? It's a nineteen sixty-six film with Donald Pleasence and Raquel Welch.'

I had to tell her I hadn't.

'It's about a group of medics and soldiers who are miniaturised and injected into the body of a comatose scientist who has defected from the Soviet Union. The unconscious man has information that might stop the Cold War, and they have to remove a clot from his brain so he can live and pass on his secrets. The team encounter all kinds of wonders and obstacles on their way to complete their mission, seeing all the amazing things that make the body function.'

'Sounds interesting,' I said.

'It is. It's a wonderful film.' She hesitated. 'Sorry, am I boring you? I can be a bit of a nerd.'

'The only nerdy stuff I like is comic books,' I told her. 'I've loved them since I was a kid.'

Which is true, as it happens.

'What kind of comics?' Charlotte wanted to know, and I could hear excitement in her voice.

As she asked the question I saw her highlighting a file named Fahlberg/Copping Due Diligence Report and dragging it to a folder she had set up, deftly dropping it in.

'Superhero mostly,' I said.

'Marvel or DC or Image or Dynamite or Epic …' she started listing publishers before I had a chance to think.

'Oh, Marvel,' I jumped in. 'I don't think I've even heard of most of the others you rattled off there.'

'DC is Batman, Superman, Wonder Woman, The Flash, Green Lantern, Suicide Squad …'

'Yes, I've heard of them but never read any comic books of theirs. I like X-Men, Spiderman, The Avengers – pretty mainstream stuff.'

'Well, it's mainstream now because of the films,' she said to me. 'What age are you, if you don't mind my asking?'

I told her I was thirty-five.

'When you were a kid, comics were far less widely accepted than they are now. And even today, I would bet that more than three-quarters of all the people who go to see movies set in the Marvel Universe have never read any of the comics they're based on. And anyway, the worlds of the films and the world of the comics are quite different, aren't they?'

I told her I supposed they were, though frankly, I never thought about it that deeply. I just assumed it was too hard to put the stories they tell in the comic books onto the screen, so they adapted them accordingly.

'So if you want to look at this from the perspective of comic books,' Charlotte said, 'what we're doing is like Tony Stark going into his AI system, J.A.R.V.I.S., to find a piece of information he lost there. Does that sound a bit more glamourous?'

'Seeing as you're the one doing the looking, doesn't that make you Tony Stark?' I said.

'I suppose it does,' she said, and I could hear the humour in her voice.

'Who does that make me, then?'

She paused for a moment, before saying:

'Well, Tony's assistant is Pepper Potts, isn't she?'

'So I'm the girl,' I said, ruefully.

'You're my attractive assistant,' she said, laughing.

'If it gets me my files back, I'm happy to be played by Gwyneth Paltrow in the movie,' I said, and laughed along with her.

It was a nice moment.

When the folder was once again uploaded and the link securely attached, it was Charlotte who checked it was operational and that everything was in the folder that was supposed to be. Satisfied, she said to me:

'I think you can press *send*, James.'

'It's safe to this time?'

'I'm certain it is, yes.'

'So you know what happened the last time, when I lost everything?'

'You accidentally deleted the folder,' she said. 'It's a simple mistake to make, and really not worth beating yourself up over.'

'Charlotte, I am working on a deal right now that involves *billions of pounds*. I cannot afford to make that kind of mistake.'

'I've seen this a lot, James. It's a common enough thing to happen.'

'I just can't believe I almost lost everything.'

'But you didn't – the backup systems did what they're designed to do.'

I smiled to myself at that.

'When I say I almost lost everything, I don't just mean the files. I'm talking about my career. A slip-up like this one could have been catastrophic. I'd have been dropped from the deal I'm working on, at best. I might have lost my job. And at worst … well, that doesn't bear thinking about …'

I couldn't believe I was talking like this. Maybe the exhaustion had torn down some of my emotional barriers, or maybe the fact Charlotte already knew I'd messed up made me feel less embarrassed about filling her in on the gravity of my situation. Or maybe I was just going temporarily crazy.

Whatever the truth was, I felt I could talk to her. I somehow, for some inexplicable reason, felt she would understand.

'That doesn't seem very fair,' she said. 'Aren't there laws about unfair dismissals and that kind of thing?'

'There are, but one of my bosses probably helped write them,' I said drolly. 'Which means they know exactly how to get around them. This is a high-stakes deal, Charlotte. The files I'm about to send will decide the fate of a company that will earn billions of pounds, influence global politics and will probably change the way financial business is performed for decades, maybe even *centuries* to come.'

She seemed to ponder that.

'Will it change it for the better though?' she said after a long moment had passed.

'As a lawyer, I don't think in those terms,' I admitted.

'Shouldn't that be what the law is about?'

I sighed. Suddenly I felt more tired than I had ever been before.

'It probably should,' I said. 'But it isn't.'

The job was done, and with a little under five hours to spare.

'Can I help you with anything else?' Charlotte broke the silence.

'Oh. Ummm – no, no thank you.'

'Well, then, I'll just say thanks for calling Tech Helpdesk, and I hope you get a couple of hours' sleep before you're due back in work.'

She was right, of course. I would be expected in the office an hour before a meeting with Fahlberg's management team, which was due to start at ten. So I could grab four hours' sleep before then.

'Charlotte, I can't thank you enough for helping me.'

'You're very welcome. I'm glad we were able to resolve the issue successfully.'

It felt as if she was reciting from a script. I reckoned everyone who worked at Tech Helpdesk finished each help session with the same sign-off.

'Yes, well, I am too,' I said. 'I'm really grateful.'

'Would you be interested in filling out a quick questionnaire about your experience with Tech Helpdesk?'

It was as if she'd switched from the person I'd been chatting with for the past two and a half hours into some kind of automaton. It was actually a bit jarring.

'Yes,' I said. 'Of course I would.'

'Thanks so much. I'll email it to you.'

'My email address is—'

As I said it, my laptop pinged.

'I'm looking at your company directory,' Charlotte said.

'Of course you are.' I laughed – ever since she had first logged onto the Astley, Clifford and Kenworthy network, it had felt as if this girl knew her way around better than I did.

'I hope your meeting goes well, James,' Charlotte said, and then she was gone.

I closed my laptop, stood up stiffly, and called a taxi to bring me home for a few hours' sleep. Once in bed, I was unconscious before my head hit the pillow.

It would be many weeks later before I recalled I had not told Charlotte I had a meeting scheduled for later that morning.

Taken from 'Controlled Rage: Mapping the physical and psychological effects of the suppression of aggression responses in professional men and women, and an analysis of socially sanctioned dominance behaviours in the corporate world', PhD thesis by Bella Murphy Fitzpatrick, City, University of London, 2010.

The case that made me want to study the impact of how aggression is controlled and channelled by our CEOs and power brokers is that of Tristan Grosvenor, CEO of Isotech, a large multinational company with its head office in the City of London. Isotech, by the time it achieved notoriety through the actions of its chief, was a business behemoth. It was considered a giant of technology, and manufactured both hardware and software, mostly for the financial sector.

During the recession of 2007–2008, as so many in his position did, Grosvenor availed of the fiscal downturn to personally fire thirty-five members of his immediate staff team, taking each of them into his office and giving them the news face-to-face, and, from what I have been informed, without sugar-coating it in any way.

What made the experience even worse for his loyal (and now unemployed) colleagues was that it was written into the fine print of their contracts that they would not be receiving severance pay if they were let go when the company's profits were below a certain level per annum.

This final indignity caused several to take their story to the media. Grosvenor himself seemed more than happy to reply to critics that this was, as far as he was concerned, standard business practice, and that he felt no guilt whatsoever about the impact his actions were having on his former employees. The fact the condition was written into all Isotech employment contracts meant that the story drifted out of news cycles relatively quickly – it was a hard-luck human interest tale, but there were so many of those during such dark times, no one was going to waste tears over a group of executives being made redundant. This was even considering the tragic fact that one employee, Julian Clarence, took his own life shortly after having his contract terminated.

A lengthy war of words erupted in the press between Grosvenor and one of his former financial controllers, Gerald Tamlyn, who accused him of gross misconduct and insisted the contracts could not be legally binding. Tamlyn also suggested there was some unethical business practices going on. He alleged that Isotech, among many other nefarious dealings, financed weapons development, and asserted that they were doing so with some nations who could be seen as enemies of Western democracy.

There was a brief hubbub about this in the more left-leaning press, but it amounted to very little, and the story died.

I think Tristan Grosvenor would have been forgotten by all but those who follow the business pages, if, five months after he was fired, Gerald Tamlyn had not decided to break into the company's offices late one evening using an old security card that hadn't been deactivated.

What Tamlyn's intentions were are not fully clear. He allegedly left a note to his wife telling her where he was going and why, but it mysteriously vanished – more of which later. She maintained that he simply wanted to air his grievances with Grosvenor face to face, man to man. Grosvenor, however, insists that his former employee physically threatened him, that a tussle ensued, and in the end there was nothing he could do but defend himself. This self-defence took the form of the CEO grabbing a granite paperweight to use as a weapon, and striking his former employee repeatedly about the head with it.

By the time security arrived, Gerald Tamlyn was missing a large portion of his skull.

Tristan Grosvenor was arrested, questioned, and twelve hours later released on his own recognisance. After six months of investigation by a team of detectives from Scotland Yard and the London Metropolitan Police, Grosvenor was charged and tried for manslaughter, and it looked very much as if he was going to spend some time as a guest of Her Majesty.

This, however, was not to be.

Several important pieces of evidence – the murder weapon itself, the security tapes from the CCTV cameras outside Grosvenor's office which would have shown the attack (Isotech's buildings all have glass interior walls, so whatever went on inside that room would have been clearly visible) and the aforementioned handwritten note Tamlyn left his wife, purportedly stating he was going to 'try to settle things peacefully but productively' with his former boss – conveniently vanished.

The case was dismissed, and Tristan Grosvenor was a free man.

A free man who agreed to be interviewed for this thesis on the proviso that he would have final approval of its contents.

Chapter 3

Bella

I never planned to be a teacher. I had lofty aspirations of pursuing a successful career in academia, with a side gig as a celebrity psychologist. I had ambition, and lots of it, perhaps due to my less than idyllic upbringing.

I grew up in a working-class family in Ringsend in Dublin. My father worked on the ferries, serving drinks to passengers as they made their way from Dublin Port to Holyhead. My mother kept the house and did some cleaning at the local primary school for a bit of extra cash.

My dear old dad did not just serve alcohol; he consumed vast quantities of it too. He was never violent and he was an amicable enough drunk when he was at home; he was just never … never *present*. I do not believe he ever saw me.

He knew I was his daughter, of course. He knew I was bright and pretty and never gave him or my mother cause for worry. But rather than being a source of pride, he simply acted as if I didn't exist. This puzzled me for a long time. I didn't ask for much, just the occasional word of encouragement. A smile when I came into the room.

As I got older, I saw that my mother craved the same thing from him.

And when she didn't get it, she shrank in upon herself. She became small.

I swore I would not follow in her footsteps.

I was going to make a difference. I was going to be *noticed*.

I could not understand my mother or my father. They were both closed books to me. But I thought maybe I could understand others. And, most significantly, I could understand myself.

That was my plan, anyway.

James and I met in 2006, when we were both students at Trinity College Dublin.

His family are originally from Knightsbridge in London, so you could say we came from slightly different backgrounds in terms of social class and wealth. He'd initially gone to Oxford to read Law, but he decided he wanted to specialise in corporate law so he applied to do an LLM in International Business Law at Trinity, where I was studying Psychology on a scholarship and working part time jobs to pay my rent in student accommodation.

I met him through the Literary and Historical Society, where he was, after only a few months on campus, heading up the committee and making a name as a force to be reckoned with. I always think his confidence stems from his upbringing; that he is entitled to be there and everyone should listen to him. Which is why, it is safe to say, I found him fairly obnoxious at the beginning.

I think I first encountered him in the canteen of the Humanities building. I heard him before I saw him, which is how it always is with James. That booming laugh of his. He was dressed that day in a green three-quarter-length tweed jacket over a red silk shirt, a long, narrow striped scarf loosely wrapped about his neck in a nonchalant manner, but which I knew probably took him thirty minutes to arrange.

James has never been particularly physically impressive. He has a blocky build, kind of like an out-of-shape rugby player, and even then, in his early twenties, his hairline was receding. He has soft facial features with a chin that some might say lacks character, but for all that, there is something arresting about him.

He is, without doubt, intellectually brilliant, and despite my reservations, I was drawn to him. I resisted getting to know him as much as I could. He certainly wasn't my usual type – he appeared brash and vulgar, and so unapologetically upper class, traits that I later found out were completely accurate.

He set his sights on me almost immediately, though.

I was ordering a cappuccino at the coffee pod in the Quad one day when I spotted him making a beeline for me through the milling students. I paid for my drink quickly and forged a path back to the library, where one of my friends was holding my seat, but he moved far more swiftly than I'd have expected and was at my elbow before I'd executed five steps.

'Hello, I'm James,' he said.

He always introduces himself as James. I've heard him called Jim or Jimmy by his friends, but to me, and indeed to himself, he's always been James.

'I know who you are,' I said, and immediately regretted it.

He was cocky enough without my feeding his ego.

'I didn't catch your name,' he said.

'That's probably because you didn't ask and because I didn't offer it.'

He said nothing for a moment, considering his next move. It made me feel good to think I'd knocked some of the swagger out of him.

'Can you at least tell me what you're studying?' he said, smiling at me, obviously recovering rapidly.

'Psych.'

'Psychology?'

'Yes.'

He nodded, slowly.

'As a psychologist, would you agree that a society requires adherence to modes of etiquette, social norms, if you will, to function smoothly? That seemingly trivial behaviours help to oil the cogs that keep our world turning?'

I knew where he was going but decided to play along and see if I was right.

'You're probably leaning more into the field of sociology than psychology,' I said. 'But yes, I'll agree with you. Agreed norms of behaviour prevent us from descending into chaos and calamity.'

'Well, if we follow that line of reasoning, you have just flouted one such social more.'

'Have I indeed?'

'I'm afraid you have,' he said, smiling cheekily. 'I gave you my name and you failed to offer yours. I feel myself teetering on the brink of anarchy as a result.'

I had to force myself not to laugh.

'Well, we can't have that,' I said, feigning a tone of mock outrage.

'Quite,' he said. 'Who knows what might follow? You should just surrender your name and we can pretend it never happened.'

'I'm Bella,' I told him.

'That wasn't hard now, was it?'

I smiled. It wasn't what I would call full wattage, but it was a nice smile, even if I do say so myself. We'd reached the door of the library by then, so I stopped and turned to look at James properly.

'Here is where our paths diverge,' I said. 'My friends are keeping my place. I need to go back in to study.'

'Why not get your books and come with me for lunch?'

'I ate lunch earlier.'

'A mid-afternoon snack, then?'

'I'm not hungry.'

He gave me a lopsided grin, shaking his head in resignation.

'Come on, you can't fault a chap for trying.'

'I appreciate your effort, but as you can see, I'm busy.'

'If you don't have time now, how about tonight?'

'I have plans.'

'Tomorrow night?'

'I'm working.'

'Throw me a lifeline!' he mock-pleaded.

'Goodbye, James.'

And I left him standing there.

For a lot of guys, that would have been that, but such a rebuff did nothing to deter James Fitzpatrick.

If anything, it made him more determined.

He mounted a campaign to win me: flowers would be delivered to my classes; he would leave little cards and notes in my mailbox; he would be hanging about at different locations he knew I'd pass, to all intents and purposes there by coincidence, looking into a shop window or chatting with friends.

Of course, I knew it was no coincidence. He was trying to be noticed.

In the age of #MeToo this would be considered stalking and justifiably frowned upon, but foolish girl that I was at that point in my life, I found it all quite charming.

I have to give James this much: he didn't ask me out again until I finally, after ten days of continued love-bombing, approached him. He was hanging about on the corner of Dame Street as I exited the main gate of the college at five o'clock on a Friday evening.

'Alright,' I said after I'd dodged through the slow-moving rush-hour traffic to reach him. 'You've got my attention.'

'Whatever do you mean?' he asked, pretending to look confused.

'You know exactly what I mean,' I said. 'So I'm standing right in front of you, and I am prepared to hear you out. So go on. Ask me.'

He grinned.

'Bella Murphy, will you permit me to take you to dinner tonight?'

I looked him up and down. I'd be lying if I said I found him attractive, but there was something undeniably charismatic about him. I *was* drawn to him. And his determination to snare me was certainly exciting. No one could say he hadn't made an effort.

'Alright then,' I said, 'you can pick me up at eight.'

'I'll be there.'

'I haven't told you where I live.'

'I'll find you.' He smiled.

I should have seen that as a warning.

But like I said, I was foolish back then.

After that, my world was James and my studies. We made a move to London, and got married in 2010. James had finished his training contract and been offered a role as an M&A associate at Astley, Clifford and Kenworthy, and my PhD studies looked as if they were going to result in a book deal and maybe a media career.

It felt like all my dreams were coming true. That nothing bad could touch us.

My heartfelt wish was to comprehend why people did what they did – to peer into the mysteries of the mind and understand its machinations, which was why I chose a degree in psychology. I wanted to see how the mind develops from early childhood, understand the building blocks that create the personality and intellect that forms who we are as adults. While I was still an undergraduate at Trinity College, I'd landed a job as a research assistant on a project that sought to map stimulant receptors in the brains of pre-school children.

It was a simple yet beautifully complex task, designed to

examine how a child comes to understand and interact with the world around them.

Sitting at a desk at the back of a creche in Tallaght, I watched on a laptop screen as different parts of the brain of a three-year-old lit up and thrummed into life as she listened to my professor read her *Hansel and Gretel*. What I found most compelling was how the amygdala, a cluster of almond-shaped cells situated at the base of the brain, began firing ferociously as the story reached the part about the witch and her house of cake and sweets and sugar icing.

The amygdala controls fear and aggression, and I understood that what I was seeing was this little girl experiencing both simultaneously. The child was frightened, yes, but she was also experiencing a powerful desire to strike back. To fight for her survival.

And the intensity of the response – the light burnt furiously in that girl's brain that morning – told me she was hungry for the confrontation. She would have stood her ground even against such a terrifying aggressor. Which would have been the end of her, of course.

But I admired her determination, misplaced though it was.

Over the course of my studies, I learned that we lose that ferocity as we get older. It is beaten out of us by the slings and arrows of outrageous fortune. I took a year to do my master's degree in Organisational Psychology at City, University of London. At this stage, I had become devoted to forensic psychology, and in 2009 I embarked upon a PhD thesis examining the evolution of the 'fight or flight' response in people in management positions.

I had a theory that the aggression reflex was highly developed, yet also tightly controlled, in people who were successful in high-pressure jobs that did not tolerate physical violence. Historically, people achieved success and position through literally wiping out their opposition: kings and lords murdered their rivals; revolutionaries overthrew their oppressors in bloody coups; even in the world of business you can see a trail of murder and devastation if you go back only about a hundred years.

There has been much work done on the presence of a higher-than-average percentage of functioning sociopaths among the upper levels of the corporate world. And to be clear, I'm not referring to that. I accept it's a fact and was not surprised when the research supported it. What I was interested in was the processes that permitted, encouraged and honed very specific forms of aggressive, confrontational behaviour while suppressing others.

I was also interested in seeing if violence seeped out into other areas of the individual's life as a result of this suppression. Do the people I proposed to study favour slasher movies? Are they more likely to engage in hobbies like mixed martial arts? Or hunting? What about sexual practices like BDSM?

It seemed to me that my thesis would continue the work I began as a research assistant, watching that three-year-old child grapple with the feelings of fear and rage that the fairy tale aroused in her.

I think it would have been a ground-breaking piece of work, one that might have informed human resource departments and cognitive behavioural therapists for years to come.

Of course, I was a year into my PhD research when everything blew up, and academia was soured for me. In fact, I thought I was finished with it for good. I had to regroup, and it was tough, with my dreams lying in tatters around me. And so, I decided to retrain as a teacher. James supported me in my decision, both financially and emotionally. I was grateful for that.

I did my PGCE course at UCL, and to be honest, after everything that had happened at City, I welcomed a change of scene. I enjoyed the anonymity of being where nobody knew what had happened to me.

I got a job teaching maths and science at Ashton Wood, an independent school in the heart of Westminster, catering for the children of the wealthy and the privileged, in the same year James made junior associate.

By the time he made senior associate, we'd fallen into the pattern where he works all hours at the firm, and I go to school and keep house. Sometimes, I wonder if I'm becoming my mother, after all.

We barely see one another. And after eight years of teaching, I'm getting thoroughly bored working with teenagers who believe the world owes them a living.

So at the start of January, after mulling it over for a couple of months, I contacted my former academic supervisor to see if I might resume work on my thesis. The furore died down years ago, and we're at the start of a new semester. He sent me over the paperwork, asked me to explain where I think the work might go after I hit the dead end I reached back in 2010. I wrote a couple of pages, setting out my ideas.

And to my great delight, he went for it. I am, once again, a PhD candidate at City.

The slings and arrows of outrageous fortune might have done their work on me.

But I am far from beaten.

Chapter 4

James

I always thought my relationship with Bella was rock solid, unshakeable. I felt like it was us against the world. We were both ambitious in our chosen career paths and I felt like I could always be honest with her about what I wanted out of life. And about what I could offer as a husband.

I was also very clear about how I feel honesty is essential in our relationship. I try to tell her what I think, and while I'm prepared to support her where I can, there comes a point where I have to draw the line, and do what's best for us as a couple. As a unit.

So when my wife told me she'd decided to return to her PhD research, I kind of lost my cool. I mean, this had nearly destroyed her, and came close to derailing all our plans, too.

I said, bluntly: 'Bella, I love you, but I think this is a really, really bad idea.'

We were having breakfast when it happened, which means it was a Saturday – we hardly ever eat breakfast together during the week. Most weekdays I leave the house at around 6.30 a.m. to get to the gym before work, if I can, so we're lucky if we pass each other in the hall. At weekends, if I'm not working, we try to have breakfast together.

She'd made omelettes and I was just pouring the coffee when she piped up.

'I'm going back to my doctoral research.'

I almost dropped the cafetiere. I mean like: *fuck sake!*

'You're doing what?' I stammered at her.

'I'm going back to school. My work was ground-breaking, and no one has gone back to it or built on it since I stopped. I'm sleepwalking through my teaching career right now. I contacted the Psych Department at City, and they're open to my picking up where I left off.'

For a long, long moment I didn't know what to say. I mean, I wanted to ask her if she was on drugs, because, as I have already pointed out, that research was not good for either of us. When it all came crashing down, she went into a proper funk, decided she was done with psychology and the world of academics once and for all.

I had to work every hour God sent as a newly qualified solicitor, trying to support us both while she got her teaching certificate. We lived in the worst bedsit in the nicest area of Notting Hill, which was all we could afford at the time. I was able to use the influence of a couple of my mates at the firm to get her a gig at Ashton Wood, one of *the* most sought-after schools in London.

You'd think she'd be just a little bit happy, wouldn't you?

But no. She's bored.

I felt like screaming.

But you have to be careful. These are sensitive discussions. I didn't know if she was hormonal for some reason, or if it was that time of the month – Bella usually doesn't act erratically, but there's a first time for everything, right? I mean, something had to explain this dramatic turnabout.

So I thought long and hard before I answered her. I'm not a fucking cave man; I reckoned Bella was just feeling a bit deflated. After all, here was me, powering up the corporate ladder at my firm, destined to have my name on the wall, earning the big bucks and getting lead roles in major deals. Whereas her career had all but stalled. She'd climbed as high as she was likely to get at Ashton Wood, as she hated the management side of the job.

I reckoned this idea of going back to her psychological research was a cry of desperation.

'This is a bit sudden,' I said, trying to look concerned. 'Can we talk about it a bit? I mean, obviously I want you to be happy, but isn't this a big jump backwards?'

See what I did there? I let her know I heard her, but stated my concerns directly. It's a classic courtroom move – lull your opponent into a false sense of security. Not that my wife is my opponent, of course. Well, she kind of was, but you know what I mean.

She gave me one of her looks, the kind I always feel could

burn a hole through a stone wall if she stared at it for long enough.

'It's hardly sudden,' she said, and that's when I knew I was in trouble. 'I've been dropping hints for about a couple of months.'

'Hints?'

'You haven't noticed me talking about taking out a subscription to the *Journal of Applied Psychology*? Or the fact I left the prospectus for the Psychology Department at City on the coffee table? Or how about my asking you to stick my application for readmission in the post on your way into the office?'

I'd like to pretend I knew what she was talking about, but I literally could not remember any of those things happening. Of course, if she'd been dropping hints for two months, that meant she'd been doing it during the time in my life where I was at my most outrageously busy.

So yes, I probably missed her not-so-subtle messaging.

'Bella, have you forgotten what that research did to you? You were a mess by the time it came to an end. I ... I don't want to see you go through that again.'

She sniffed at me.

'I'm a different person now than I was then,' she said.

'Yes, but is *he*?'

'That's what I want to find out,' my wife said dispassionately.

I felt a coldness wash over me.

There was more to all of this than my just not paying attention, you see. I probably hadn't wanted to believe she was actually thinking about going back to her psychological work. Her thesis involved researching an alleged murder committed by a man called Tristan Grosvenor, and she … well, she became kind of obsessed. She ate, slept and breathed that man, and in the end, it all came crashing down on her and got very nasty.

Bella's reputation as an academic researcher was ruined.

I'm about to make partner, it's within my grasp, and I cannot tolerate any negative publicity.

Right now, I need to do everything right.

It is hugely important I maintain my billable hours as a senior associate in the law firm. I'd been clocking up eighteen-hour days at least five days a week, and it's not unusual for me to work most of the weekend too, replying to urgent emails as we attempt to go for a walk or out for dinner.

I know my wife is getting tired of this, but Bella knows what it will mean not just for me, but for *us*. This is what we've dreamed of. If I can get my foot on that ladder, I'll be making not just good money, but really good money.

Okay, so I'll be expected to sustain a certain level of performance for a few years, and it'll mean sacrificing some personal time for a while longer, but in the long run, the rewards will be huge. I could retire by the time I'm fifty. Bella could too, if she wanted to. I know she won't, but won't it be nice for her to have the option?

This business of going back to her studies, it knocked me for a loop.

I kept my tone calm, though. Understanding. But I wanted to let her know that she was moving the goalposts in the middle of a fucking game, you know what I'm saying?

'I really don't think now is the time,' I said. 'We've got too much in play.'

'What do you mean *we've* got too much in play?'

'We've got a plan, babe.'

'No,' she said, and she was shaking her head vigorously. 'You've got a plan. It's *your* plan. Not mine. It was never mine.'

That was bullshit, and we both knew it. I couldn't *say* it was bullshit, not with her in this weird mood, but I wasn't going to pretend, either. So I went for:

'You never said you disagreed.'

'I never said anything because you wouldn't have heard me if I had. You only hear what you want to.'

At that point, I was thinking my omelette was getting cold and I just wanted the conversation to be over.

'Love, can we just file this under "to be talked about another time"?' I suggested to her, in the kindest voice I could muster. 'Come on, we have a nice day planned. Let's not spoil it!'

'You're playing squash with Ralph at eleven and I'm going for coffee with Claudette,' Bella said, and her tone was not kind at all. Not one bit.

'We're going for dinner together later!' I countered, but I could see her shutting down as I said the words. It's something she does, and you can actually see it happening right in front of you. It's like a computer going into sleep mode. Her eyes just go dead and you know she's gone inside herself.

'Can you pass me the Arts section of the paper?' she asked, picking up her fork and stabbing her tepid omelette.

I did, and she opened it and then all I could see was a headline about some musical or other. Which was a relief, to be honest.

I took the opportunity and finally tucked into my breakfast, and within three minutes she was chatting about some business going on at school (don't ask me what – one of the other teachers talking crap about her in the staffroom maybe), and I reckoned the whole nasty business was forgotten.

I made a mental note to get her some jewellery or some of the lingerie from Agent Provocateur the next time I was in town.

That's the good thing about Bella – she blows up but it's over as fast as it begins and she doesn't bear a grudge.

I thought I was a lucky guy.

Seems I was wrong.

Chapter 5

Bella

Our apartment is in Chelsea, just a five-minute walk from the heart of London's action, but tranquil and serene in its own grounds, accessed through an electric gate. The building is surrounded by grass and trees and there are benches to sit on and read, little paths to walk and nooks to discover.

It's quite beautiful.

Once you're inside the apartment, it's just as special.

I can't believe we can afford to rent a place like this in the centre of London, but James has a generous salary, and combined with my wages, we have a very comfortable life. This apartment, though ... it's beyond what I could have ever dreamt of, considering where I came from.

The Alvar Aalto designed living space is minimalist yet sophisticated, with floor-to-ceiling windows that flood the room with light and provide views of the bustling and trendy locale – there's a gorgeous old-school pub on the corner, perfect for a quick glass of wine on the way back from shopping on the King's Road, or an afternoon spent poring over the artwork in all the local galleries.

I love to cook, and one of the things that attracted me to the apartment was all the high-end appliances in the kitchen, and the stylish dining table where I visualised James and I enjoying an evening meal. It's safe to say that scenario has been a rare occurrence.

We've got two bedrooms. Three bathrooms. The whole thing laid out over 110 square metres. I've decorated the place with original art bought from some of the small, but interesting, galleries in the area, and I designed themes for each of the four seasons for our soft furnishings: in spring we have yellows, oranges and greens; in summer reds and blues and champagne whites; in autumn russet browns, powder greys and darker greens; in winter purples, silvers and snow whites.

I make a ritual of changing them as each season rolls around. I quite enjoy it, pouring myself some wine, putting some appropriate music on and really indulging in the process of moving my home along with the year.

It would be grand to be able to tell you James had anything to do with choosing this fantastic place in which we live. That he shared my vision for the colour scheme, chatted with me about the outdoor space or even once went shopping with me and stopped for a drink on the way home.

But I cannot say such a thing, because it simply isn't true.

I chose where we live, and he came for the final viewing, although he had to leave early to get to a client meeting. I asked him what he thought of the colour palettes I'd put together, but he'd barely looked up from his laptop, and just said: 'Whatever you think, babes.'

He pays the rent.

I'll give him that.

It just feels as if I'm the only one really living in this apartment he's mostly paying for.

Maybe that's one of the reasons I started to notice Caleb Westlake.

Caleb was drafted in as a substitute physical education teacher back in September. Since then, my days at school have been a lot brighter.

Caleb is attractive. This is a demonstrable truth. And he is not subjectively attractive. His beauty is thoroughly *objective*.

Anyone who looks at Caleb cannot but immediately notice he's gorgeous. He is simply a beautiful man. Like Johnny Depp is beautiful, or Brad Pitt is beautiful.

Caleb is sexy all in his own way. He is clearly no stranger to the gym, although I heard him mention to Bob, one of the newly qualified bunch who started last year, that he attends one of those outdoor affairs where you lift breeze blocks and flip tractor tyres and run five miles up to your knees in mud, so gym might not be the right word.

He has a beard, as most men do these days, which he keeps trimmed fairly close to his face. He has fine features: a straight nose, dark, well-set eyes and prominent cheekbones. But I'm not all about his looks. Caleb is kind and he's funny and he really listens when I talk to him. We chat about anything and everything – books, films, recipes we like and our favourite restaurants. We've tried the nicer restaurants near the school if we manage to get an extended lunch break. Does it seem strange that I've been for meals with a male colleague? It might draw a few raised eyebrows, but we're friends, and God knows, it's not like James ever asks about my day. Yesterday, he got home from work late, as usual. I was in bed already reading my book. I mentioned that I'd stayed late in school and gone for dinner with some of the staff. I mentioned Caleb and there was no reaction from James. I don't even think he was listening … it's a bit depressing really.

Oh yeah, and Caleb can also make me laugh, like in a way I haven't laughed since, well, university.

The teaching staff, all the women and some of the men, are a-flutter over him.

Bea confided in me in the staffroom the other day that she wouldn't ever date Caleb because no one would be looking at her when she was with him. That is Bea all over, of course. She's so in love with herself she could never be with a guy or a girl more attractive than she is. Bea likes to remind everyone who will listen to her that she swings both ways.

Of course, the fact that she claims that she doesn't want to date him doesn't mean she isn't looking for his attention.

It is deliciously ironic that Caleb never so much as looks in her direction, even though she has taken to wearing low-cut tops in spite of the unseasonably cold weather for early March.

His lack of interest is driving her to distraction. That's possibly a bitchy thing to say, but actually, I don't care.

If I'm being completely honest, I enjoy the distraction. Things between James and me haven't been great. I feel invisible and it's affected my confidence. His absolute horror and disdain when I told him I wanted to restart my PhD research knocked me for a loop, and I just don't know where things are going with us.

I used to spend a lot of time getting ready for the day but now the most I can do is pull my hair into a ponytail, applying only the barest hint of make-up. With everything that has been going on with James and me lately, looking my best does not seem important. I would have to think hard to remember the last time we had any real physical contact, never mind sex.

James, I sometimes think, can only get turned on by his work. I might as well be a roommate he passes in the hallway. So yes, I've been enjoying the attention from Caleb but it has always been just a flirty friendship. Or that's what I thought.

Yesterday, though, things changed all of a sudden.

Because yesterday, Caleb asked me out. Not on our lunchtime collegiate breaks, but a proper date.

It was late in the midmorning break and I was at the Nespresso machine, half asleep after an hour of teaching applied maths to a group of bored sixteen-year-olds. I was watching the slow trickle of my second shot when I sensed, through the dull chatter that is always the ambient sound of the room, that someone was standing behind me.

And standing close, at that. Not touching but near enough

for me to feel the warmth of them through the material of my silk shirt. I knew it was Caleb before I even turned around; he always smells really good. It wasn't a heavily masculine scent, either: expensive soap, a cologne that had a citrus edge to it, giving it a freshness a lot of aftershaves lack.

It was like breathing in the most perfect Tinder profile.

I still didn't turn. The last drops of coffee eased into my cup, the crema forming slowly, and a voice at my shoulder said:

'A double espresso. You like to live dangerously.'

Caleb also has one of those voices that is meant for radio, all soft and velvety and resonant. That's funny, isn't it? A voice for radio and a face and body for the big screen.

'What makes you think I'm dangerous?' I asked, surprised to find my heartbeat quickening.

I didn't want him thinking he made me nervous. We were friends so why did this morning feel different?

There was no one else within earshot. It was just him and me. With the short break nearly over, everyone else was bundling books together, hefting laptop cases onto their shoulders and quaffing back the remnants of their oat milk-laced hot drinks. No one was paying attention to us.

'Do you know how many people in this room opt for decaf?' he continued with a smile in his voice. 'Only me and old Felicity over there drink our coffee leaded, but, cowards that we are, we just take good, old-fashioned Americanos.'

'You mean black coffees,' I heard myself saying.

'Precisely,' he continued. 'But you, Ms Fitzpatrick, are the *only* one of the teaching staff who is courageous enough to ingest not just a single, but a *double* espresso every morning.

I have to say, I'm impressed. It's nice to meet an even worse caffeine junkie than me.'

I had to smile. There was a coyness about his tone of voice, and the fact he was as close as it was humanly possible to get without actually touching me added an intimacy to the exchange I found thrilling, in spite of myself.

'You know what they say,' I said, and I took the cup from its little platform in front of the machine and turned so I was facing him. I thought he'd step back, but he didn't. We were almost nose-to-nose.

'No,' he said. 'What do they say?'

'That we're given caffeine from Monday to Friday to energise us enough to make us productive members of society, and alcohol from Friday to Monday to keep us too stupid to figure out the prison we're living in.'

He laughed.

'I love that. Who said it?'

'Bill Hicks, I think.'

'He could have been talking about me.'

I took a sip of my double shot. I was due to teach maths to sixth formers in two minutes, but I didn't want this tête-à-tête to end.

'Me too,' I said, giving him my best smile. 'He had another good one. Something about him being skin covering coffee and some very nervous teeth.'

He guffawed then, and a few heads turned to study us for a brief moment, but the gravity of classes to be taught was drawing everyone from the room in a rapid river of movement, so no one gave more than a glance.

'You're a fan of Mr Hicks' work then, I take it?'

'Well, he'd be considered desperately politically incorrect by today's standards, but if you can tolerate that without getting too offended I think the topics he talked about are still relevant.'

'You'll have to enlighten me. I've heard of him but I don't really know his material.'

'He was interested in personal freedom and how society is determined to rob us of it.'

Caleb pondered that for a second before saying:

'I'm in favour of personal freedom. I mean, if something seems like it might be fun, don't we have an obligation to ourselves to try it?'

'I think that would depend on what it was,' I said, downing the last of my coffee. 'There are one or two people I think it would be fun to run over with my car, for example, but that doesn't seem like something I should follow up on.'

'I dunno' – he laughed – 'I mean, if there were no witnesses …'

With a supreme effort of will I tore myself away from his hazel eyes and his scent, which seemed to be infusing me with energy, as if the oxygen around him was somehow purer than anywhere else in the room, and went to wash my cup in the sink. He followed.

'Come out with me for dinner after work, and we can draw up a cunning plan to evade arrest,' he said as I turned on the hot tap.

I am not going to pretend for even a second that I didn't get a little bit dizzy when he asked me. We'd been out to eat plenty of times before – friendly lunches discussing the school show or fundraiser, but this was different. There was a stretch of time, which can't have been more than a second but seemed to last an eternity, where I had a full and detailed conversation with myself, examining the pros and cons of accepting. But then, as if I was watching events from somewhere above, I saw myself turn to him and smile sadly, and I said, in a fun, jokey way:

'I'm married, Caleb. So thanks for the offer, but if you're suggesting a date, I'm going to have to politely decline.'

He eyed me up and down very deliberately, and I felt the hunger in his gaze.

'What's being married got to do with it?' he asked, a smile playing about his lips. 'We're friends, right?' His eyes locked with mine. 'I think we'd have a good time, is all,' he continued. 'Don't you?'

I did. I thought we'd have an absolutely fantastic time.

'That's not really the point, though,' I said, and trying to project a purpose I really did not feel, I went past him, grabbed my bag off the table and speed-walked to my class.

As I switched on my iPad to mark the register in my next class, I saw my hand was shaking.

Chapter 6

James

I let Bella choose our apartment. We'd been living for years in what was really just a big bedsit in Notting Hill. It wasn't great, to be honest, and there was a problem with damp Bella kept going on and on and on about.

I told her to get on to the landlord about it, but he didn't seem to give much of a fuck, so I suggested she go online and see if there was anything she could do herself about it.

I mean, I listened, you know what I'm saying? I didn't just nod and smile.

She got this plastic sheeting to put down over the floorboards, and it helped for a bit, but mould kept on showing up here, there and everywhere, so it clearly wasn't working as a long-term solution.

Then, thank heavens, I was given a promotion, and a raise along with it. And, maybe most importantly, I got my yearly bonus payment, and that gave us the funds and impetus to move. We'd never have gotten a deposit together for anything decent if we didn't have that, as we were definitely splurgers and not savers.

I knew Bella had a few places in mind, so I just told her to book some viewings, and when she had somewhere narrowed down, I'd organise time off and go and have a gander.

She didn't let me down. The place in Chelsea is fucking smashing.

I thought we'd been really happy there.

And I think we were. For a while, at least.

I love being a lawyer, but I wouldn't exactly say I'm completely happy with the actual job. I know damn well that every lawyer in London wants to work at Astley, Clifford and Kenworthy. Its reputation precedes it. I never take it for granted, because the second I do, I'll take my foot off the accelerator, and there'll be twenty other hungry corporate lawyers just waiting to fill my position.

The firm is housed in a beautiful old building in Temple, which has been the centre of the British legal world for centuries. You can almost feel the sense of history as you walk down the warren of narrow cobbled laneways and courtyards, with barristers in their powdered wigs bustling past with an air of self-importance. It's almost like stepping back in time, and I love it. Our offices have kept their period features, so the lights are electric but look like they're powered by gas. The carpets are so deep you think you're going to sink into them, and every desk is topped with green leather and has an inkwell, which is never used, but is cool if you're into that kind of thing.

I have an office on the second floor. It's tiny, and just about holds a desk and a rickety filing cabinet, but I fucking love it and I've made it my own. I have my degrees on the wall, and a framed photo of me and Bella at my qualification ceremony on my desk. We look so happy, young and in love.

I am paid large amounts of money to make rich people richer. We lawyers sometimes operate in morally grey areas, but this is what happens when vast sums of money are involved, and I've had to make my peace with it.

I've worked fucking hard for this office.

I served two years in the bullpen with thirty other trainee solicitors. Astley, Clifford and Kenworthy only take the cream of the crop. Most of us have first-class honour degrees, followed by LLMs, and a wealth of other accolades adorning our CVs. We are worked like dogs, and you need to be tough, ruthless and hungry.

There's no room for error in a job like this. A simple drafting mistake could cost a client millions. I spend hours reading, re-reading and redrafting agreements to ensure that I am not going to be that person who fucks up.

The bizarre thing is that this doesn't make me exceptional at Astley, Clifford and Kenworthy. Every single person there, from the goblins in the mail room, all the way up to the three old codgers with their names on the wall, are busting their balls to work harder than the guy in the next office. It would be a cliché to say it's dog-eat-dog, and, what's more, it wouldn't even be true. The culture at the firm goes *way* beyond dogs ripping chunks off one another.

It's more like piranhas in a feeding frenzy.

And you cannot afford to lose focus for even a second at Astley, Clifford and Kenworthy, because as soon as you do, you're finished. There's always a leaner, hungrier, more aggressive fucking fish hanging about just outside the feeding scrum, waiting for his chance to destroy you so he can take your place at the table.

The senior partners have encouraged the fear this engenders, teaching every single new employee at the firm to be constantly looking over their shoulder, watching out for the person who is waiting in the shadows to take them down. It'll keep you awake at night, if you're not careful.

It certainly has me.

I was two and a half years at the firm before I believed the partners had any confidence in me. I mean, I knew I was good at my job, but that was it. I was just … satisfactory. I kept my head above water, worked diligently and did as I was told, but never had that big deal, the one that would make my name.

What I didn't know was that they'd been watching me and had decided I was that rare thing among legal eagles – I was an excellent team player.

In my early days at the firm, I put myself forward to do some menial work on one or two big transactions, and those deals brought in a lot of fees. I got no credit, and I didn't think anyone had even noticed I was involved, but to my great surprise, Clifford has a hard-on for administration; he believes the devil is in the detail. My work on these big transactions was mostly in the area of document review and creating bibles of documentation and deal information, but this seemed to make him very happy indeed.

So happy, in fact, that he asked me to call to his office to talk to him. This had never happened before, and I was convinced I was getting the sack. It was quite the opposite, though.

'The boys doing the negotiating get all the kudos,' he told me as he guzzled a very expensive Scotch whisky from a bucket-sized crystal glass, 'but we both know they couldn't do what they do without someone doing all the grunt work.'

'I just wanted the experience of working on a high-profile transaction,' I told him. 'I thought it would be good to see how the big hitters do their business.'

'What did you learn?' he asked me. 'The most recent deal you worked was a big one. Tell me what your takeaway from it was.'

The big deal he was referring to was a global oil company acquiring a renewable energy company in order to swallow it and prevent it taking any of its market share.

If you think this sounds grim, you'd be right, but there was nothing illegal in what we did. Without a doubt, we skirted close to the line. But we stayed just the right side of it.

'That the client doesn't care about anything other than getting the result they want,' I said. 'Everything else gets pushed aside, after which they take the shortest path to the end goal.'

Clifford narrowed his eyes at me.

'Not exactly subtle, is it?'

'No,' I said, 'but it's damned effective. Some people got hurt along the way, but no one significant. And the clients were pleased as punch. We saved them millions over the short term and the safeguards we put in place will keep billions in their pockets in years to come.'

Clifford nodded and took a long pull on his drink.

'That's probably the most important lesson of them all,' he said. 'Know what you want, and then go out and get it. Do what you have to, and don't give a fuck for anyone who tells you that you can't have it. That's the difference between the big boys and the also-rans.'

It's also the difference between sociopaths and normal people, I remember thinking, but I kept that to myself.

Over the following couple of years, I was given bigger and bigger roles. I still wasn't leading the teams, but I wasn't bibling any more either. I was at the table with the other high-fliers, and when I spoke, people started to listen to what I had to say. I was climbing, and the sky was the limit.

When I was offered the chance to work on the team representing Fahlberg Financials in their merger with Copping International Insurance, I knew I'd finally made it.

It's ironic it was also the deal that nearly finished me.

Taken from 'Controlled Rage: Mapping the physical and psychological effects of the suppression of aggression responses in professional men and women, and an analysis of socially sanctioned dominance behaviours in the corporate world', PhD thesis by Bella Murphy Fitzpatrick, City, University of London, 2010.

I asked Grosvenor, in an interview conducted in 2010, if he felt that running a company that funded weapons development had prepared him for physical confrontation. He was a tall, slim man with blond hair brushed back from his forehead, cut long at the back so that it curled at the nape of his neck. He had a cold, steely demeanour that could be intimidating at times. He seemed very happy, however, to discuss the incident that has gained him such notoriety.

I found his response interesting.

'When I understood that I was under physical threat from Mr Tamlyn, I used the same line of reasoning I do in any business situation. I weighed up the pros and cons and decided that the only sensible line of action was to retaliate. Tamlyn had clearly lost his reason, and I felt that only one of us was going to be leaving my office alive. It was a simple matter of whether it was going to be him or me. I have seen this in many business deals, where the only way to move forward is to take a risk. This was no different, except here the dangers were to life and limb rather than to my profit margins. I looked at my adversary, and I rationalised that while he probably weighed more than me and was certainly agitated, I had the advantage as I had my wits about me. As it happens, my instincts were correct.'

I can assert that while Mr Grosvenor was animated when he discussed the experience, he did not seem particularly emotional or in any way traumatised by it.

He told me about it the same way he would any business deal.

There was nothing in his manner that made me think he felt any remorse, any sense of shame, any self-disgust or personal reproach, all of which are emotional responses reported by individuals who have committed acts of violence, even acts mainstream society considered justified.

Tristan Grosvenor seems to view what happened that night as just another managerial interaction, an engagement that was needed to address a staffing problem. Gerald Tamlyn's death was, as far as Tristan Grosvenor is concerned, simply a by-product of doing business. An operating cost.

'Why should I lose any sleep when what passed was solely the result of a decision Tamlyn made?' Grosvenor asked me.

It is apparent the CEO of Isotech sleeps soundly.

I wonder if the same can be said for his employees.

Chapter 7

Bella

Today, I discovered that, when it comes down to it, men are all the same.

There are etiquettes in teaching that just make life a little easier for us teachers. When you're finished your class, you ask your students to take all their litter with them, for example. You'd be amazed how many sweet wrappers, plastic sandwich cases, cardboard takeout coffee cups that an average group of students will generate during one hour of learning. Particularly when you consider that it is college policy that they do not eat or drink anything during class time.

Another accepted rule is that the teacher leaving the class wipes down the whiteboard before they go, leaving a clean slate. I was doing this at the end of a physics class today when I realised, as is so often the case, that one of my students, Philo Armitage, was still in the room, although the rest of the class had already left.

I knew he was still there because he cleared his throat loudly. I was in a world of my own, thinking about what I was going to get for dinner that night and if James would be home, so the unexpected sound made me jump. He saw my discomfort and laughed, which annoyed me. I turned, and he was sitting in his usual seat at the back of the class, his feet up on the desk, staring at me.

'You need to get to your next class, Philo,' I warned.

'I'm right where I want to be, miss,' he said, grinning.

'Though not where you should be,' I shot back.

'Aren't you supposed to be someplace else too?'

Philo is the definition of a privileged public school boy. Sixteen, blond hair, which he wears long. He has large blue eyes and a long face with a big mouth and full lips. Like most of the students he takes grave liberties with the school uniform and his shirt is usually untucked and mostly unbuttoned. Sometimes Philo wears t-shirts underneath, usually advertising some band or other. Today he was sporting a vest, which clung to his body.

'My itinerary is none of your business,' I said primly.

'Well, mine isn't any of yours, neither.'

The young man sprawled in front of me was from a very wealthy family who lived in Belgravia, yet he adopted the slang of the market traders from *EastEnders*. I should have found it annoying, but there was a bit of me, a part I am not proud of, that found it charming.

Objectively, you would say he was attractive. I could certainly see how he was popular with the female students at Ashton Wood, and he always seemed to have some girl or another on his arm.

I put the whiteboard cleaner back on its shelf and picked up my bag.

'If you don't have anything to do, I certainly do. I'll see you tomorrow, Philo.'

He was up and out of his chair in a trice, stepping in front of me as I made my way to the door, blocking my path.

'Don't you think it's time we stopped mucking about, Miss?'

I stopped in my tracks. I was a little scared, but my primary reaction was surprise and outrage. On what planet did he think he was ever going to walk away from this one unscathed?

'I have no idea what you mean, Philo,' I said, the warning evident in my voice. 'Now please get out of my way so I can get to my next class.'

'Come on, Miss. You know we have a vibe going on.'

'I know nothing of the sort. Now get out of my way or I am calling the principal right now.'

He laughed. He actually laughed in my face. Instead of standing aside, he walked slowly towards me, holding me with his eyes the entire way. He stopped inches from me. The sweet, slightly nauseating smell of marijuana smoke clung to his clothes.

'I want it,' he said, enunciating each word carefully. 'And I *know* you want it. I'm not going to wait forever. You know what I'm saying?'

I was fighting hard not to let him see I was shaking. I wanted to kick him in the balls and tear his eyes out. I could see myself leaping at him, ripping out chunks of his luxuriant hair and smashing the heel of my hand into his perfect nose.

But if I'm being completely honest, and I would never say this to a single soul, I was also more than a bit excited by it too. His absolute confidence in himself. The sense of authority he had assumed, which he actually had no right to claim at all, but which he seemed very comfortable with. I saw myself jumping on him and doing other things, too. Still violent. But it was a different kind of aggression.

'Are you going to get out of my way?' I asked again.

'Are you going to consider my proposal?'

In that moment I knew damn well I was looking at a future CEO or MP. The type of guy I'd written about in my thesis, probably. Entitled and arrogant, a young guy for whom everything just dropped into his lap, a kid who was privileged but had no sense of it. Everyone he knew was rich, and he saw the world he lived in in terms of sliding scales of opulence.

In that moment, I realised he saw me as a commodity. I wondered how many housemaids and cleaners he'd propositioned since he'd hit adolescence. And how many times he'd been knocked back. I figured I was just another in a long line of what he saw as easy conquests.

Disgusted at myself for responding in any way to the spoiled brat, I held up my phone so he could see it.

My eyes were glued to Philo, but just for a second I could see myself reflected in the glass of the screen: my long dark hair was pulled back into a loose ponytail, and strands of it had fallen out to frame my slim face. I have quite prominent cheekbones, and my green eyes are large and were wide, now, their pupils dilated in anger I was trying to control.

I was surprised at how tired I looked.

'If I hold down the number four, it speed-dials the number of the porter's office, which, as you know, is just a few yards up the corridor from here. It's a special line that is only called when a staff member is in need of immediate assistance. My name will come up on their screen, as well as the classroom I'm currently in, which will bring two large men thundering in here. Would you like me to make that happen?'

He smirked and stepped aside, indicating the clear passage to the door with a flourish of his hand.

'No need for aggro, Miss. I was just being friendly.'

I went up to him this time, looking him dead in the eye.

'You have a strange understanding for what passes as friendly, Philo.'

He shrugged. The energy he was getting off me now was not flirtatious, or uncertain, or shy, but was in fact angry, and authoritative and very much in control.

'I am warning you this, and I want you to listen well: if you ever approach me in anything other than a respectful and courteous manner in future, I will make it my business to see you are expelled from this school.'

'You can't do that, Miss,' Philo sneered. 'My old man donates heaps of money to this place. The library was built with his cash. His name is up on a plaque and everything.'

'My husband works for one of the biggest law firms in the City. Do you think he'd be happy if I told him you'd refused to let me leave my classroom while you made lascivious suggestions?'

'I didn't say anything, Miss. All I said was that we had a vibe. I meant no harm in that. Like I said, just being friendly.'

I added lawyer to the list of jobs Philo might aspire towards.

'We both know what transpired in here,' I said. 'As my husband always says, the law isn't about what happened, it's about what you can make a judge and jury *believe* happened.'

Philo suddenly seemed a lot less brave. I almost felt sorry for him.

Almost.

'You've made your point, yeah?'

'Good. I'm glad we understand each other.'

And giving him one last hard look, I stalked out.

Chapter 8

James

My success has come at a cost.

Fahlberg Financials has decided to proceed with the merger with Copping International Insurance after the meeting in which the due diligence report was presented and the client satisfied themselves that the risk of combining their companies was one worth taking. Nobody knew how close that meeting came to not happening at all, but then, no one needed to know. I didn't have to participate in the meeting, but I sat there looking attentive and took some notes, and when the meeting was over, I went to my office and pretended to work.

In actuality, I was sleeping at my desk. No one bothered me, and why the fuck would they? The meeting had obviously been a success; we were due a tiny bit of respite from the hamster wheel of the deal before we had to start drafting agreements.

We still had a distance to go before we got to the finishing line, but we had just jumped a major hurdle – the deal was going ahead, and that meant we could celebrate, as the firm would be raking in millions in fees. As the partners were wont to do in such circumstances, they decided to throw a party at the Ritz as a morale boost. Attendance was obligatory, and we were expected to bring our spouses along. Generally the partners didn't give a damn if we brought our significant others, but there are some occasions where it is frowned upon if they don't attend.

I've never really understood why. I think it's about creating the sense, fictitious though it so obviously fucking is, that Astley, Clifford and Kenworthy is a big happy family. I've been to several of these functions, and it's always painful to see everyone pretending to have a nice time. What usually happens is the lawyers end up clustered around the bar getting pissed, while their spouses gather around a couple of tables and complain about how tough it is to be married to lawyers who are, really, married to their jobs.

Is that me? Probably. I might as well admit it, the job *has* become my main focus over the past twelve months. Did it make me push my wife away? Probably. But goddam it, I did it for her too. I did it for both of us. This was meant to be our fucking dream. It was how we were going to get everything we'd ever wanted.

I thought she wanted it too. I really did.

How did I get to this place? How did it all go wrong?

When I got word about the party, I called Bella.

It was a short conversation.

The call rang and rang and I was convinced she was ignoring me. Just as I was about to hang up, she picked up. Except she didn't speak. I could hear the hiss of the open line, and the sound of what I took to be the corridor at her school. Footsteps and voices and echoes.

After a few seconds I said:

'Bella, are you there?'

'Yes, James. I'm here.'

'Okay. Good.'

'Why are you calling me, James?'

That was unexpected. She's never asked me that before. I mean, I'm her husband. Do I need an excuse to call my wife?

'I … I need to talk to you.'

She laughed, that short, staccato snort she does when she's pissed at me. Which is pretty fucking rich, seeing as I'm the one with a reason to be angry – I hadn't forgotten about her plan to reembark upon her thesis, the same research that had nearly destroyed her, and, to an extent, almost finished our marriage before it had begun.

'You're speaking to me for the first time in more than a week and that's the best you've got – you need to talk to me? I've passed you in the hallway at home and you've barely acknowledged me.'

She had me there and I knew it.

'Fahlberg and Copping are proceeding with the merger,' I said. 'The deal still has a way to go, but this is a huge milestone. And it happened because of all my work.'

'Congratulations, but why would I care about that?'

'They've booked a function room at the Ritz for tomorrow evening. To celebrate. Spouses and partners are expected to be there.'

She didn't answer for the longest time, and then she said:

'Well, I am going to have to disappoint those expectations this time, James.'

I felt sick.

Yes, because her absence would be noted and that would raise questions I absolutely did not want to answer, but also because of the tone she used. It was emotionless. Empty. And it hurt me to hear it. What had I done to make her so angry with me? So devoid of giving a shit about what should have been one of the greatest achievements in my life?

'Bella, I'd really like you to come.'

'Well, I really wouldn't,' she said, and hung up.

And that was that.

I sat there at my desk, feeling dead inside. I didn't know what to do. How to respond. I was gazing into space, on the verge of another panic attack, when there was a knock on my door.

'Come in,' I called, hearing my voice as if it was being spoken by someone else.

I was on autopilot.

Kenworthy stepped in, his blocky form filling the space between my desk and the door.

'Mr Kenworthy, great to see you. Is there anything I can do for you?' I said, suddenly wondering if I'd forgotten something important and was in trouble.

'That's okay, Fitzpatrick,' Kenworthy growled. 'This won't take long.'

I waited to find out what was going on.

'You've worked hard on this merger so far,' Kenworthy said. 'All of the partners have noted your work ethic over the past few weeks, and management at Fahlberg singled you out for a mention. They're more than happy with everything you did.'

'Thank you, sir,' I said, completely blindsided by this. No one at the firm ever gave praise for *anything*. This was totally unexpected.

'You're going to get a significant lump sum in your end-of-year bonus in April to reflect our recognition of your hard work and dedication to the firm.'

'Thanks sir, much appreciated,' I said, although I had expected I would. That was standard, really.

'And here's a little something extra, from me,' he said, and reverently placed a bottle of Macallan 25-year-old Scotch on my desk, his very expensive tipple of choice.

'I don't want you to get ahead of yourself yet, but I wanted to formally let you know that you are being put forward for partnership. You have the backing of all the senior partners. I don't see why we won't be officially announcing your partnership come December, unless you majorly fuck things up for yourself,' he said brusquely.

We were in March, so he was telling me that in nine months I could be looking at my name on the wall. That was a very big deal.

'That's really great to hear,' I stuttered, slightly stunned by this news. Kenworthy turned and marched out of the office before I could say anything else. I sat there for a minute, completely stunned by the brief exchange. I couldn't believe it. I had been working towards partnership, but I certainly hadn't expected it to come so soon. I was going to be the youngest partner at Astley, Clifford and Kenworthy. And it was nothing short of what I deserved.

I suddenly knew beyond a shadow of a doubt that I had done something that was not just good, but was actually significant. I had knocked one out of the park.

And I was entitled to some happiness for that.

Even if that came in the form of a massive bonus and a promised promotion, rather than the respect and admiration of the one person I really cared about.

Chapter 9

Bella

The next incident with Philo happened in a corridor full of students and teachers the following day, yet no one afterwards would admit to having seen anything.

I suppose I shouldn't be surprised by that, but if I am to be honest with myself, it rankled a great deal, probably because it made me feel deeply, echoingly alone. And nobody wants to feel like that.

We were in the middle of that between-class rush in Ashton Wood, that time where everyone is tumbling from one room to another, students grabbing books from lockers, teachers queuing for the photocopier or pouring a hurried cup of coffee down their gullets, everyone wrapped up in their own little worlds in

74

this curious in-between moment, a brief island of nothingness that will blink out of existence once the next bell rings and the new session of learning begins.

I had just taken my fourth form maths book and notes from my own locker in the staff area and was making my way through the broiling mass of students who clogged the artery that was the main ground-floor corridor of the school. The class I had planned for the next session involved explaining Theorem 11, and then getting the students to do a number of thought experiments to demonstrate the proof.

My mind was on the lesson ahead, and suddenly, I felt someone press right up against me from behind, a hand cupping my left breast, and I was immediately aware that that someone was in a state of arousal. I could feel his hardness jammed against my thigh.

'How do you like that, Miss?' I heard Philo whisper menacingly in my ear, squeezing my breast painfully. 'Because I like it a lot.'

I was in such a state of shock, it was all I could do but gasp.

I felt affronted. Violated.

And *angry*.

If my brain responses had been attached to a laptop, my amygdala would have been lighting up like a Christmas tree.

What happened next was almost an unconscious response. I brought the full force of my elbow into his stomach.

I felt air explode from his lungs and he made a kind of muted squeal, and then he folded as if he was a human deckchair and went down. All this had taken place in the space of mere seconds, and, despite my fury, I kept on walking to my class, leaving him where he fell.

When I had imparted as much wisdom as I could about Theorem 11 to my students I went to the principal's office.

'Joel, Philo Armitage sexually assaulted me on the A corridor. I want him expelled,' I said as I burst into the office without knocking.

My boss looked abruptly up from his computer screen with a look of surprise and panic.

'What did he do?' he asked with a note of fake sympathy, his voice struggling to conceal his alarm. 'I'll have to make an incident report immediately.' He worriedly loosened his tie.

'Like I said, he sexually assaulted me, Joel, in broad daylight. He approached me from behind and grabbed my left breast.'

'Shit, Bella, are you okay? When did this happen?'

'In between the classes at eleven thirty.'

'On the A corridor?'

'Yes. I just said that,' I said, barely hiding my frustration.

'Are you sure it wasn't an accident? It gets quite crowded there in the mornings.'

I shook my head in wonderment.

'I'm absolutely, one hundred per cent *positive*. He groped me, Joel, and I won't stand for it. This is an absolute breach of the Code of Conduct.'

'This is a very serious allegation, Bella. And you do know his father is one of our most generous benefactors—'

'I don't care who his dad is or how much money he's got. This is exactly the problem. The entitled little prick thinks he can do whatever he wants with zero consequences because his dad will buy him out of trouble. Not this time, Joel. I'll go to the police myself if you don't,' I hissed. 'For the moment, expel the little fucker!'

Joel Borden blinked.

'I'll ... I'll look into it, I promise. Please don't do anything hasty, Bella. I give you my word.'

What his investigation resulted in – his findings were presented to me the following day – was a short section of CCTV footage that seemed to show Philo bumping into me, and falling backwards. Philo denied having ever touched me outside of an accidental collision, and no one saw or heard anything inappropriate.

That was when I probably should have pressed charges. I suppose I didn't think there was any point.

It might have saved me some anxiety later on if I had, though.

Chapter 10

Charlotte

People can be mean.

As a tech support worker, a lot of the calls I get are from individuals who are stressed out and annoyed, frustrated that the technology designed to help them has failed, or an important piece of work has disappeared, seemingly into thin air. They're pissed off and, even though they're calling on you to help, the likelihood is that they're going to treat you like shit.

I've seen this so many times, and I pretty much expect that it's going to be the case on every call. I'd have to say that, more often than not, I'm right. So, I go into each assist emotionally guarded.

A few months ago, a guy called because he'd been shopping online on his work computer, and had somehow ordered a load of sex toys that he insisted he never clicked on. Not only did he want me to cancel his order, but to also cleanse his laptop of any signs of the not-safe-for-work nature of the websites he had been browsing.

You would think that someone in this situation would be polite to the person who could potentially help them out of this tricky situation. But not in this case. I like to believe it was the fear of being caught that made him obnoxious and ungracious. Even when I talked him through cancelling his order and deleting his history and cookies, he still didn't show any gratitude. I did get a sense of pleasure letting him know that there was a remote backup that records all activity, and that I didn't have the authorisation to access it and delete the information.

'But ... but I didn't search most of the stuff in the browser history. It's a ... it's a mistake. Like a virus or something,' he spluttered down the phone.

'I'm sure your boss will believe that's the case,' I lied.

His history, going back fourteen months, was a litany of porn, gambling, escort sites and some deeply unsavoury pursuits I was certain weren't legal.

'If you can't help me, what fucking good are you?'

'Sir, I do not work for you,' I pointed out. 'My company is kept on retainer by your employers. It's their interests we serve.'

He began to curse me from a height, telling me in no uncertain terms what he would like to do to me if our paths ever crossed. I cut across him.

'Might I warn you that this call is being recorded for training purposes?'

At that point the connection seemed to drop out. Or perhaps he hung up.

Callers rarely disappoint.

But sometimes you meet a nice one.

The other evening I received a cry for help from one of the sweetest people I've encountered in a long time. He'd made a simple mistake and lost a hugely important piece of documentation that was critical in a multi-billion pound corporate transaction, and we only had a few hours to retrieve it. Despite the fact that he was stressed, anxious and sleep deprived, he was polite and easy-going. We even had a chance to talk about our shared interests. I felt like I had made a genuine connection with someone – a feeling that I haven't experienced in a long time.

It's clients like this that you remember. They're the ones you think about long after the calls are over.

And, sometimes, they reach out to you again.

Chapter 11

James

My body was buzzing with adrenalin after my meeting with Kenworthy that afternoon, and I couldn't relax when I got home to my empty, silent apartment. On a whim, I decided to take my metallic blue Aston Martin V12 Vantage for a drive. It's my pride and joy, bought with the proceeds of last year's hefty bonus, and the most beautiful vehicle I've ever had the pleasure of owning. I didn't pay much attention to where I was going once I pulled out of our secure garage, but somehow ended up down by the river, following the curving road that runs beside the Thames. I drove until I reached Battersea, and stopped in view of the old power station.

I felt empty inside, and angry. Angry with Bella. Angry at

myself. Angry because I didn't know what to do to make things better. It seemed as if I was surrounded by people who didn't really give a fuck about me one way or the other, and I was sick of it. This should be my proudest moment, but instead I felt like a piece of shit.

What killed me was that in my work life, in the professional sphere, I was doing so well. Everything was lining up, things could not, in fact, have been going better. I wasn't just in line for promotion, Kenworthy had more or less guaranteed that I would be making partner within the next nine months. Okay, the merger was not complete as yet, but as soon as it was, the job would be mine.

Now I'm not an idiot, and one of the qualities I possess is an ability to be honest with myself. I knew damn well that my making partner had nothing whatsoever to do with anyone at Astley, Clifford and Kenworthy actually *liking* me. They wanted me to step up because I was earning them money. Nothing more and nothing less.

But I could live with that. I didn't *need* them to like me.

I did expect my wife to be proud of me, though. To be grateful for the sacrifices I was making. To want to encourage me and congratulate me. To share in my success.

That she could not bring herself to do that was a bitter thing. It made me feel worse than I ever could have imagined.

A big part of that dark feeling was the looming shadow of Bella going back to school. I'd seen, among the pile of mail that sits on a console table just inside the front door of our apartment, a letter from City, accepting her application to continue the doctoral thesis she had left unfinished eight years ago.

I simply could not understand why she wanted to go back to it.

It nearly finished her – I am convinced she considered taking her life, even though it was never said as such – and she and I came perilously close to separating. Tristan fucking Grosvenor became a third person in our marriage, and by the time Bella's name was being dragged through the mud she was still mentioning him in every third sentence. Despite all the signs to the contrary, Bella seemed convinced he was going to sail in and rescue her from all the shit that was coming down, even though it was painfully obvious he was behind all of it.

I was terrified of her stepping back into all of that.

I didn't think I could take it. And I am *damn* sure our relationship couldn't.

I had tried to tell her all of this, but it had fallen on deaf ears. So here I was, finally getting everything I wanted professionally, but I was without a friend in the world.

The only person I had encountered lately who had shown me any kindness was the girl who had answered my call to the Tech Helpdesk. She'd said her name was Charlotte. She'd been really sweet. And she'd had a nice voice. Kind of shy. Gentle.

The complete fucking opposite of everyone else I had around me.

It didn't take me long to find the number – a simple Google search did the trick. I dialled without even thinking, and to my horror, a man's voice answered.

'You're through to Tech Helpdesk. How can I help you this evening?'

'I was hoping to speak to Charlotte,' I said, realising she might not be working that day.

'Charlotte is not in the office today. My name is Edward. Can I help instead?'

I thought about just hanging up, but I had come this far, I figured in for a penny, in for a pound.

'She helped me on an important job. Because of what she did, my firm made a really significant step forwards on a major deal. I just wanted to let her know, and thank her again for her assistance.'

'That's very kind of you, sir. I'll be sure to pass on your kind words.'

'I'd really like to do it myself. Will she be working later tonight?'

There was a pause while he tried to decide if I was a nutjob or not. He must have come down in my favour, because a moment later he said:

'Hold for a tick please,' and then I was listening to a classical guitar version of The Beatle's 'Help'. Which I thought was a nice touch.

He was back maybe thirty seconds later.

'Putting you through now.'

I heard the texture of the sound change, and then:

'Yes, hello?'

It was her. I'd know the voice anywhere. Which is weird to say, because we'd only spoken that once, but it had been an intense night for me, and as I've already said, I felt we bonded.

She was different this time, though.

I mean, she was still nice, but it felt as if she didn't have much to say, that I was distracting her from some important task, which in fairness, I probably was. I think I came off as gushing and that I was trying too hard, and in the end I just felt stupid. I offered to send her a present to thank her for what she'd done. I was sitting in a sports car that cost as much as most people's houses, looking ahead at a glittering career, which was partly down to her help that fraught night. I felt I owed her something.

But she shut it down right away. Something about it being against company policy. She was nice but firm. There wasn't much else for me to say, so I thanked her again, and said goodbye.

There was something else, though.

And I've thought about this a lot, turned it over in my head and I believe I'm right.

When I was saying goodbye, I thought I detected a slight sense of ... I don't know ... of hesitancy in her. I negotiate for a living. I'm used to the different tones and subtle changes in the flow of the conversation. I know if the other side is waiting for you to do something or offer something. And I know when they have something they're holding back, too.

And that is what I felt here. It seemed to me she was holding back. That she wanted to say something but was reluctant to for some reason.

I don't think I've heard the last of Charlotte from the Helpdesk.

I have a feeling there are a few chapters left in our story.

Taken from 'Controlled Rage: Mapping the physical and psychological effects of the suppression of aggression responses in professional men and women, and an analysis of socially sanctioned dominance behaviours in the corporate world', PhD thesis by Bella Murphy Fitzpatrick, City, University of London, 2010.

F. Scott Fitzgerald famously once wrote that the rich are different to you and me.

Tristan Grosvenor agreed with that sentiment whole-heartedly.

'What most people don't understand,' he told me during our interviews, 'is that, in a capitalist system, being rich is a right. If you are prepared to create something that others value, a product or a service, you have every right to charge for it and make a profit. Getting rich is as much about believing you can as it is about anything you actually do.'

I put it to him that for the majority of people, the value placed on their labours is set by employers, people just like him, which of course limits the capacity of such individuals to achieve great wealth. In fact, wasn't it him deciding that Gerald Tamlyn's services were no longer of value that caused the altercation that had brought us together in the first place?

Grosvenor scoffed at this suggestion.

'There is not a thing in the world that prevented Tamlyn, or any of the others, from setting up their own businesses. I would have encouraged any of them to do so. The average worker sees setting up a business as too risky. They want the safety and security of a steady pay cheque. What they don't see is that the risk is a calculated one. You have to be prepared to take a chance, and live hand-to-mouth for a year or two. But if you work hard, the rewards can be huge. That's the difference between someone like me and someone like Tamlyn. I'm not scared of taking those risks.'

'Is it a matter of intellect?' I asked him. Is it about knowing what risks are worth taking? Being able to read the markets? Understand the latest business trends?

'It's not about brains,' Grosvenor said firmly. 'If it was, every boffin and geek who comes top of their class would be a billionaire, but most of them are still living in their mothers' basements.'

'What is it about then?' I wanted to know.

'It's about a certain kind of guile,' he said, winking at me. 'It's about watching what other successful people do and learning their tricks. It's about ruthlessness, being prepared to go for the jugular in deals, and not worry about offending competitors. It's about being a *survivor*.'

'So you do what you need to protect yourself,' I said. 'To the detriment of everyone else around you?'

'You protect who you need to,' Grosvenor said. 'If I have someone working on a project for me and I know their skills are essential to getting it done, I'll do what I have to do to keep them. You need a good team to become rich. It's not possible on your own. But never forget who is in charge, and who the buck stops with. Yes, my team is important, but success is made or broken by me.'

And that, in some ways, sums up an important difference. Research into the wealthy shows that a key factor that separates them from the rest of the population is that their approach to problem solving is deeply internalised. Rich people like Tristan Grosvenor look at aspects of their environment that are not working optimally and seek solutions within themselves. They seek to actively alter their world, and to be sole agents of change.

Which brings us, yet again, to Gerald Tamlyn. He became an environmental threat to Grosvenor, and Grosvenor responded by eradicating that threat.

I asked him about that.

'Of course I was responding to a situation that was unfolding before me,' he said. 'Yet how I chose to respond was completely up to me. I could have tried to delay him, hide behind my desk and called security. I could have attempted to make a run for the office door. I might have even negotiated – see if I could talk him down. All of those possibilities occurred to me.'

I asked if he was happy with the decision he made.

'Oh, very,' he said, smiling. 'I wouldn't have had it any other way.'

Chapter 12

Bella

I should have seen it coming, but I didn't.

On Fridays I teach a class on calculus in a small classroom, situated at the rear of the school campus. A narrow passageway facilitates your return to the main building, and it runs between the sports centre and the science block. I've made the trip hundreds of times since I started working at Ashton Wood. This Friday I left the classroom, my tummy rumbling a little as I thought about the three-bean salad I'd brought for lunch waiting for me in the fridge in the staffroom.

Other than lunch, my mind was on a biology class I had later that afternoon, and I was paying little attention to the world around me. I didn't immediately see the three students who were waiting for me, one in front and two behind, blocking the narrow walkway.

'Hey Miss Fitzpatrick,' a voice said, and looking up, I saw Philo, his shirt hanging open as usual, revealing a Ramones t-shirt beneath, though I doubted he'd ever heard a single song the punk group had recorded.

'Hello Philo,' I responded, and seeing the look of contempt on his face, I realised I was in trouble.

I didn't know the names of the two kids behind him. I'd seen them around. I thought one might be a student in an advanced language class Bea taught – he was a tall, bulky young man with acne scarring his face, his blond hair shaved at the sides and worn long and gelled back on top. The other was short, perhaps only five foot three or four. He was skinny with a heavy brow and a hollow-cheeked, hungry look to him.

'I think it's time we had us another chat, Miss. What do you reckon?'

I tried to look blasé. Maybe even a bit bored.

'I think we said all we needed to the other day,' I said, folding my arms across my chest. 'Principal Borden has decided not to investigate the incident further, and as long as you behave like a gentleman, I don't think we have a problem.'

'See, there is a problem though,' Philo said, and began to advance towards me, his friends keeping pace behind him. 'Respect goes both ways. And I don't think you have any respect for me.'

He made a grab for me, and I pulled back, causing his fingers to close on air.

Swearing, he lunged at me, but I had already turned and was

sprinting the way I had come, cursing myself for not putting on my trainers this morning.

'Get her!' I heard Philo yell, and then there were pounding steps behind me, which were almost drowned out by the ferocious thumping of my heart.

This could not be real. How was I being chased in broad daylight by three students in a school for posh kids? I hadn't led Philo on. Had I?

The thought echoed around in my head, and later, I was angry with myself for that. Isn't it funny how male pride, once rebuffed and angry, can make us women feel we've in some way behaved unfairly by choosing to say no to their advances?

I rounded the corner at full pelt, and as I did I felt a hand closing on my shoulder, and one of them had me. Turning, I lashed out with my nails, not even registering who it was, raking them down the forehead as hard and as viciously as I could.

I think I was screaming and my eyes were full of angry tears, so as soon as the hand let go I charged on. I hadn't made three steps though before I was grabbed again by the back of my jacket, and I was lifted off my feet for a moment before being hauled backwards. I felt another hand catch me by the front of my shirt and then I was slammed so hard onto the ground all the breath was knocked out of me.

Then they were on me. I felt a hand grab me between my legs and fingers were ripping at my shirt. A face rammed into mine so hard my nose was crushed and more tears poured from my eyes.

I tried to fight. I screamed. How could nobody hear my screams? I thrashed and I attempted to bite the nose that was directly in front of me, but I was physically overwhelmed, and I knew it.

'*Oh God, this is happening,*' I thought. '*This is not supposed to be happening to me, but it is. How could it be?*'

Without warning, then, something changed.

Some of the weight was gone from me. I half-heard a scuffle and then more of the weight disappeared, and then all of it.

I lay where I was for a second, unable to move, breathing heavily. Then as if by magic I felt power returning to my limbs, and I pushed myself upright. It took me a moment to work out why I was free of my attackers, but then I got it: someone had come along and interrupted them in their attempted assault. I had been rescued.

From where I was now sitting I could see Philo on the ground, looking as if he'd fallen awkwardly – he was more or less lying on his face with his butt in the air, a weirdly ungainly pose for a kid who spent all his time posing. The small student seemed to be gone, and the fat one was squaring off against someone, presumably my rescuer. His wide back was blocking my view, and at first I couldn't see who my saviour was.

But then Fatso, in his fighter's stance, shuffled to the side, and I saw it was Caleb.

The big kid tried to loop a right hook at Caleb, who caught the blow easily on his forearm, before stepping in and punching Fatso once, twice, three times on the nose, and following with a left that caught him squarely in the jaw and put him on the ground beside his friend.

I saw Caleb dance back a few steps, showing a grace of movement that was almost beautiful. He still had his hands up, en garde, and I understood he was waiting to see if either of them was going to get up again. When he saw they weren't, he dropped his hands and rapidly came to my side.

'Are you okay, Bella?'

I nodded, and, crying bitterly now, devasted and in shock, I threw my arms around him.

The police were called.

The principal asked me if I wanted him to ring James.

To my surprise, I heard my own voice saying 'no'.

Caleb stood beside me, attempting to comfort me with an arm around my shoulder. With him beside me I felt safe, secure, grounded. I should have wanted James, but I didn't. It sounds awful to admit, but it's the truth.

The three kids' parents were called. I didn't see them, as Caleb and I were kept in the principal's office, away from everyone, which was probably for the best. Despite the fact that their progeny had sexually assaulted me, I knew they would be furious.

The smaller kid, whose name was Bill Kincaid, was still missing. A uniformed officer told me they'd put out an all-points warning, which meant he'd more than likely be picked up by evening.

Caleb and I were brought to St Thomas's hospital, where we were checked and given clean bills of health. A social worker spoke with me, and offered leaflets with information about where to call to arrange therapy. I said I'd think about it, but had no intention of doing so. I didn't want to talk about what had happened any more than was absolutely necessary. Maybe at some stage in the future, but not now.

After we left the hospital, Caleb and I went to Charing Cross police station to give our formal statements.

'Are you hungry?' Caleb asked me as we walked out into the night, hours after we had finally given our statements.

'I didn't think I would be, but I am,' I said.

We made our way, hands in pockets and heads down against the chill March air, onto the Strand, which was a hive of activity as bustling crowds streamed out from the various theatres that lined the street.

'I know it's not fancy, but …' Caleb looked sheepishly at me and nodded towards McDonald's.

'I'd murder a burger,' I said, smiling, and together we jogged across the road.

'Are you sure you're okay?' he asked, as we sat down at a table by the window. 'You've got the clean bill of health from the medics and you've fulfilled your civic duty by cooperating with the police in their inquiries, but are you actually okay?'

I tried to smile and had to really force it, because, emotionally, I was still quite raw.

'Thanks to you, yes,' I said, giving my voice a firm, steady tone. 'It was scary, and I can't say I'm not shaken by it. I'm just glad you were nearby.'

He shook his head in disgust.

'Still,' he said, sighing in annoyance, 'we should be safe in the schools where we work. I can't believe what happened today. Those little *fuckers*!'

'They'll claim I led them on,' I said, shaking my head ruefully.

'Somehow, this will come back on me.'

'You were assaulted,' Caleb said. 'How is that your fault in any way?'

'These kids come from money,' I said. 'Their folks donate generously to Ashton Wood and I'll bet the Police Benevolent Fund will be their next beneficiary.'

Caleb looked at me, aghast.

'That's a horrendous thought, Bella.'

'I know, but it's true. When I was doing my PhD, I carried out extensive research on people just like Philo and I am here to tell you, Caleb, that for him to be the way he is, his parents are to blame. They'll already be doing damage control.'

'But what happened to you is indefensible.'

'It'll be painted as boyish high jinks. I hate to say it, but you probably won't walk away scot-free either. They'll try to get you on assault charges.'

Caleb shrugged.

'I was acting in your defence, that has to count for something. Anyway, I don't have much to lose,' he said. 'I'm only a supply teacher. I can do other things.'

'Oh,' I said. 'Like what?'

'I've got a few strings to my bow.' He grinned, munching on a fry.

'Secretive much?' I asked.

'You can't blame a bloke for wanting to be just a little mysterious,' he said.

I looked at him. He was ridiculously handsome. He was kind. He had put himself and his career on the line to help me today. He looked up and met my eyes.

'Thank you, Caleb, for saving me,' I said, reaching over and squeezing his arm.

'I did what anyone would have,' he said. 'You don't need to thank me.'

'You took on three teenagers, two of whom are bigger than you are,' I said. 'I'm not sure many of the staff would have done that, if I'm honest.'

'Well, lucky I came along when I did then,' he grinned.

I got home at eleven thirty that night.

James still wasn't in.

I went straight to bed.

I never told him what happened that Friday afternoon.

Chapter 13

Charlotte

He called me out of the blue after I helped find his missing files.

It was early evening. I was eating noodles and watching *Buffy* Season 6 Episode 7, 'Once More, With Feeling', the musical episode. I have seen it thirty-five times, and I will watch it again. It's a great episode.

I answered my phone and it was Edward Flood, one of my colleagues at Tech Helpdesk.

'Charlie, there's a geezer here asking for you. Switch put him through to me, but he says he wants to talk to you.'

I was not on shift, and I told Edward that.

'Bloke says he wants to thank you for something.'

I thought that was weird, but I told Edward to put him through.

'Hello, is that Charlotte?'

I thought I recognised the voice, but I was not immediately sure.

'Yes, this is she.'

'Charlotte, it's James at Astley, Clifford and Kenworthy. From the other night. You helped me find my file in the cloud.'

I knew right away who it was. I had thought about him several times. Most callers are not nice. But he was. He was not rude or aggressive or mean. That is unusual, in my experience.

'Yes, James. I remember you.' I couldn't help but smile to myself. Had he been thinking of me as much as I had been thinking of him over the past few days?

'I wanted to tell you, the deal is going through. It was a success. A really big success.'

'That's good,' I said. 'I'm glad it went well.'

'I … I don't think it would have happened if you hadn't helped me.'

'You already thanked me,' I said. 'I was just doing my job.'

'I wanted to thank you again, though. I am really grateful to you.'

'You're very welcome,' I said, trying to stay as professional as possible.

'Is there a way I can send you something? A card or a gift?'

I told him that really wasn't necessary.

'I'd like to.'

'It's against company policy,' I said.

That was a lie. I did not know if there was a policy of that

98

nature, but I felt there probably should be. I made a mental note to send the idea to Edward.

'Okay then,' he said. 'I just ... I just wanted to talk to you. Tell you how much what you did meant to my firm. To me.'

'That's very kind.'

And I did think it was.

He hung up and I put back on *Buffy*, but try as I might, I could not concentrate. I usually sing along and I have tried to teach myself some of the dance moves. That evening, after James called, I was unable to think about anything else.

I paused the episode and opened my laptop, going to the website of his firm, and clicked on the M&A practice group link. It didn't take me long to find his name on the list of lawyers on the team.

James is not a typically handsome man. In his corporate photo, he looks a bit stiff, but his eyes are kind and his smile seemed genuine. I sat and looked at him, wondering what it might be like to sit with him in person.

The text underneath his photograph told me that he advises corporate clients on mergers and acquisitions, reorganisations, joint ventures and general corporate advisory work. I was not completely sure what all of that meant, but it sounded impressive.

I am not always good with people in real life. I can talk to them on the phone and I can send messages on social media and chat forums but when I am in the same room as someone, I find it hard to talk. My brain freezes up and I often find I'm unable to speak. I thought, for some reason, that might not be the case with James Fitzpatrick.

I suddenly wanted to be in the same room as him very much.

His biography said he had studied at Oxford University and Trinity College Dublin.

I sat and looked at the photo with its kind eyes and pleasant features for a while longer, then clicked out of it and closed my laptop.

I decided I would try to forget about James Fitzpatrick.

People like him did not end up with people like me.

Chapter 14

Bella

My union rep suggested I take some time off, so I told James I'd been given some leave to prepare a new subject I was going to be teaching next term, and he didn't question it. Sometimes it helps that James is so self-involved. I was secretly delighted with this, as it gave me some much-needed space and time to get deeper into my research for my PhD. A wealth of new research had been published that linked in with my work, and I planned to use my time reading up on new developments.

And I wanted to see what Grosvenor had been up to in the intervening years. It didn't take me long to see that Isotech had gone from strength to strength. Their CEO's net worth had increased from £34 billion in 2010 to £40 billion in 2019. Making him number 7 in the richest CEOs in the world.

I found photographs of him at various global functions and events, usually in the company of beautiful models or actresses. The fact he was married was never referred to – another example of the usual rules not applying to Grosvenor. He was often pictured with other world-renowned business leaders or politicians, shaking hands and slapping backs.

In each image he was beaming from ear to ear, apparently as pleased with himself as a man could be.

The time off was supposed to help me get over what had happened, but in reality it just ended up making it worse.

If I wasn't seeing Grosvenor playing up for the cameras, I kept on seeing Philo's face leering over me. I'd be in the crush of the Tube and I'd be sure I could feel hands on me. I'd wake in the middle of the night smelling the awful, sweet-scented energy drink-laden breath blasting into my face and I'd scream, but of course, there would be no one there.

Not even James. He was staying late in the office most nights, coming home in the small hours of the morning and going straight into the spare bedroom. I was so wrapped up in my own pain, I didn't care.

I was shocked at how hurt I was by the whole thing.

You might find that surprising – I'd almost been raped – but I'd spent my life telling myself I was made of sterner stuff. I'd studied aggression, I had an understanding of the darker side of human nature, and had even explored a bit of it myself in my younger days.

When I was much younger, in my first couple of years at Trinity and before I met James, I'd dabbled in some purely physical relationships where I pushed my own sexual boundaries.

I wanted to see what I liked and didn't like, how turned on I could get by certain stimuli and where my lines were in terms of pleasure and pain.

It was an interesting period of exploration and self-discovery. I enjoyed most of what my partners and I experimented with, and now I've been there and done that, I probably wouldn't wish to revisit most of it again.

It's funny. There were times back then when I'd allowed myself to be placed in vulnerable positions by sometimes more than one man, and I'd never felt threatened. I'd always believed I was in control. Yet, after the attack by Philo, I was forced to re-evaluate those experiences, and now I found myself wondering if I had always been reckless and placing myself at risk without even knowing it.

Had I been blind to the pitfalls and dangers around me?

I had admitted to myself that I was spuriously attracted to Philo, even though I never had the slightest intention of doing anything about it. But had I unconsciously projected that unspoken want?

The truth was, I had no idea.

And that frightened me.

I spent two weeks agonising over it all, and then decided it was a waste of time.

I needed to go back into work and face my fears.

Chapter 15

Charlotte

I tried to stop obsessing over James Fitzpatrick.

To do so, I did what I have spent the last ten years of my life doing: I sat at the desk in the corner of the living room of my apartment and I answered calls from people having computer-related problems. I updated and moderated the two websites I run, Buffyfanpage.org and Browncoat.org, a *Firefly* fan page. I visited my mother, who was a resident at St Hilda's Nursing Home in Earl's Court, and I went to my Saturday art class.

I did all these things, and as I did, I struggled not to think about James Fitzpatrick.

Except I was thinking about him all the time.

I found this fact disturbing. I consider myself self-sufficient, and I take pride in not being dependent on anyone else for any of my needs. Yet suddenly, without warning, I find myself wanting something from another person.

And I do not know what that something is.

I thought about it last night as I ran on the treadmill I keep in front of the bay window in my living room. I do forty-five minutes every evening, starting at three miles per hour and building up to eight before dropping back to five, then three, then one. I usually listen to a podcast as I run: *Imaginary Worlds* or *Hello From the Magic Tavern*. Since James has come into my life, I haven't been able to concentrate on anything, and I find that I get to the end of an episode and can't remember anything I've just listened to.

To pass the time as I ran, I pondered what's behind my fixation.

I decided that, while I certainly am attracted to James, it's not just a physical longing. I don't consider myself to be a deeply sexual person. I have had boyfriends, and one girlfriend while I was in college, and these experiences were all satisfactory, but I have been without a physical relationship for five years and I don't particularly miss it. If I ever become aroused, I masturbate and that usually makes the feelings go away so I can get on with my day.

This has not worked with James. As soon as I climax, he is on my mind again.

So I don't think the connection is purely a sexual one.

My next thought was that I might be lonely. The majority of my relationships are with individuals with whom I interact online, and most of these I have never met in the physical world, nor do I have any desire to. My visits to my mum in the nursing home and my art classes fill in any gaps, and usually only serve to remind me why I do not enjoy being around people.

The part of my life where I spend most time in direct contact with others is through my work, and most of that contact isn't with good people.

I do not let it stop me providing an excellent service, though.

As this thought crossed my mind, I realised I had failed to adhere to this policy when James called that night. I had explained what he had done and even outlined how it could be rectified, but I had mostly done it for him. I told myself I took this course of action because he had an important meeting and time was limited, but in truth, I believe I was showing off. For a reason I still do not comprehend, I wished to impress him.

And it seems he was impressed. The fact he called me again suggests he was very impressed indeed.

But why was that so important to me?

I am still none the wiser.

What I find particularly alarming is my desire to know everything I possibly can about this man. I have never felt drawn to social media. If you had asked me one week ago what social media I use, I would have told you I do not have a Facebook page, I do not tweet and I have never indulged in the falsity of Instagram. TikTok seemed to me to consist of bad lip-synching videos, and Snapchat seemingly a platform for the transmission of dick pics.

None of these sites held any attraction for me.

But this past week I have created accounts on all of them so I can find out what James Fitzpatrick's life is like.

Something many people don't realise about social media is that it can provide a doorway into any of the user's personal email addresses. I already had access to James's work emails. It was a simple matter to get into his personal account.

To my bemusement, it was a mess. It seemed James Fitzpatrick never deleted a single email, nor did he put them in folders and archive them. His entire life was laid out like a dismembered jigsaw puzzle, and it was such a mess I almost logged off and went elsewhere to try and find out the information I was after.

I spent three nights running various searches, delicately picking through the communications that languished in his scatter-gun email dump.

And of course I had a good look at his social media, too.

And to my disappointment, I gleaned very little.

He has a Facebook page he has not posted on since 2015. His Instagram is more up-to-date, but even here he has not added anything to his grid in three months. His Twitter account is all retweets, mostly of headlines from various legal journals and the *Financial Times*, with a few sports-related tweets too. He has neither a Snapchat nor a TikTok account. His LinkedIn page is a simple work biography, similar to the one on his firm's website.

By piecing together snippets of information, I learnt about Bella. She is thirty-four years old and is a teacher. She is stereotypically beautiful. He and Bella do not have children. This was good news; it meant less baggage. They live in an apartment in a prestigious gated complex in Chelsea that it seems they rent.

James has one picture of himself with a friend, Ralph Bastible, at a rugby match. Ralph is on every social media platform, and James features in a lot of his posts. Ralph likes posting photos of him and his 'mates', out drinking, usually at sporting events. Ralph tweets a lot about both rugby and cricket. I do not understand the rules of either. I tried to google what some of these tweets might mean but got bored. I noted that James likes almost everything Ralph posts. And almost nothing his wife does.

After a thorough analysis of James's emails and social media posts over the past five years, I know that his interests are, in descending order: his job; the legal profession; the Conservative Party – I cannot discern if he loves them or loathes them, because it is difficult to tell if he is celebrating their behaviour or being ironic in some of his posts; sports cars; rugby; American alt-country music – he seems to like an artist called Gillian Welch, whom I googled and while I like some of her songs, her image and the lyrics she writes seem completely at odds with what I know about James (perhaps he is more complex than he seems); Marvel comic books and their associated movies.

The main thing I have learned from my research is that James is very focused on his job. I am not sure how much time he really devotes to anything else. I took it, however, that the fact he had mentioned the Marvel universe to me that night while we worked together shows that it means something to him.

I do not know what knowing all this random information about James means.

But I am glad I know some things about him.

I hope the knowledge will help me to sleep better.

Chapter 16

Detective Sergeant Harvey Brennan

Police Report – Detective Sergeant Harvey Brennan, Violent Crimes Task Force, London Metropolitan Police 19th March 2019

The facts of the case:
Joel Borden, the principal of a private secondary school, Ashton Wood, which is situated in the City of Westminster, dialled 999 at 13.43 p.m. on Friday, 8th March 2019, reporting that an employee of the school, Bella Fitzpatrick, a 34-year-old science and maths teacher with an address in Chelsea at Flat 3, Elm Park Gardens, London SW10 9QW, had been attacked by three students at the school.

- When the uniformed officers arrived on the scene, they found that Caleb Westlake, 33-year-old physical education supply teacher with an address at 32 Byrd Park, London, KT2 5LU, had come upon the students in the act of assaulting Ms Fitzpatrick, and had intervened, using physical force to subdue them. Two of the boys, Philo Armitage and Algernon Asquith, were injured. William Kincaid fled the scene.

- Mr Westlake corroborates Ms Fitzpatrick's story. The location where she was assaulted is a narrow walkway between two buildings and is the only route she could have travelled to get from the classroom where she was teaching to the main school campus. Mr Westlake asserts he decided to go to meet her, with the intention of walking with her to the staff room so they could eat lunch together. This caused him to disturb Ms Fitzpatrick's attackers during the alleged assault. Mr Westlake is an accomplished mixed martial artist, fighting at middleweight for an amateur team based out of the Fighter's Gym in Twickenham.

- Philo Armitage, a 16-year-old student at Ashton Wood, with an address at 32a Cadogan Lane, London SW1X 8PH, asserts that Ms Fitzpatrick has been having a sexual relationship with him since the start of the school year.

- Algernon Asquith, 17, with an address at 15 Warwick Way, London SW1V 1AA, was present at the scene, and has been named by both Ms Fitzpatrick and Mr Westlake as being involved in the assault. He states that he witnessed Armitage and Ms Fitzpatrick together in an intimate capacity on numerous occasions.

- A third boy was at the scene: 16-year-old William (Bill) Kincaid, also a student at Ashton Wood, with an address at 18 Archbishop's Park, London SE1 7DG. He managed to get away when Mr Westlake came upon the scene, and was reported missing for two days, but has since returned home. We are in the process of arranging a formal interview with William and his solicitor.

- Armitage asserts that Ms Fitzpatrick asked him to meet her at the classroom to the rear of the school at 12.30 p.m. on Friday, 8th March, and to bring two friends along. The plan was to have group sex in the classroom as it was isolated from the main school building. Armitage notes that he was slightly delayed, as his previous class finished a few minutes later than scheduled, and Ms Fitzpatrick came in search of him. They had just met and were on their way back to the classroom when Mr Westlake happened upon them. According to Armitage, he, Asquith and Ms Fitzpatrick were already engaging in consensual sexual activity, and Westlake became angry and attacked them.

- Mr Westlake states that when he arrived on the scene, Ms Fitzpatrick was on the ground and the three students were assaulting her: specifically Asquith and Kincaid were holding her down while Armitage was in the process of attempting to rape her. Westlake asserts that when he pulled the boys off his colleague they became aggressive and he had no choice but to retaliate using physical force.

- All four parties were taken to St Thomas's Hospital, London, SE1 7EH, where they received medical attention and where a full forensic examination was performed upon the four individuals involved. The results of the examinations were as follows:

o Mr Westlake had grazing on the knuckles of both hands consistent with his statement that he had been forced to strike both Armitage and Asquith about the head and face.

o Philo Armitage's jaw was dislocated and was reset by medical staff. Bruising and abrasions on the soft tissue matched the shape and size of Mr Westlake's hand, and some skin fragments with Mr Westlake's DNA were found in the wounds.

o Algernon Asquith's nose was broken and had to be set and packed. He had one broken tooth and another two had been knocked out. Saliva and fragments of tooth belonging to Asquith were found in striations on Mr Westlake's knuckles.

o Bella Fitzpatrick was found to have a wound in the back of her head, which was consistent with landing badly when she was knocked off her feet and thrown to the ground. There was also a pattern of cuts and scratches to her face, which are consistent with an assault. She was found to have bruising about her pelvis, which matched her report of being genitally groped by one of her assailants.

o As part of the forensic examination, skin and blood cells were taken from beneath Ms Fitzpatrick's fingernails. On testing, the DNA in these cells was found to be a match for DNA taken from a hair follicle taken from a comb in William Kincaid's home. Ms Fitzpatrick reported scratching the student during the assault.

- Beatrice Muldowney, a 34-year-old teacher at Ashton Wood with an address at 14 Tothill Street, London, SW1A 0RS, provided a statement alleging that Ms Fitzpatrick has been having an affair with Mr Westlake.

- There is no CCTV cover of the walkway where the assault is alleged to have taken place. I have advised Mr Borden, the principal, to rectify this situation.

I finished typing, printed out the report, and signed my name. Stretching my arms, I wondered what exactly was going on at Ashton Wood.

DI Bodhua was at her desk in the squad room, her eyes scanning something on the screen of her laptop.

'All is not well in our esteemed public school,' I observed.

My colleague did not remove her eyes from the computer but said:

'The principal, according to my initial investigation, is a very poor manager of both staff and students.'

'How so?' I inquired.

'The students seem to be permitted a remarkable amount of leeway in their conduct, which seems to be both harmful for their character development and terrible for staff morale.'

'Not exactly a glowing indictment of our education system,' I agreed.

'I don't see a lot of respect on display,' Bodhua went on. 'It's as if the teachers are barely worthy of consideration by the students.'

'Agreed,' I said. 'During my interviews with both Armitage and Asquith I witnessed them speaking about Ms Fitzpatrick using the coarsest of language. I was forced to remind them they were speaking to a member of Her Majesty's Constabulary, and that everything they were saying might be used in a court of law.'

'How'd that go down?'

'Alas, it did not seem to discommode them.'

'Can't say that I'm surprised.'

'Have your efforts uncovered any intelligence on the nature of Ms Fitzpatrick and Mr Westlake's connection?'

'The rumours among the teaching staff is that they're engaged in some kind of extra-curricular relationship, but no one is certain how long it's been going on, or precisely what the nature of it is.'

'Ms Fitzpatrick is married,' I observed, 'but I'm told her husband did not come to the school on the day of the assault.'

'I wonder if they're estranged,' Bodhua said. 'Or maybe she didn't want him to know what happened, as it would highlight her shenanigans with Caleb, or Philo or both.'

'Perhaps we should follow up on that,' I mused.

'We should,' Bodhua said, closing her laptop and gazing at me. 'Another valid theory is that she and her colleague started an affair, he found out about her also being involved sexually with students, and in a fit of pique beat said students up.'

'Which is, more or less, the story we are being asked to accept by the students themselves,' I said.

'It's a bit of a reach, isn't it?'

'I'll admit I am uncertain of its veracity.'

'It is,' my colleague said, shaking her head ruefully, 'a bit of a shitshow.'

'There is too much we still do not know,' I said. 'All we can say for certain is that there is something very wrong going on at Ashton Wood.'

'And Bella Fitzpatrick is at the centre of it,' Bodhua said, finishing my thought for me.

Chapter 17

Bella

As soon as the two weeks were up, I forced myself to go back to Ashton Wood. I'd received a call from my rep to tell me there would be no problem in extending my paid leave, but that felt to me as if I'd be letting *them* win. And I couldn't do that.

Someone must have told the police I was returning, because they were waiting for me at reception when I arrived. They were there, I was informed, to re-interview both me and Caleb.

The two detectives hastily stood up from the comfortable leather armchairs when they saw me come in through the door. The male police officer introduced himself as Detective Sergeant Harvey Brennan. He was probably in his fifties, a fair-skinned short, skinny, sandy-haired man, with a stubbled chin and sharp, darting eyes. He was wearing a suit that had gone out of fashion fifteen years ago, and a blue anorak. The female detective was Detective Inspector Carol Bodhua. I would guess she was around thirty-five, maybe six inches taller than her male counterpart. Her skin was a deep dark brown and she wore her hair in braids. Her suit might have been taken off the rail in a very trendy boutique just that morning, and she had the build and coiled energy of an athlete.

Caleb was already there, and he caught my eye and gave me a tight, reassuring smile, before they whisked us away to separate empty classrooms. I tried to ignore the students craning their necks as we walked past. Clearly, we had been the main topic of gossip and intrigue over the past couple of weeks. Bodhua took Caleb, so I got Brennan. As we settled down on the uncomfortable plastic desk chairs, the detective took a wrinkled and grimy-looking notebook from the pocket of his anorak, and then fished about in his trouser pocket until he found the stub of a pencil.

'You could keep notes on your phone,' I said. 'There are loads of apps that would make it very easy for you.'

He put a pair of wire-rimmed glasses on, looked at me solemnly and said nothing for a while.

'Do you trust those devices, Ms Fitzpatrick?'

I didn't quite know what to say.

'Do you mean phones?'

'Yes,' he said. He had a slight Irish tinge to the edge of his accent. I suspected he'd been in London for most of his life, but Ireland was definitely in his past. Somewhere out west, I thought. Kerry, or Clare, maybe. 'Phones, computers, tablets. All of those things. Do you feel you can trust them?'

'Well, I've carried a phone for years at this stage, detective, and none of the ones I've owned has ever exploded in my pocket.'

He made an odd sound, a kind of wheezing hiss. I thought he might be having a coughing fit, but then I understood he was laughing.

'No, I'm not asking if you trust them *physically*. I'm asking if you think they're secure. I've heard it said we're all carrying around surveillance devices. They listen in on our conversations, record our movements, and can even be used to influence our behaviour.'

'Yes, I've heard all of that,' I agreed. 'But these days it's hard to live without one.'

'You could be right,' Brennan said, and gave one of those wheezes again. 'Now, if you don't mind, and I appreciate this will be stressful for you so we can take our time, but I would like to go through what happened to you here at the school on Friday the eight of March?'

'I already gave a statement,' I said, not wanting to rehash the events of that awful day.

'Oh, I know that,' Brennan tutted. 'I'd just like to hear for myself what occurred. I may bob in and out with a few questions here and there, but that's just my way. Don't be put off by it.'

'Alright,' I sighed, realising I really didn't have a choice in the matter. 'Where do you want me to begin?'

'Tell me about your relationship with Philo Armitage.'

'I was … *am* … his maths teacher. He's my student. That's all there is to it.'

'Have you ever been assaulted by a student before, Ms Fitzpatrick?'

'No, not by any student other than Philo.'

'And how long have you been teaching?'

'Around eight years, I've been here since two thousand and eleven.'

'What did you do before that? If you permit me to be so bold, eight years suggests you started in the education game a little bit later than usual.'

'Before that I was doing a PhD and lecturing in psychology in City.'

'So you're *Doctor* Fitzpatrick then?'

'No. I'm afraid to say that I never completed the research.'

'Might I ask why?' he asked.

'My husband got a job at a very auspicious law firm, so money wasn't an issue, and I experienced some … health issues.'

He nodded and scribbled away in his dog-eared little notebook.

'What was the nature of those health issues?'

'They were not physical, per se.'

'You had a mental breakdown?'

I shrugged. 'Crudely put, detective, but I suppose it sums it up.'

'What was your doctoral research on, Ms Fitzpatrick?'

'The suppression of aggressive behaviours in people in executive positions in large companies. I was interested to see if aggression would seep out into other areas of their lives.'

He stopped scribbling for a moment and looked up at me sharply.

'Well now, I have to say that sounds very interesting. What did you learn?'

'I told you, I never got the chance to finish my work.'

'No, but I'll bet you a nice shiny pound coin you drew some conclusions, though,' he said, laughing.

'Well. Well, yes, I did.'

'Would you do me the honour of sharing your informed opinion? I have my own theories, you see, but I'm always open to hearing other perspectives.'

'I came to believe it depended very much on the person,' I told him. 'Some people can channel their aggression quite successfully into safe methods of expression – music or art or sports – and these people can stay in high-pressure jobs for a long time and not suffer any ill effects. Others bottle their feelings up, and these are the individuals who end up having ulcers, heart attacks and strokes. And then there is a third group.'

'And what do they do, this third group?' Detective Sergeant Brennan asked, leaning forward, seemingly enthralled by my exposition.

'They can't control the limits society places on us. Their innate violence has to come out somewhere, and they finally explode and people around them get hurt.'

The little man nodded vigorously.

'Yes, yes indeed. I find that most interesting. Very astute.'

'Thank you.'

'Now, might I ask you to direct that informed perspective to your own situation, and that of young Mr Armitage and his friends.'

'Algernon Asquith and William Kincaid.'

'You remember their names.'

'They tried to rape me. I'm not likely to forget them.'

'That is your assertion.'

'That is what happened. What possible reason do I have to lie about it?'

'We're getting ahead of ourselves,' Brennan said, raising his hand as if to slow me down. 'Using the theories you developed during your research, why do you think a young man like Philo Armitage – a lad who has everything money could buy, and a bright future ahead of him – why would he want to throw all that away by committing a violent crime on school property in the middle of lunch hour, the time he was most likely to be discovered and interrupted?'

'He did it because he wanted to and thought he could get away with it,' I said firmly. 'It's as simple and as complicated as that. Philo Armitage had never been made face the consequences of anything he did in his life. He made a pass at me a few days before the attack, which I rebuffed, then sexually assaulted me in a corridor, which I reported to the principal. I don't think Philo liked that someone had said no to him.'

'Do students usually make sexual advances on their teachers?'

'Detective, I don't believe for a moment that you're naïve or innocent. It's not unheard of; sometimes they develop crushes, but it can be managed with the right support from the school.'

'I don't dispute that, Ms Fitzpatrick, but there is a world of difference between fantasy and reality.'

'For the majority of students, I would agree with you. But here, at Ashton Wood, we cater for the children of the wealthy. The idle rich. For these kids, the line between fantasy and reality is often blurred, because they never really have to fantasise. If they want something they have the means to make that desire a reality within a very short space of time.'

'For material things, yes,' Brennan said. 'But isn't it different when that wish involves being intimate with someone?'

'Philo is good-looking for a kid of his age,' I said, choosing my words carefully. 'He's smart enough, in his way, and he is rich beyond most people's wildest dreams. I doubt he gets refused very often when he sets his sights on a girl.'

'Yet you decided not to accept his attentions.'

'I'm his teacher. I wouldn't go there.'

'You've just told me you think he's a good-looking young man.'

'I said he was good-looking for a kid; I was being objective. It doesn't mean I'm attracted to him and willing to risk my career and marriage on a quick fling.'

'He's sixteen. Hardly a kid. He is, in fact, at the age of consent.'

I sighed and rolled my eyes. This was juvenile.

'Yes, but in my eyes, he's a child. And even if I were interested in conducting a sexual relationship with Philo, which I am not, as a teacher it is one of the worst abuses of power, and also illegal.'

'Can I then ask why Philo Armitage alleges that you have been in a relationship with him for a year. That it was you, in fact, who suggested he and his friends meet you in that walkway on the lunch break that Friday.'

'This is unbelievable,' I spluttered 'Let me get this straight: he's saying I *wanted* to have sex with all of them? In school? During class time?'

Brennan shifted uncomfortably on his chair.

'I agree it is distasteful, Ms Fitzpatrick. But these young people – they have a different set of values. And really, who are we to judge? I've been married to the same person for thirty years. I've never been with anyone else. Childhood sweethearts, we are.'

'That's nice, detective,' I said. 'But it doesn't really do much to enlighten my situation. I can promise you that I did not invite those three boys to meet me for an illicit lunchtime orgy.'

'It has also been mentioned by more than one person I've spoken to, that you and Caleb Westlake have been having an affair, too.'

I felt my face flushing and did my best to hide it. I don't think I did, though. I saw him register my discomfort.

'I actually can't believe this,' I said. 'Caleb and I are friends, and nothing more. This is a school. People love to gossip. I must have lots of spare time if I'm managing to have simultaneous affairs with a teacher and a student.'

'Ms Fitzpatrick, would you please accompany me to the security office for a moment?'

'Yes, of course,' I said.

But I didn't really want to. Because I knew what was coming.

'The good thing about a crime occurring in a school is that there are lots of closed circuit security cameras for us to examine,' Brennan said as we left the classroom and headed down the corridor towards the office. 'Now, I want to show you a couple of different clips our boys in the Tech Squad were able to isolate for me.'

A few minutes later, we were sitting in front of the bank of CCTV monitors.

'Here's the first clip I want to show you,' he said. 'This was taken in the corridor outside classroom 5A on Tuesday, March fifth at twelve twenty-eight. You have class, with Philo's group, from eleven thirty until twelve thirty. So here we are, twelve twenty-nine and the students are all coming out. There, that seems to be the last one. No sign of you yet, though.'

I knew exactly where he was going with this.

'Now I'm just going to roll the tape forward a smidgeon. So you can see no one comes out, no one comes out, and then … well, you can see for yourself, here *you* come. In quite a hurry too, looking a bit flustered. And then, two minutes later …'

He moved the tape forward again.

'Here comes Philo. Am I right that his shirt appears to be open?'

'He always wears it like that,' I said. 'They all do. He's got a t-shirt on underneath. It's a flagrant breach of the uniform policy but the students always get away with it. Just look around the building.'

'You'll agree it looks suspicious, Ms Fitzpatrick.'

'Not really. I already told you. He waited back after the rest of the class had left, and he tried to come on to me.'

'Ms Fitzpatrick, I am not going to waste your time by making you sit through them, but I can show you half a dozen recordings from outside that room over the past few weeks, and in each of them you leave five to ten minutes after the other students, and shortly after you do, Philo emerges.'

I felt my stomach turn over.

'He made a habit of hanging around and asking me stupid questions,' I said, not even finding myself believable. 'I'm a teacher. If a student asks for help, you endeavour to give it to them.'

'Okay. Allow me to show you these next two items of interest.'

He hit a button and the screen changed.

'This one was taken from a camera in the staff room,' he said. 'As you can see. And we can now clearly make out you and – that is Caleb Westlake, is it not?'

Caleb and I could clearly be seen chatting. And then he put his arm around me. It was a friendly gesture, not sexual, but as I watched, I saw myself slipping my own arm about his waist. I couldn't even remember doing it. But there was no denying I had.

'I won't linger on that one,' Brennan said, hitting the button to change the reel again.

'It means nothing,' I said, though there was nothing but resignation in my voice. 'Caleb was comforting me. I'd just been attacked!'

'Here's what I think could have happened, Ms Fitzpatrick, and I'll admit, it is just a theory, and someone with your knowledge might laugh at me, but I'll ask you to hear me out.'

I said nothing. I knew what he was going to posit, and I was sick to my stomach at the thought of it.

'I think it is not beyond the realm of possibility that you and young Mr Armitage had been engaging in a secret affair for months, maybe even longer. I think somewhere along the line you also began a relationship with Mr Westlake. Westlake, of course, had no idea he was sharing you with at least one member of the student body. You arranged to meet Philo – maybe you asked him to bring some friends, maybe that was an idea of his own, I can't be sure – and somehow Caleb Westlake found out.'

'This is absurd,' I said, suddenly feeling very tired.

'Did you know Caleb Westlake is a mixed martial artist? He trains at a gym in Twickenham, and has quite a successful track record, too. Those lads didn't stand a chance against him. He came across you in a clinch with the kids and lost his cool. Gave them a right good hiding.'

'You're wrong,' I said. 'You are so wrong about this, it's not even funny.'

'I assure you, Ms Fitzpatrick, I do not find anything about this situation funny. The three lads involved have been asked to remain away from the school pending the outcome of this investigation, as I'm sure you're aware. Did you know that William Kincaid went missing for two whole days after the alleged assault? Whatever your Mr Westlake did to him scared him so much, he went into hiding and only emerged once he thought he was safe, much to everyone's relief. We didn't know if he was still alive. Luckily for you and Mr Westlake, he showed up physically unscathed save for some scratches. Had his injuries been of a more serious nature, I shudder to think of the consequences. As it is, there are a lot of questions that require answering, Ms Fitzpatrick, but what I can be sure of is that this case is getting more and more complicated the closer I look into it.'

I felt like screaming.

There is no such thing as secrecy in a school, and the arrival of the police on that Monday and both mine and Caleb's classes being cancelled for the morning meant that we were officially the talk of the school.

It seemed opinion was split down the middle. Some of my colleagues tiptoed around me, behaving as if I might burst into tears at any moment. Others I caught taking furtive glances at me, acting as if I might have caught some kind of transmittable flesh-eating virus. Nobody approached me that day to ask how I was.

I gritted my teeth and just got on with things as best I could. Until three o'clock on Monday afternoon, that is.

Because at that precise time, I walked into my applied maths class to find a picture pinned to the middle of the whiteboard. It was a screenshot scene taken from a porn movie. My face had been photoshopped onto the woman, and the grinning visages of Philo and his two cronies had been placed on the men. I looked at it and heard the sniggers from the assembled yobs behind me, and felt a rush of anger and resentment that surprised me in its intensity.

In one motion I ripped the picture from the board and crumpled it into a ball, and then walked briskly out of the room and straight to the principal's office. Joel was on the phone when I walked in, but the fury on my face told him it was time to hang up.

'Is everything alright, Bella?' he asked with a mix of concern and anxiety written across his face.

I tossed the bunched-up page onto his desk.

'Ummm …' he said, looking nervous. 'What's this?'

'Take a look for yourself,' I said, trying to get my breathing under control.

He looked at the ball of paper warily, keeping his hands

suspended in the air, as if even touching the desktop it was sitting on might infect him.

'It's not going to bite you, Joel,' I snapped.

Gingerly, using his thumb and forefinger, he picked up the offending article and tentatively unbunched it. When it was open he gazed at its contents for a second, and then placed it face down. He had gone pale.

'Gosh,' he said. 'That's really quite distressing, isn't it? Where did you find this?'

'Yes, Joel, it is quite distressing,' I said with a hint of contempt in my voice. 'I could add offensive. Abusive. Twisted. And very possibly illegal. The fourth form applied maths class thought it would be super fun to stick that on my whiteboard. I think you might find that creating that and posting it in a public place is tantamount to publishing pornography.'

'Perhaps we're getting a little ahead of ourselves,' Joel said. 'It has been a very fraught few weeks and emotions are running high.'

'You're making excuses,' I said, 'for the inexcusable.'

'As educators, we also have to be mindful that images of those three boys were used as well. Their parents will have to be informed *again*.'

'Seriously?' I said, my tone becoming shrill. 'I come to you with this, and you're worried about those evil little bastards?'

Joel blinked as if I had just slapped him.

'There's no cause for that type of language,' he said. 'As principal of Ashton Wood you must know I have a duty of care to both staff and students.'

'And it is outrageous those three were not expelled!' I said, and I was shouting now.

'You are fully aware that an investigation into precisely what happened is ongoing,' the principal said stiffly. 'No decisions can be made until that has been accomplished.'

'So the word of two of your staff is worth nothing?'

'Both your and Caleb's accounts will be taken into consideration.'

I wondered if I might be going mad.

'I cannot believe what I'm hearing.' I sat down on the chair, cradling my head in my hands.

'Are you aware Philo Armitage was brought to hospital with a dislocated jaw and Algernon Asquith sustained a broken nose and lost two teeth? Not to mention the fact that Bill was so terrified that he disappeared for a few days. This is gravely serious, Ms Fitzpatrick. The school is being sued by the parents. A criminal investigation may well be pending.'

'A criminal investigation?' I said, not believing what I was hearing.

'Yes. Of course.'

'Against whom?'

'I would have thought the answer to that is obvious,' Joel said. 'You and Caleb.'

That was the straw that broke the camel's back.

I pressed my hands on the desk and leaned in close, so we were almost nose to nose.

'Fuck you, Joel,' I said slowly, making each word count.

And then I turned and stormed out.

I found Caleb in the sports centre and motioned for him to come over.

He shouted some instructions to the kids, who were playing dodgeball, and jogged towards me.

'How's it all going?'

'They're hanging us out to dry,' I said, and then the tears came.

'Oh Bella,' he said, turning me around so the kids didn't see me crying. 'Come on, let's pop into my office for a second. Give you a chance to recover.'

'Now, what's happened?' Caleb asked, and in reply I threw my arms around his neck.

He returned the hug and held me.

It was the first time I'd felt safe all day.

His body was pressed against the length of mine, and I could feel the hard muscle of his chest, and beneath it the soft rhythm of his heartbeat. The rise and fall of his breath was soothing, and as we embraced, he stroked my hair. Gentle, delicate brushes of his fingers.

Breaking away from him for a second, I put my hands on his slim waist and looked up at him.

'I don't know what I'd have done without you,' I said.

'You don't need to worry about that' – he was stroking my cheek now – 'I'm right here.'

We gazed at one another. I saw a deep longing in his eyes. And something else. It was that something else that puzzled me, because I didn't have a notion what it was.

'Bella,' he started to say haltingly, stretching my name, elongating the 'l' sound.

'Yes, Caleb?'

'Bella, you're in trouble.'

'I know. I just told you that.'

'No … I … I think it's much more than that. I believe you're in real danger.'

'I know you're just trying to help,' I said, and then, almost without realising, I raised myself up on my tiptoes, and I saw he was leaning down towards me, and our lips were almost touching …

And I couldn't do it. At the last moment I pulled away, stepping back so we weren't touching any more.

'Caleb, I …'

'No. No, this was me. I'm so sorry, Bella. I don't know what I was thinking.'

'Please don't apologise,' I said.

'I'd best get back out to the kids. I'll … I'll talk to you later, yeah?'

He left me standing in the office, breathing in the scent of mouldering sports gear and stale sweat.

Chapter 18

The feelings I had for Caleb alarmed me.

I didn't want to call them feelings. I told myself they were simply urges. Lusts, perhaps, would be a better term. Animalistic drives. Wanton desires. Whatever phraseology you choose to adopt, the end result was the same.

I did wonder if, after the attack from Philo and his crew, I was just trying to experience a healthy, positive sexual connection. Or maybe it was simply because Caleb had saved me? I wondered briefly why, after an assault, I would want any kind of physical connection with anyone at all, but the truth is, sensible or not, I did. But seeking such a thing from anyone other than James just seemed wrong.

I'd be lying if I suggested I wasn't dumbfounded by this turn of events, and I made a concerted decision as I left the school (despite having walked out of one class and still having two more to teach) that I was going to do something proactive to combat the compulsion.

So I did the only thing I could think of, and redirected it. Towards my husband.

I tried to call him as I drove home.

I tried his mobile first but it went straight to voicemail.

I could have left a message, but to be honest, I really wanted to talk to him. I thought it was time I told him about the attack. About how I'd been feeling. About my reasons for wanting to get back to my research. About everything. Leaving a message on his voicemail, which he would probably listen to in three days' time, seemed a waste of effort. That was if he listened at all – I thought it likely he'd just skip over it when he heard it was me, and after our last few conversations, I wasn't sure I blamed him.

So I tried calling the office.

'Astley, Clifford and Kenworthy, Mr Fitzpatrick's office.'

'Hello Delia, it's Bella. Can I talk to James, please?'

'Oh, hi Bella! I missed you at the Ritz. How have you been?'

'I've been good, Delia, just really busy with work. Is James available?'

'I'm afraid he's on a conference call at the moment.'

'Do you think he's likely to get off it any time soon?'

'How long is a piece of string? I wouldn't bank on it. Can I give him a message?'

I thought about that. But said:

'No. I'll see him at home. Thanks, Delia.'

'Any time.'

And she was gone.

I stopped by the off-licence on the way home and picked up a bottle of Sancerre, James's favourite wine. The brand I bought wasn't the most expensive – I went for a Cherrier, which only set me back just a little over twenty pounds, but this was a wine we'd loved when we first got together, guzzling glass after glass as we stayed up all night talking and laughing and planning our future.

I got home and put the bottle in the fridge and then, without even taking off my coat, I opened my laptop and sent an email to James's work address. I knew he'd check it, so I figured this was the best way to get my message to him.

Bella Fitzpatrick bellfitz1@gmail.com
Mon 25/3/19 16:58

To: James jamesfitzpatrick@ack.co.uk
Subject: Sancerre and a Chat

Hi James,
The last time we spoke, I know I didn't respond in the way you wanted me to. I was hurt and angry, and I wanted to hurt you too. That wasn't fair. You've been working so hard and I know you are so close to your dream of making partner, and even though I probably haven't expressed it, I really am proud of you.

James, I've been having a tough time recently. When you told me you were scared of my resumption of my doctoral research, I did hear you, and I'd really like to sit down and talk about the reasons why I want to, and why

I think now is the time to do it.

I also want to talk about some things that have been going on at school, and, more importantly, how things have been between us.

When I married you, James, I wanted it to be a forever deal. I still do. But unless we change how we've been treating one another, I'm scared we're not going to make it.

I love you. I believe you love me.

So let's put that fact front and centre, and have a chat about how we're going to rescue what we've got.

I've bought a bottle of Sancerre. When you get home tonight, why don't we have a few glasses and just talk, honestly and openly, about how we've both been feeling, and what we'd like from one another going forward? No bullshit, no recrimination, just two people who deeply care for one another doing what they can to make each other happy.

I know you're very busy, but if you could even send me a text to let me know what time you'll be home, I'll be here with the wine chilled.

I love you very much.

Bella

Xx

After I pressed 'send' I took off my coat, hung it up and then hoovered and dusted the apartment, even though Chen, our cleaner, had just been in the day before. I had a lot of nervous energy to expend, and needed to keep myself busy. I put clean sheets on the bed, and lit some candles here and there, giving the whole place a nice, warm glow.

I checked my phone sporadically. No text came through from James.

I pulled up Miles Davis's *Kind of Blue* on Spotify. There's a track called 'Blue in Green' that James played to me on one of our first dates, and even though a good deal of water has passed under the bridge, it still makes me think of him fondly.

After a shower, I blow-dried my hair and put on just enough make-up, liberally applying Coco Mademoiselle, which I know my husband particularly likes. This done, I put on a dress, a black flowing, silk number that I'd worn to the last firm party we attended.

James had complimented me on it all night, and I liked the way he looked at me when I wore it. He hadn't looked at me like that in a long time.

I wanted him to look at me like that again. In that moment, I knew I wanted us to recover what we'd had.

I started *Kind of Blue* at the beginning, playing it through the speakers on the smart TV. The gentle sound soothed me, and as I listened I set out a dish of olives and a bowl of smoked almonds, and arranged a wheel of brie, some Parma ham, a few slices of good chorizo and some sun-blushed tomatoes on a chopping board, and placed it on the coffee table. I stepped back, considered my display, and added a few grapes from the fruit bowl, along with a small loaf of sourdough and a good bottle of olive oil.

Now it was perfect. Checking my phone, I saw there was still no text from my husband. I took a look at my own email account, but there was nothing there, either. I gazed at the bottle of Sancerre, languishing unopened in the ice bucket I had placed on the table alongside the food.

I reached over, opened it and poured myself a glass.

The clock told me it was ten fifteen.

I felt annoyance prickling at the edge of my consciousness, but tried to push it aside. Any kind of crisis could have hit since I sent the email. He probably just hadn't had time to message me. I could be patient.

I'd only bared my soul to him in an email. A fucking email. Because he was too busy to talk to me.

I took a deep breath. This was important. I could wait.

Five minutes later, *Kind of Blue* was over. Spotify, as is its wont, continued to play, giving me 'So What' again, the album's most recognisable track.

I got up and went into the bathroom, turning on the light and gazing at myself in the mirror, striking a few different poses, examining myself from various angles. I decided, after consideration, that I am worth coming home to.

Kicking off the high heels I'd chosen because I knew they made my legs look good, I went back into the living room and poured myself another glass of wine. Charlie 'Bird' Parker was on now, playing his staccato, free-form bebop. Not romantic at all. In fact, I always find Bird's music difficult to listen to. There's something anxious about it.

But I did not switch it off.

I stood at the window and looked out at the beautiful gardens of the walled, gated complex where James and I lived in lonely luxury, and wondered what I was going to do.

By eleven thirty, I had come to the inevitable conclusion that James wasn't coming home. Feeling deflated and rejected, I went to the bedroom and removed the dress and lingerie I had put on under it, one of the sets James had bought me as a 'gift', although I tell him repeatedly such items are really only presents for him. Leaving the discarded garments on the floor, I pulled on a t-shirt and pyjama bottoms, then climbed into bed and pulled the duvet up to my chin.

I never heard James coming in.

He never apologised for standing me up.

Chapter 19

Charlotte

My feelings for James Fitzpatrick did not go away. If anything, they became more intense. Trying not to think about him did not work, and in the end, my fascination for him caused me to do something I always swore I would not do.

Something I am not proud of.

The work tech support workers do has a raft of ethical implications.

We are gatekeepers, guardians and warriors. I bet many who do the job don't think of themselves in those terms, but they should. What we do demands a wide skill-set and personal qualities most people do not possess. We are a special breed.

Think about it for a moment: every single one of us has the capacity to wreak havoc across the networks and systems of the companies we serve. We have access codes that would enable us to shut down trading and production, hold entire corporations to ransom if we chose to do so. We could easily become the most effective cyber terrorists the world has ever known, because we know the technology behind industry and finance from the inside out.

We know where the bodies are buried.

We are the ghosts in the machine.

I have always been proud that, like a medic who has taken the Hippocratic Oath, I, first of all, endeavour to do no harm to the companies and individuals I serve. Usually, I can help, and can solve whatever issue my clients are dealing with. Sometimes I can't, and when that occurs I know I've reached my limits, and I send them on to someone who can solve their problem.

I never do anything that might have a detrimental effect on the people I am supposed to serve, or on their employers.

At least I never did until Thursday March 28th, 2019.

I was on call that evening and had just finished assisting an accountant who had somehow changed the codes he needed to access his online filing system without knowing he had done so. I went through my usual sign-off, asked him if he would be prepared to fill in our short customer satisfaction questionnaire, and had only just hung up when a notification flashed across the bottom of my laptop screen.

New email received at account jamesfitzpatrick@ack.co.uk

I had set these notifications up while I was going through James's correspondence and hadn't yet switched them off. Since I had come online that evening, I'd received about fifteen of them, all relating to James's work email – I had similar alarms set up for his personal email, but he didn't seem to use it.

I decided, in an impulsive wish to rid myself of my burgeoning obsession, to deactivate the notifications. The less I was hearing about James Fitzpatrick, the better. To do so, I had to log into James's account and switch them off at source.

I was in Astley, Clifford and Kenworthy's system within the space of thirty seconds and had James's emails in front of me within another fifteen. I was genuinely about to click on the settings icon, which would take me to the notifications menu, when I found my eyes drawn to the list of communications. Almost unconsciously, I scanned the Subjects and Senders. Most related to the merger James told me he was working on – I could see the senders were either from Fahlberg Financials or were internal emails from staff at Astley, Clifford and Kenworthy. These messages were labelled F&C Merger.

All were like this until I came across one, sent at 16.58 (as I read it I checked the clock in the corner of the laptop and saw it was 17.05) from Bella Fitzpatrick. It had the subject line: *Sancerre and a Chat.*

I looked at the email and blinked.

I had been through all of James's emails going back more than five years, on both his personal and work accounts, and had found only three from his wife. One had been to remind him to pay a gas bill and had included a jibe about her having to resort to email to get his attention, as he was not answering his phone. Another had been simply a link to a meme of a jubilantly boogying Baby Groot from *Guardians of the Galaxy*, which had the caption: Dance as if nobody is watching. I assumed this was a private joke between James and his wife. The third one was also a link, this one to an Instagram post about a gig by the New Orleans singer, songwriter and guitarist Chris Smither which was taking place on June 2nd in King's Place. There was no supplementary text, so I took that at face value. She was simply letting James know about the concert.

This email looked different. The subject matter suggested a deeper sense of intimacy. As I looked at that subject line, my heart began to pound in my chest. I wanted to read it and I didn't want to read it. The cursor, as if it had a mind of its own, hovered over the email, and then, as if that arrow made the decision for me, I found myself clicking on it.

Text materialised on the screen before me.

I read it but my eyes covered the lines so quickly I might as well have been reading gibberish. I retained not a word. I took a deep breath and read again.

And this time, I absorbed the information. And wished I had not.

Isn't it funny how even a short email can tell you so much about the sender?

Bella was articulate. Thoughtful. Honest.

She loved her husband, and believed he still loved her.

I wanted to cry at that. It made me feel sick to my stomach.

Yet all was not lost. They were having difficulties. That much was also clear. The email was a request for what struck me as a crisis talk. Bella wanted to save their marriage. She asked James for an open and honest conversation. She called it an attempt by two people who cared for one another to make each other happy.

As I read, I felt myself getting angrier and angrier. I was, I realised, experiencing something I had not felt before. I was *jealous*.

Really, really jealous.

I did not want this conversation to happen. And suddenly, I realised I could do something about that.

With one click of my mouse, the email vanished. For good measure, I deleted ten others, chosen at random – this way, if it became an issue and James investigated why he had missed his wife's communication, it would look like a simple software glitch.

Another click opened the account's Trash folder. A third emptied this of its contents, including the offending email from Bella.

Feeling satisfied and guilty all at the same time, I logged out of Astley, Clifford and Kenworthy's system.

I never did switch off the notifications.

Chapter 20

James

It had been a busy day, but not in a bad way.

It was one of those days where you're rushing from one job to the next; you never quite have a chance to slow down, but it's okay, because you can see your goals stacking up in front of you, and you know it's all going to be fine, that you're on top of things, in the zone.

Delia popped her head around my office door once I came off my conference call at around 5 p.m. to let me know that Bella had called, but hadn't left a message.

'She said she'd see you at home,' she told me.

I took this at face value. I'd love to say I considered calling her back, but I didn't. I figured she was calling to add some kind of hassle or stress to my day, and I didn't need it.

So yes, I reckoned I'd find out about whatever it was when I got home, and I didn't think about it again.

I was about to leave for the evening at 7 p.m. – I mean, I literally had my bag on my shoulder and was heading for the door when Clifford barged in to my office, uninvited.

'Where the hell are you going?' he asked me without preamble.

'Home,' I said, although as the word escaped my mouth, I felt something drop in my stomach. I knew I had given the wrong answer. Clifford has always had a threatening presence around the office, but there was a darkness and anger to his tone that I hadn't had directed at me from any of the partners in a long time.

'James, I just received a call from Blake in Fahlberg's LA office. They're urgently looking for an answer on that liability query raised in the due diligence report.'

I tried to look as if this wasn't a surprise to me, but I think my face gave me away to Clifford. I wracked my brains, trying to remember a phone call or a conversation across the course of the day in which this had been brought to my attention, but nowhere in all the fuss and bluster I had experienced could I recall any mention of it.

'Um …' I said, stalling for time.

It was a tactic that didn't work. Nothing came. Tumbleweed blew across my mind's landscape. I was completely blindsided.

And Clifford knew it.

'Can you liaise with Stephanie in litigation and get a response over to Blake tonight?'

'Yes, yes of course,' I stammered.

I knew I was blushing now. I'd fucked up and fucked up

royally, and I didn't know how it had happened. And that scared me. I made a mental note to go back over my diaries and my notes, and have a conversation with Delia, to see where this critical communication had been missed.

As this thought crossed my mind, Clifford gave me the answer.

'Blake said he sent you two emails, both marked urgent, but hasn't heard back from you. I realise you're busy and have a lot of irons in the fire in this deal, but you *cannot* take your eye off the ball for even a moment. Do you hear me, James?'

'Yes, sir, of course.'

'Do you hear me?'

'I do!' I said, louder this time. 'I'll get right on it. Immediately.'

'Missing something of this magnitude has the potential to cost this firm dearly,' Clifford growled. 'In terms of our reputation but, more importantly, *financially*. Now, put down your bag, order in some Chinese in and *do your job*.'

He stalked out without saying goodbye.

I didn't bother to order food. I wouldn't have been able to eat even if I had. I immediately went to my email account, but could find no emails from Blake, or anyone else for that matter, referring to the liability issue.

I checked every folder, including the Junk filter and the Drafts list, but if Blake in LA had sent me urgent communications, I could see no sign of them.

Abandoning my search, I picked up the phone and called the LA office of Fahlberg Financials myself, but of course Blake was unavailable. I left a message for him to call me on my mobile and hightailed it down to the litigation department on the first floor.

Stephanie Billman, my equivalent in the litigation group, was already at work on the problem – it seems Clifford had already been on to her, which made me feel even worse. I should have been the one coordinating all of this.

I'd been with Stephanie for an hour when Blake rang, and I discovered that Clifford had saved my tail. He told Blake that I'd been speaking at a conference on behalf of the firm, and that it was a job I'd just been handed that day, so while he was mildly irritated at having to wait, it was still only 1.30 p.m. in Los Angeles, so there was no real harm done.

Stephanie and I listened as he talked through the aspects of liability he was concerned with, and then Stephanie and I worked solidly until midnight, drafting a proposal for Copping Insurances that laid out which liabilities Fahlberg was happy to take on, and which it would like to see addressed before the merger went through.

It was 1 a.m. by the time I gave the document one last read-through, and 1.15 a.m. precisely when I emailed it over to Blake.

I waited ten minutes, and then called Blake's office to ensure the email had arrived, and was relieved to learn it had.

Then I sat back in my chair, closed my eyes, and took some deep breaths.

I was exhausted and genuinely scared. Where had those emails gone?

I was on the verge of calling Charlotte, but as I was about to do so, something occurred to me. There were probably people within the Fahlberg organisation who were not in favour of the merger. People who, for reasons of politics, personal animosity or just good, old-fashioned fear, would do what they could to slow the cogs and jam up proceedings.

Maybe I had just fallen foul of something amounting to in-fighting.

I had enough brownie points saved up from my work on the merger so far to be able to absorb a bump in the road like this.

Feeling a bit better, I went home. I could hear Bella snoring gently in what had once been our bedroom. I experienced a moment of sadness, but then weariness took hold, and I fell into the bed in the spare room, and knew nothing until my alarm woke me four hours later.

Chapter 21

Transcript of Interview with William Kincaid at the Offices of the Violent Crimes Task Force, London Metropolitan Police.

Interview conducted by Detective Sergeant Harvey Brennan and Detective Inspector Carol Bodhua.

Also present Jeremiah Kincaid, suspect's father and his solicitor, Franklin Weatherfall.
28th March 2019

DS Harvey Brennan: Interview commencing 6.22 p.m. William, do you know why you have been called in for a formal interview with myself and DI Bodhua?

WK: Because he brought me in.

HB: Let the recording show that William has nodded towards his father, Jeremiah Kincaid. Why do you think your dad brought you in to see us, William? Or should I call you Bill?

WK: My friends call me Bill. So you can call me William.

HB: Very good. William it is.

WK: He dragged me here because of all that shit that went down at the school. With Philo and that slutty teacher, Ms Fitzpatrick.

CB: By which you mean Ms Bella Fitzpatrick. Your teacher.

WK: She never taught me. She was Philo's science teacher. I think Algy had her for maths when he was in, like, third form or something.

HB: We are aware that some events transpired between you, your two associates, and Ms Fitzpatrick. Can you tell us more?

WK: Yeah. And that maniac Westlake.

HB: And Mr Westlake, of course. Can you explain why you characterise him as a maniac, William?

WK: Because he's mental. If I hadn't been quick on my feet he'd gave beaten the snot out of me. He came out of nowhere and like ... well, he just went for us.

CB: Could you back up a bit, William, and help us to put things into context? What were you and your friends doing when Mr Westlake allegedly attacked you?

WK: I don't like talking about all of this with my dad here.

HB: I'm afraid we have no choice but to have an adult present with you, William. If you're not comfortable answering questions in front of your father, we could get your mum? An uncle, a teacher maybe?

WK: Fuck no. That'd be worse.

HB: Then I'm going to need you to answer the question DI Bodhua has asked.

WK: We were meeting Bella for like ... well ... she was going to *do* us, you know what I mean?

CB: By which you mean she wanted to have sex with you, Armitage and Asquith?

WK: Yeah.

HB: Had you engaged in this type of interaction with Ms Fitzpatrick before?

WK: No. Philo had been banging her since September, though.

HB: And you saw them together?

WK: I didn't, but everyone knew. It wasn't really a secret; he told everyone. She's hot. If I was shagging her, I'd have probably done the same.

HB: So, as I understand it, Philo Armitage informed you and young Mr Asquith that Ms Fitzpatrick wanted to have sex with you over the lunch break on that Friday afternoon.

WK: Yeah. It was gonna go down in that old room at the back of the school. No one ever goes there, so we knew we wouldn't be disturbed.

HB: But things didn't go according to plan?

WK: No they fucking did not. Philo was late finishing up his last class, and Algy had to take a shit, and by the time we got underway, I think Bella reckoned we'd stood her up. Like that was going to happen!

CB: Why do you think she believed you weren't going ahead with the plan?

WK: We met her walking back towards the school.

HB: But you reassured her you had simply been delayed?

WK: Philo talked to her. I don't know, it was like she wasn't into the idea any more.

FW: I think what my client is suggesting is that Ms Fitzpatrick was engaging in some … foreplay. *Not* that he believed she was withdrawing consent.

HB: Is that what you're saying, William?

WK: She tried to walk past us. Told Philo to get out of her way. That if he didn't, she'd call the principal. As if old Borden was going to do anything! Philo's dad fucking *owns* him.

FW: I think I would like to consult with my client, detectives.

WK: I want this done. I want to tell the truth.

JK: Son, maybe we should stop for a few minutes and talk to Franklin.
WK: Dad, I didn't do anything. I think she knew what she wanted. It was all a game to her.

FW: I can't protect him unless he allows me to, Jeremiah.

JK: The boy says he's innocent of any wrongdoing and I believe him.

HB: So to be clear, you're indicating that Ms Fitzpatrick *did not* in fact want to engage in a sexual encounter with you boys?

WK: She was just playing hard to get.

CB: Did she say no?

WK: Yeah, but …

CB: That meant she didn't want to. Don't they teach you about consent at Ashton Wood?

FW: Are you speaking as a police officer or a woman, Detective Bodhua?

CB: Both.

HB: So Ms Fitzpatrick expressed that she did not want your attentions. What happened then?

WK: Philo went to put his hands on her, and she tried to stop him, and I … I guess me and Algy tried to get her back in the mood, too.

HB: How did you do that?

WK: I dunno. We put our arms around her a bit. Let her know we were still good to go and that she would have a good time.

HB: How did you get those scratches on your forehead, William?

WK: What?

HB: You have three long scratch marks that run right across your forehead. They're faded, almost healed, but I was wondering how you sustained them?

WK: I don't know. I've been living in a fucking shed for the past few days. Anything could have happened. It was like a … a survival type of situation. Would you ask Bear fucking Grylls where he got a few scratches?

HB: Ms Fitzpatrick did not give you those in an attempt to defend herself?

WK: Fuck no.

CB: You and your friend were trying to encourage Ms Fitzpatrick to return to the classroom for your pre-arranged bout of lunchtime sex. You were doing this through petting and fondling. Was she asking you to stop touching her?

WK: She didn't really say anything.

CB: Did she try to get away from you?

WK: (laughing) She ran back towards the classroom where we were meant to be shagging her. What were we supposed to think? If that's not a come-on, I don't know what is.

HB: And you pursued her?

WK: It was like a game. No one was threatening her or anything.

HB: Did Ms Fitzpatrick, in the course of this game, end up being thrown onto the ground?

WK: Algy pushed her down onto the ground. He wasn't rough. It was like he was taking control. Girls like that.

CB: You've been seriously misinformed, William. Where did you do your research? Pornhub?

JK: Is that really necessary? The lad is here answering your questions.

HB: When did Mr Westlake arrive?

WK: Right then. He must've been with Bella in the classroom, cause he came around the corner, the way she'd come.

HB: He didn't come from the school?

WK: No. I saw him before the others did, cause I was kind of kneeling up.

CB: Kneeling up? Why?

WK: It's difficult to explain.

CB: Try me.

WK: You ever done, like, a threesome?

CB: I have a good imagination.

WK: Okay then. Let's just say I was waiting my turn.

HB: You saw Mr Westlake coming towards you?

WK: Yeah. He was moving fast. Running, like. I tried to warn the others but it was too late. He was shouting, saying he'd fucking kill us.

HB: You managed to get away though?

WK: He actually grabbed me first, threw me off Bella. I landed quite a bit back from her, about three or four yards from where we'd been. I was going to go back and fight him, but by then Philo was up and Algy got involved too.

HB: So you ran?

WK: He was like a man possessed. I thought he was going to kill one of us. He was shouting and screaming, not even words, just noise. It was scary. I wanted to get away, and I thought if I came back to the school, he'd come after me. He's not normal.

HB: William, don't you think your decision to go into hiding shows you knew your actions were wrong? That you were afraid what the consequences might be?

WK: I was not and am not afraid of you guys. It was fucking Westlake who scared me. As I was running away, he shouted after me he'd kill me if he ever saw me again.

HB: And you took that literally.

WK: He took Philo out with a punch and a kick, and I thought I heard something break when he hit him. Poor old Philo went down like a sack of potatoes.

CB: And Asquith?

WK: I didn't wait around to see what happened to him.

HB: Is there anything else you want to tell us, William? Anything I forgot to ask you?

WK: Just that the whole thing was weird.

HB: You were there to have an inappropriate and illegal interaction with your teacher. That's bound to raise some moral conundrums for you.

WK: No. I was cool with that. It was just like … I remember Bella's eyes just before I ran away. It was like she was enjoying the whole thing.

CB: Has it occurred to you she was elated because she had just been rescued from a sexual assault?

WK: No one assaulted anyone.

CB: Did you once hear Ms Fitzpatrick say she had arranged this 'gangbang' with you and your mates?

WK: No, but Philo told me!

CB: And, in your experience, Philo is honest to a fault? You've never heard him boast about anything you thought might not be strictly true?

WK: Well …

CB: You've just answered my question.

WK: I want to say this, and then I'm done on this subject. Bella Fitzpatrick wanted to be with us. And I think she wanted mad fucking MMA head Westlake to witness the whole thing. I reckon it was all a setup, and me and Philo and Algy, and even you two, have all fallen into her trap. We've all done just what she wanted.

HB: Interview terminated at 6.48 p.m.

Chapter 22

Bella

I really tried with James. I reached out, and he refused to take my hand. I made it clear that I wanted to talk to him, to try and rebuild the aspects of our relationship that were crumbling and damaged, but he did not share my desire to do so.

I woke up the day after my husband stood me up, and I felt empty. Bereft. Lost.

And as I lay there in the bed I used to share with James, I decided I needed to do something about those feelings.

A voice in my head reminded me that James worked ridiculous hours for us, for our future. But then, I never asked him to do that. I would have been happy continuing with my studies, living a less lavish lifestyle. He could have worked in-house for a company, where he would be guaranteed regular hours, and have a great work/life balance.

The future I saw for myself was as a lecturer in a small college somewhere, teaching undergrads by day and perhaps doing the odd bit of commissioned research and media work in my spare time. I thought the occasional piece of funded work might pay for a holiday. I'd always wanted to go to Iceland to see the Northern Lights.

James hadn't said much when I mentioned this to him in the early days of our relationship. But then, he often didn't react when I told him about my hopes and dreams. They didn't seem to hold much interest for him. I asked my husband about this – wasn't he interested in my inner world?

'Of course I am,' he'd said. 'I'm just filing all those little nuggets away, until the moment we can make them real together.'

I'm still waiting for that moment to arrive.

So after James left me sitting alone in our luxurious apartment, sipping wine that he was never going to share with me, I decided it was time I made a few dreams come true for myself.

The next day, I left my first class a few minutes early so I was in the staff room before anyone else. I made my usual double espresso and positioned myself on a seat right inside the door. Caleb was, irritatingly, five minutes late and the place was already full when he came in, but I still managed to catch his eye.

I looked good, and I knew it. My hair was perfect, my make-up flawless. I'd worn a pair of jeans I knew fit me well, and while I'd kept all the buttons on my shirt closed during my first class,

I'd opened the top two as soon as I arrived into the sanctity of the staff area, showing a tasteful, but still eye-catching, amount of cleavage.

Caleb noticed. I could see him taking it all in. But I had now rejected him twice and we had the allegations hanging over our heads, so he let his eyes rest on me for a moment but didn't linger for long.

'Hi Caleb,' I said.

He came to a stop right in front of me, looking and smelling as good as he always did.

'Hi Bella.'

'Can you chat a minute?' I asked, nodding at an empty set of chairs beside the door.

Much to my disappointment, he raised his reusable coffee mug and gestured to the coffee machine. 'I'm just going to grab and run, sorry, Bella. I promised I'd fill in for Jason. He's got a doctor's appointment.'

Jason was one of the phys ed teachers.

'I want to get in there early to set up some games. So I'll get a coffee and head right to the sports centre.'

'No worries,' I said, and he whisked past me.

I watched him add milk and sugar to his coffee while trying to work out what I should do next. Should I just let him go? Admit that I'd had my opportunity and had allowed it to slip through my fingers?

Mug in hand, he made his way through the crowd, nodded at me as he went by, and was almost out the door when I heard myself say, 'Caleb?'

He stopped and looked back at me.

'Yeah?'

I almost froze at that point. No one was paying any attention, but I was still somehow convinced the entire room was listening. Shaking the feeling off, I ploughed onwards.

'Any chance you want to go out for dinner with me tonight?' I said sheepishly.

He grinned.

'I do. Very much.'

'Ask me then.'

'Would you like to go out with me, Bella?'

'Tonight,' I said. 'I want to go out with you tonight.'

'Okay. Dinner and drinks.'

'That sounds perfect.'

'Where will I pick you up?'

'I'll meet you at Fellini's in Notting Hill,' I said. It was the first place that came into my head, and I wanted to be far away from Chelsea, and from Temple. I didn't want us to run into anyone we knew.

'Cool. I'll see you then.'

I gave him a look full of promise.

'You can count on it.'

He smiled at me, and it was full of potential, too.

And then he disappeared to his class.

That night I wore a dress I'd bought for an evening out that James and I were meant to go to but had to cancel at the last minute when a work thing came up. The outfit, a beautiful red ruched Isabel Marant dress, had hung in my wardrobe since then, gathering dust. I figured now was the time for its maiden voyage.

When he met me outside Fellini's at 8 p.m., Caleb was dressed in a charcoal-grey suit with an open-necked black silk shirt. He looked at me, his eyes consuming me hungrily. I saw him register that I was doing the same.

Then, without saying a word, he leaned over and kissed me.

It wasn't a long kiss. It was actually fairly chaste. The only part of us that touched were our lips. But I can say, without fear of exaggeration, it was one of the hottest, most arousing kisses I have had in a long time. With that one gesture, Caleb took my breath away.

He guided me in through the doors into the cosy, candlelit restaurant. The place wasn't busy, and as soon as we sat down I relaxed. Caleb doesn't drink as he's so into his fitness, and ordered a sparkling water. I ordered a glass of Pinot Grigio, but just sipped at it, not wanting to get even a little drunk. I fully intended to have all my faculties about me. I wanted to *feel* everything.

Over dinner of a shared creamy burrata, fresh ravioli gamberi for me and a spicy crab risotto for Caleb, we talked. I barely tasted a thing.

Caleb came from a long line of teachers. He'd always known this was the job he was destined for, and he loved working at Ashton Wood.

'I already feel like I'm part of the place,' he told me. 'Everyone has made me feel very welcome. Until recently, that is. But I'm hoping the charges against me will be dropped, considering I was acting in your defence. I don't feel like I used unreasonable force. I thought those guys were going to rape you. I have faith in the law.'

'You sound like my husband,' I said, and his face dropped.

I could have kicked myself.

'I don't know why I said that,' I said. 'I'm sorry.'

He waved it off.

'You've fitted into Ashton Wood really well,' I said, eager to keep the conversation going. 'I think a lot of the female teachers would love to make you feel even more welcome.' I gave him a suggestive wink in an attempt to get the flirty conversation back on track after my gaffe.

'Well, your friend Bea, maybe,' he grinned.

'Oh, so you noticed, did you?' I teased.

'I'm not blind,' he said. 'It'd be hard not to.'

'I think she's quite insulted you've not taken the bait,' I pointed out.

'Oh, she's certainly pretty. It's just that she's …'

'A bit too in-your-face?'

He made a *comme ci, comme ça* motion with his hand.

'Little bit.'

'And I wasn't?' I said, taking a sip of my wine.

'You were barely in my face at all!' he said, shaking his head in mock annoyance. 'I was trying to get your attention from the first day I arrived.'

'I genuinely didn't notice,' I said, and that was true.

'Well, I was. Just so you know. I was drawn to you from the first time I saw you.'

I liked that. The fact he didn't faff about with suggesting we were soul mates or that it was love at first sight. He was telling me he was attracted to me, and whether the fact was convenient or not, I was attracted to him. And my being there told him I'd stopped fighting it.

'All it took was a violent, hideous crime to get us together,' I said, deadpan.

He stared at me agog for a moment, then burst out laughing.

'Yes, I don't think either of us could have seen that coming!'

He had such a good laugh.

'How have you been,' he asked me, 'since the attack?'

I sighed.

'It rocked me,' I said honestly. 'It never occurred to me that something like that *could* happen in the kind of school we work in. Yes, the kids can be awful, sometimes, but did I believe they could be *that* awful? No. I didn't.'

'I think it's the sense of entitlement,' Caleb said. 'Sometimes it's like they think they own us.'

'I agree,' I said. 'The whole experience, and the build-up to it, has sort of pushed me back to some research I was engaged in a few years back.'

'Yeah?'

'Yes. I was studying the links between power and aggression. Have you heard of a man named Tristan Grosvenor?'

'No. Should I?'

'Probably not. He's a very wealthy CEO of an extremely large company. He killed one of his employees, allegedly in self-defence. My thesis took that event as a starting point, and tried to look at the wider problems such behaviour might pose to our society.'

'Sounds really interesting.'

'It was. Interesting and exciting and, at times, terrifying too.'

'Looking at the awful things human beings are capable of?'

'Yes, but it was more ... personal than that. I got to know Tristan Grosvenor really well. He's brilliant and charming and handsome and ... we became close, for a time.'

Caleb was watching me closely.

'I can see how working closely with someone could cause a sense of intimacy to develop,' he agreed.

'Yes,' I said. 'I thought we had an understanding. A mutual respect for one another.'

'But you didn't?'

'No. I did something he didn't like, something I thought he would actually be really pleased with, and he turned on me and it was ... it was awful. Frightening.'

'I'm very sorry,' Caleb said, reaching out and taking my hand.'

'All of this has really ... well, it's brought a lot of that back up again. I haven't felt so threatened, so scared in a long time, and it has triggered not just an interest, but a very powerful desire to understand what turned those boys, kids I thought I knew, children I've passed on the corridor every day, into a pack of predators.'

'I can see how it would,' he said. 'I ... I wish it hadn't happened.'

He squeezed my hand, and I realised we were gazing into each other's eyes.

'You know I'm married,' I said, slowly.

'You're wearing your ring,' he said. 'As I already pointed out, I'm not blind.'

'So you know what this is, then.'

He shrugged.

'I'm not sure I do.'

'What do you think it is?'

'Well, it could be two colleagues going out for a bite to eat.'

'In one of the fanciest restaurants in town?'

'If you're going to eat, it might as well be somewhere decent.'

'Do you think I'd wear this dress if all I was interested in was eating? I'm not even sure I can consume much more without bursting out of it.'

'That's a risk I'm more than willing for you to take.' Caleb grinned.

And that was when I saw Ralph coming up the street.

Caleb saw my expression change and looked at me quizzically.

'What's up?' he asked, craning his neck to try to see what I was looking at.

I shook my head, but as I did so, the trio arrived into the restaurant, and I saw Ralph clock me instantly.

'That's my husband's best friend and colleague,' I said.

'Oh.'

A concerned expression passed over Caleb's handsome features.

'We're not doing anything to be ashamed of,' he said. 'I mean, we're not holding hands, we're not kissing. It's just two work colleagues eating together. That's not so awful, is it?'

I grimaced, involuntarily.

'Do two work colleagues go to an expensive restaurant for a casual dinner?' I asked.

'They might.'

I gave a dry laugh that held no humour at all.

'Do these casual work colleagues dress up in their finest attire for this casual dinner?'

'I don't see why not.'

'Come on, Caleb. This looks exactly like what it is, and you know it.'

I don't know why I was getting so angry at him. It felt as if I had planned a wonderful night, which had gone off exactly as I would have hoped, and then suddenly James and his world had intruded upon my reveries. I was seething, and was upset that the night had to end like this.

He knew it, too.

'Do you want to leave?' he asked.

'That wouldn't look one bit suspicious, would it?' I snapped. I was immediately sorry when I saw the injured look on his face. 'I'm sorry. I'm just upset. So, we'll sit here as if it is the most normal thing in the world,' I said. 'We finish our food, we finish our drinks, and then we leave.'

'Okay. As long as you're sure.'

'I am.'

'Let's finish our food then.'

He took up his fork and ate some of his crab risotto.

'I really am sorry, Caleb.'

I felt awful. He hadn't done anything wrong. I knew I was

feeling shame and guilt. It was as if my husband had walked in and found me *in flagrante delicto*. Which I was aware I would have been, a little later, if the delightful Ralph hadn't put in an appearance.

'That's quite alright,' he said, and tried to smile, although I could see he was hurt and disappointed. 'Occupational hazard of setting my sights on a woman I knew was married. I don't know what I was thinking.'

'I don't know what *I* was thinking,' I said glumly.

'I expect you think I'm a proper player, but I'm really not,' Caleb said. 'I was in a long-term relationship up until just before I came to Ashton Wood. You're the first woman I've been out with since Claudia left.'

'Well, at least you waited until she left,' I said. 'My husband is currently at work. And if I know Ralph and his big mouth, by tomorrow, James will know I was here with you.'

Caleb sipped some water.

'You've really not done anything. Yes, we kissed, but it wasn't for long and it was closed-mouth, if you really want to get forensic about it. It could be passed off as friendly. We came here, we ate, we talked. If you want to spend a few minutes covering a project we might double up on at the school, you can honestly say it was a work meeting.'

I put down my knife and fork and smiled wanly at him.

'You're very kind. Which I probably don't deserve.'

'I like you, Bella,' Caleb said, and I could hear the sadness in his voice this time. 'I really do like you. I don't want to be something you look back on with upset or unhappiness. So let's just write this evening off as a misfire, and I hope we can still help each other out at work, get through the investigation, and have a laugh in the staff room.'

'I hope so too,' I said.

He insisted on paying the bill, and stayed with me until I flagged down a black cab.

'See you in the staffroom?' he said sadly. I gave him a quick kiss on the cheek goodbye, and climbing into the back seat of the cab headed home alone to my empty apartment.

Chapter 23

James

I'm so angry. Furious. My wife is seeing another man.

I was having a much-needed coffee in the office canteen with Ralph, a fellow senior associate on the M&A team. Ralph and I had met on our first day of our training contracts at Astley, Clifford and Kenworthy and had quickly become good friends. We knew the realities of working in a firm like this, and to be honest, sometimes I felt he understood me much better than Bella.

We'd both been at a meeting, yes on a Saturday morning, and Clifford had ripped the whole team a new one over unbilled hours, and we were both feeling pretty raw and tired.

We were both sitting there, next to each other, mugs in hand, with Ralph chewing on a croissant and getting flakes of pastry all down his shirt, as he always does, when he turned to me.

'I hate saying this to you, mate, but I saw Bella last night.'

'Did you? I didn't know she was out last night, but I was in here trawling through a pile of documents as per usual. At least one of us has a life,' I replied absentmindedly, not really acknowledging the warning in his tone.

'Yeah. In *Fellini's*.'

That kind of gave me pause, because Fellini's is a high-end Italian restaurant in Notting Hill. Very expensive, very fancy. Definitely not a jeans and trainers kind of place.

'Must've been a work do,' I said.

Ralph did this shrugging motion he does, which means *'Yeah, like fuck it was.'* I sat up and looked at him.

'What aren't you telling me, Ralph?' I said, getting a bit vexed now.

'She was at a table for two, mate,' he said.

'So?' I asked.

Ralph looked at me as if I was the thickest kid in the class, and the teacher had just given me the simplest sum to do, and I'd still fucked it up.

'It didn't look like she was with a friend,' he said.

'Who was she with then?' I asked, wishing he would stop dragging this out.

'She was with a bloke,' Ralph said. 'And he was … well, he wasn't exactly Shrek, if you get my meaning.'

'Oh,' I said.

I couldn't think of anything else to say. After a few moments I suddenly had an idea:

'You know, that was probably Bob she was with. He's one of the teachers in her school. Bob's gay, so no worries there. She's been mates with him for ages. Goes out with him every now and then to blow off steam.'

Ralph thought about that.

'Haven't I met Bob? At your Christmas party?'

I realised that he had.

'Yeah,' I said.

'This wasn't Bob,' Ralph said, firmly. 'And mate, I don't think this chap was gay, either.'

'How do you know?' I asked.

'Because this guy and Bella looked close. They looked like they were having a good time together, and not in the platonic sense. I'm telling you now, Bella was out to dinner with a pretty damned good-looking guy who was not her gay best friend. And if you don't mind my saying so, she looked like she wanted to be noticed.'

I didn't know what to say to that.

'What … I mean how …' I raked my fingers through my hair, trying to grasp the enormity of the situation.

'I think maybe you should ask her what was going on,' my friend said. 'I mean, I didn't see them holding hands, there was no kissing or canoodling or anything like that, but that doesn't take away from the fact your missus was out for dinner in a very nice restaurant with a good-looking guy and she was dressed like she wanted to impress him. If I were you, I'd want to know more about it.'

Ralph was wrong.

I didn't want to find out about it at all. Sometimes, ignorance is bliss.

Taken from 'Controlled Rage: Mapping the physical and psychological effects of the suppression of aggression responses in professional men and women, and an analysis of socially sanctioned dominance behaviours in the corporate world', PhD thesis by Bella Murphy Fitzpatrick, City, University of London, 2010.

Swiss psychiatrist Carl Jung posits the idea that each person carries within them the capacity for bestial, animalistic violence. He calls this aspect of the psyche The Shadow, and maintained that it is an evolutionary heirloom, a feature of our psychological make-up left over from before our species walked upright.

At one time, Jung suggests, we had claws and very sharp teeth, and we used them to fight for survival.

The concept of The Shadow is a reminder that, if you trace your family tree back far enough, you will reach a branch in which your ancestors were not human. That is a salient point when we are talking about violence and aggression.

At one time, the ability to perform sudden, dramatic acts of violence was essential for survival. In fact, it still is, though now we subcontract the unpleasantness out to someone else so we do not have to watch. Our food is rarely hunted any more. We farm animals so they can be herded to their deaths, docilely walking towards a 'humane' end, performed with surgical precision so the animal experiences as little distress as possible.

The adrenaline will spoil the flavour of the meat, we are told.

No one wants to taste the fear, these days.

Everything we do has become sanitised.

Almost everything. Shows like *Love Island* and *Big Brother* suggest we still enjoy violence as entertainment, we just prefer it to be emotional in nature.

And I'm no different.

Please indulge me for a moment. I'd like to tell you a little bit about myself and how I fit into this research.

I learned when I was in my late teens that I find violence exciting, and that fantasies involving aggressive acts were stimulating for me. I was at first ashamed of these feelings, and it took me some time to integrate them into my sense of self and lose the guilt I associated with them.

But it was a process, and it is one I am still working on.

Yet I discovered it in a relatively unassuming way.

When I was a student, there was an anime society in the university. Anime is Japanese animation, and it runs the gamut from standard science fiction and comedy to ultra-violence and pornography. Every taste is catered for, and I was amazed at how the college was more than happy to facilitate the viewing of very graphic material in its classrooms after hours.

The first time I saw sexually violent material I was appalled. I watched my first such animated movie with my fingers covering my eyes, too horrified to watch for more than a few seconds at a time. Yet I discovered that, after the screening was over and I went home, I couldn't stop thinking about what I had seen.

It took me some time, but before long I had to admit, I

found the material intriguing. Arousing, even. I was turned on by it.

I finally decided it was the forbidden nature of such material. This was the type of thing we had been conditioned into believing was unacceptable, taboo. Our culture had pushed us into thinking that there is only one kind of erotica that is acceptable, and even that was perceived with a certain degree of blushing.

In Japan, where society enforces huge levels of compliance and where there are rules and etiquette to almost everything, entertainment is one of the few areas where the imagination is allowed to run unfettered. Almost nothing is off-limits, which Western culture considers disturbing but our Eastern counterparts view as a safe and controlled way of letting off steam.

During my interviews with Tristan Grosvenor, we discussed intimate relationships, and he was characteristically candid.

'My wife and I have an understanding,' he told me. 'When I am at home, I adhere to what I think of as the rules of domesticity: I am polite, I am not overtly aggressive, I am, to an extent, loving. I make every effort to ensure my wife and family are protected from the more excessive traits I know I possess.'

'You compartmentalise,' I suggested.

'I suppose you could say that.'

'Is that an easy thing for you to do?' I wanted to know.

'I do not need to indulge my sharper impulses at home,' he said. 'I can do that at work where it is appropriate, and I also engage in other … relationships … where I can express some of those wishes and wants when I feel compelled to.'

'So would you agree the death of Gerald Tamlyn was not appropriate?'

'I would not agree. Under the circumstances of what occurred, it was wholly appropriate. I was physically assaulted and believed my life was under threat. So responding physically was, within those parameters, completely appropriate. However, if someone disagrees with me at a staff meeting or in the board room, a physically violent response would not be acceptable in that instance.'

'You mentioned other relationships where you can express your more aggressive tendencies.'

'I did.'

'Would you care to expand on those?'

He smiled at me, and there was humour and warmth and … possibly something else in that smile, too. It caused me to tingle, that smile.

'Suffice to say my wife and I have always had an understanding,' he said. 'If I feel a compulsion to engage in certain types of physical intimacy which my wife would find distasteful, she is content for me to find someone who is happy to participate in such physical acts with me, so long as it is done quietly and does not impact on our home life.'

'Would you characterise these as long-term relationships?'

He thought about that.

'Some. Not all. There have been people I have returned to, but in this age of the internet it is not difficult to find people who share similar tastes.'

'And your position as a relatively well-known figure in

international business doesn't make you vulnerable to people who might wish to make your tastes public?'

'I am not unaware of that risk,' he said. 'Only two individuals have ever tried to blackmail me.'

'What happened?'

'It was dealt with.'

'Did you pay them off?'

He smiled again.

'I did not.'

'But it was resolved satisfactorily?'

'It was for me.'

Western society has made some steps forward in accepting that many of us harbour violent kinks. Horror has become much more mainstream and shows like *American Horror Story* and movies like the *Hostel* films have normalised the idea that enjoying dark stories as entertainment need not be a dirty secret.

The explosion of interest in light BDSM with the *Fifty Shades of Grey* novels, which started out life as *Twilight* fan fiction, showed that what had been believed to be niche sexual practices were actually much more commonplace than was previously accepted.

And the public conversation about consent ensured that everyone was aware of how to approach rough sex and potentially violent role play. Once such things are safely planned with a full and frank discussion of what each partner wants and expects, there is no reason not to explore all kinds of fantasy.

Danger only exists where consent is not sought and if participants do not know what they are agreeing to.

By denying The Shadow, we are denying ourselves.

It struck me as I talked to Tristan Grosvenor that he rarely denied himself anything. And by adopting a highly compartmentalised lifestyle, he had found a way to (usually) keep his activities away from his family and out of the press.

Chapter 24

Detective Sergeant Harvey Brennan

Detective Bodhua and I met at 9 a.m. on the 30th of March to discuss our progress on the case.

'Caleb Westlake is clean,' my colleague told me. 'No criminal record, and I spoke to two schools who had employed him previously, and they've got nothing but good things to say.'

'It would seem he suffers from White Knight Syndrome,' I said, more to myself than to her.

'That doesn't make him a bad bloke.'

'No. Just an overzealous one.'

'What have you got on Bella Fitzpatrick?'

'She told me that she is originally from Ireland, but I couldn't find much information about her family situation before coming to London. I sent an email to our garda colleagues in the National Bureau of Criminal Investigation in Dublin, to see if they might be able to turn up anything on that front.'

'What about her professional career? Surely that's easy enough to track down.'

'Yes, absolutely. Through the Department of Education I was able to confirm she studied first at Trinity College Dublin, before moving to London to study at City, University of London. I made a call to the registrar at City and was informed that Ms Fitzpatrick completed an MA in Organisational Psychology followed by an unfinished PhD in Psychology that was funded by the Department of Psychology at that institution.'

'So she's a smart cookie.'

'Yes, but all did not go well for our Ms Fitzpatrick.'

'Do tell.'

'This research was discontinued for a period of a little over eight years.'

'So you're saying she'd gone back to it?'

'I am. It appears that she completed a PGCE before taking up her teaching post at Ashton Wood. However, it seems that her PhD studies resumed in January of this year, meaning that Ms Fitzpatrick is currently a postgraduate researcher once again.'

'On the same topic?'

'She's continuing her research, picking it up where she left off. I asked if a copy of any work done was on file, and was informed that, as the research was funded by the university, they own all findings. I requested that the unfinished thesis be pulled, and informed the registrar I would be over directly to have a look at it.'

'And?'

'I was met by the Dean of the Psychology Department, who seemed distressed as to my presence.'

'How so?' Bodhua asked. 'That seems like a strange reaction.'

'It seems this is not the first time Ms Fitzpatrick has brought unwanted attention down on the university.'

'What exactly is this woman studying?'

'Her thesis is entitled' – I pulled a wad of pages towards me – '"Controlled Rage: Mapping the physical and psychological effects of the suppression of aggression responses in professional men and women, and an analysis of societally sanctioned dominance behaviours in the corporate world".'

'Snappy title.'

'I won't pretend the work isn't technical, and I was unable to understand much of what I read. I was, however, able to glean that the work had been inspired by a case I was involved in earlier in my career, the murder of a young business executive named Gerald Tamlyn.'

'She was looking into a murder?' Bodhua asked, coming over and picking up Bella's thesis from my desk. She began flipping through the pages, her interest piqued.

'She was. Tristan Grosvenor, the billionaire who had beaten Tamlyn to death, seems to be held by Ms Fitzpatrick with some degree of fascination, and she refers to him in virtually every chapter, comparing and contrasting the works of other sociopaths, and referring to an interview she did with him at some length.'

'Are you saying Ms Fitzpatrick is like one of those lonely women who become fixated by prisoners on death row and end up marrying them?'

'I'm not sure. Possibly.'

'Is this Grosvenor guy still at large?'

'He is. His case was thrown out on a technicality.'

'Don't you just hate it when that happens?'

'Very much. I have met him, many times, and I believe him to be a seriously dangerous criminal. I am, in fact, convinced we have not caught him for any other crimes only because he is too clever to have been caught and has the funds to hide his actions effectively.'

'Interesting, but where does that leave us?'

'Here is a case involving violent crime and Tristan Grosvenor's name has come up. I cannot believe that is a coincidence.'

'So what do you want to do about it?'

'His offices are in Mayfair. How about we pay him a visit?'

'It's a Saturday, Sarge.'

'He'll be there,' I said. 'Tristan Grosvenor is always there.'

Grosvenor made us wait for an hour before seeing us.

'I want it noted for the record I am agreeing to a meeting with you under grave sufferance,' he said, reclining in his enormous leather chair, as his secretary meekly ushered us into his office. 'Who's your new friend? I haven't met *her* before. What happened to your old partner?'

'DS Granger retired. This, as I told your receptionist, is DI Bodhua.'

'Charmed, I'm sure,' Grosvenor said.

'Hello,' Bodhua said flatly.

The room reeked of money. He was sitting behind a beautiful antique mahogany desk, and had – what looked to my untrained eye – valuable art work hung on the walls, and a huge Persian rug covering the floor. A drinks cabinet in the corner was laden down with crystal decanters and glassware, making me yearn for a stiff drink as I took a glance at his smug face.

'Can we get on with it?' Grosvenor said, drumming his fingers on the huge desk. 'I'm very busy and police officers bore me. Even hot ones like DI Bodhua.'

'Your feelings about our being here are really of no consequence,' I told him. 'I just want to know one thing.'

'What?'

'What is your relationship with Bella Fitzpatrick?'

'The name rings a bell,' he said, yawning. 'Buggered if I could tell you why, though.'

'She began a psychology thesis in two thousand and nine focused on you and your predilections,' I reminded him.

'Oohhhhh,' he said, sitting forward for the first time since I'd been admitted to his inner sanctum. 'Her. Yes, I remember her. Pretty little thing. Fascinated by me and what made me tick. Which I found a most attractive quality.'

'I can see how you would,' I said. 'Did you read what she wrote about you?'

'Yes. It was part of the agreement for her being permitted to do the interview. I insisted on prior approval of everything that she wrote.'

'And you were happy with her analysis of your character?'

I saw something flicker in him then. It was only small. Just a short flash of something. But it was there.

'I was quite content, yes. Her prose struck me as a bit lurid in places, but in the main, I found it all very complimentary.'

'And you have had no contact since then?'

'None. I am quite a busy man, as I'm sure you understand, detective sergeant,' he said as he picked up a gold fountain pen, opened a leather folder and began signing the documents inside. It was an abrupt sign that our meeting was over, and we were still in the dark about the true relevance of Bella and Grosvenor's connection.

When we finally returned to the station after fighting our way through the busy London traffic, I called the Dean of Psychology at City at his home. I was determined to get to the bottom of this and I was missing some vital facts. When he answered the phone, I told him that I had spoken to Grosvenor and wanted to clarify a few things he said, namely about his final approval on Ms Fitzpatrick's research.

'He did have final approval, that is correct, yes,' the dean confirmed.

'Is that usual?'

'It's not *un*usual. Obviously we prefer that students are permitted to write what they choose, but for a research subject as influential as Mr Grosvenor, there didn't seem much choice.'

'Did he utilise his power of veto at all?'

'That's an interesting story, actually.'

'Please tell me the details.'

'Bella – Ms Fitzpatrick – was publishing pieces as she wrote them, mostly in journals and other academic publications, but as word got out that she had interviewed Grosvenor, she received some requests from less high-minded corners of the publishing world.'

'Such as?'

'*The City Grapevine* asked Bella to write an article for them about high-profile murderers.'

'I take it from your tone she accepted the commission?'

'Against our advice, she did. I think Bella had certain aspirations and I felt that she may have taken this commission to raise her profile.'

'Was the article widely read?'

'Within certain circles. The magazine is popular among true crime fans, conspiracy theorists and fans of the seedier side of celebrity culture. It's *not* a publication in which we would like to see our PhD candidates' names printed.'

'Am I to take it that Ms Fitzpatrick published this article without allowing Mr Grosvenor to first approve her … her copy … is that the correct term?'

'Yes, quite right. I fear the guidelines of writing for *The City Grapevine* contradicted her agreement with Mr Grosvenor. They would never have accepted him editing her work before them. So yes, it went to print before he was able to influence what was published.'

'Which made him unhappy?'

'In the piece, Bella suggested Grosvenor killed that man, Tamlyn, simply because he wanted to know what it would feel like to do so.'

'Rather damning, possibly libellous,' I suggested.

'It was. Do you know, it caused Isotech's share price to plummet. There was an emergency meeting called in which a motion was tabled to have Grosvenor removed as CEO of the company. He barely survived it with his position intact.'

'Did he contact the university?'

'I spoke to him personally.'

'And how was that?'

'He … he made threats.'

'Of what nature?'

'Mostly legal.'

'Mostly?'

'Well … he was angry.'

'Can I remind you that I am a police officer, and also, perhaps more pertinently, that this is a man who beat another to death with a lump of stone?'

'He said it would be a pleasure to know what it felt like to destroy both me and Ms Fitzpatrick.'

'That's the word he used? "Destroy"?'

'Yes.'

'When I spoke to Mr Grosvenor he said he thought Ms Fitzpatrick was fascinated by him.'

'I see.'

'Did Ms Fitzpatrick maintain a … a scientific objectivity in her research?'

There was a lengthy pause, so long I enquired if he was still on the line.

'Yes, I'm here. There was a rumour among the faculty that Bella had become emotionally involved with Grosvenor.'

'Are you suggesting they were having an affair?'

'That is what I heard, yes.'

'Who was supervising Ms Fitzpatrick's research?'

'I was.'

'Did you confront her about this?'

'I did, but by then it was something of a waste of time.'

'Please explain.'

'Once that article was published, Grosvenor had Bella blacklisted across all media outlets in London.'

'Was that a blow for her?'

'She tried to pretend it wasn't, but everyone who was close to her knew it was. Bella had ideas about becoming something of a celebrity. She thought she could be a pop psychologist, one of those people who appear on TV shows talking about motivational ideas and helping people overcome emotional trauma. Perhaps like that American fellow – Dr Phil.'

That surprised me.

'Having read some of her work, isn't that all a bit lowbrow?'

'Oh, she would have been punching way below her intellectual weight, but Bella Fitzpatrick is a complicated woman. She wanted success and she was prepared to do what she had to do to achieve it. She was devastated when the pathway to a media career was blocked for her. She abandoned the thesis after that.'

'I was under the impression she ceased her research because she decided to pursue a career in teaching?'

'That's what she told everyone. But it wasn't true. No. It was Grosvenor's revenge that caused her to give up her academic dreams.'

'Yet she has returned to them.'

'That puzzled me. But there you go. Perhaps time has given her some perspective.'

I thanked him and hung up. *Fuck*, I thought. I leaned back in my office chair and pushed the door open onto the bustling police floor. 'Bodhua,' I yelled, 'I need you in here, now, please!'

Chapter 25

Bella

James came home early on Saturday evening. I mean technically he should have been at home all day, but again, work is always the priority.

Continuing the irony, he was actually home before me, and was sitting on the couch in the living room when I came in after a day spent researching in City's library. When I pushed open the door, I nearly fell over his briefcase and suit bag, which he had abandoned on the hall floor.

I was surprised to see the unexpected items there, and even more surprised to see my husband sprawled out in his mostly unused spot on the couch, looking sheepish. I didn't say a word. He got up and went into the kitchen and clattered around in there, finally emerging with a glass of whiskey for him and wine for me.

He handed me the drink and sat back where he had been.

'Can we talk, Bella?' he asked after he'd taken a sip of the golden liquid in his tumbler.

'I'm listening,' I said.

'Who was the bloke you were with in Fellini's?'

And there it was. I didn't try to come up with a story. I knew there wasn't any point. The truth is supposed to set you free, so I decided to see if it would.

'His name is Caleb. He works at the school.'

'Are you sleeping with him?'

'No.'

'What was it Ralph saw then? Are you going to tell me it was a work thing? Please don't lie to me, Bella. If there's something going on, will you please just tell me and we can try and deal with it.'

'It wasn't a work night,' I said. 'It was … it was a date, I suppose. He asked me out. I said no, of course, but then, when I tried to arrange a night in with you so we could talk things over, you didn't even bother coming home. I sat here all alone, wine getting warm and food drying up, and you didn't even have the decency to ring and say you'd be late. So I decided that, if you didn't want to spend time with me, I'd go out with someone who did.'

He blinked, and I could see he was breathing quickly and his colour had gone very high.

'I … I don't know what night you're talking about, Bella. What night was this?'

'That is exactly my point.'

'Did you screw this guy?'

'I already told you no.'

'I don't believe you.'

I spluttered a loud laugh.

'He kissed me, James,' I said. 'Not a long kiss, no tongues and he didn't try to cop a feel or anything pathetic or adolescent like that. But it was a fucking *amazing* kiss. It really did rock my world, and do you want to know why?'

He looked at me, and I saw there were tears in his eyes, and he didn't answer.

'It rocked my world because I could feel how much he wanted me. You haven't kissed me or touched me in … I have actually stopped counting, that's how long it's been.'

'Bella …' he started to speak and then choked, a sob coming out, a sound of pain and misery.

I was hurting him and I was glad. I wanted him to feel the loss and the anguish I had felt for so long.

'I thought about going to bed with Caleb,' I continued relentlessly. 'He is a beautiful man, and I was sorely tempted.'

'Why didn't you?' he managed to blurt out. 'What stopped you?'

'I do not have a fucking clue,' I spat. I could feel myself getting annoyed, and his outrage, which struck me as completely unreasonable under the circumstances, was making me even worse. 'I'm starting to think I should have just gone for it. Let off some steam and have a good fuck while I'm at it. It would have been a win-win for me.'

'What the fuck is wrong with you?' he said through his teeth, and that was when I saw red. I threw my glass, wine and all, at the wall above his head. It smashed into a thousand pieces, and while most of it ended up soaking into the wallpaper, I know a good deal of it splashed onto James.

He sat there, wine and some splinters of glass glistening in his hair, his drink held in a trembling hand, his eyes red and his cheeks flushed.

'What the fuck, Bella,' he said. 'How did we end up back here again?'

He was breathing rapidly, and I could see tears welling in his eyes.

'I don't know what to say to you right now.'

'Then don't say anything,' I shot back, still in the grip of the fury that had overtaken me. 'I am not looking for forgiveness. I know I shouldn't have kissed him, but to be honest, you got off damned lightly. I think I am a saint not to have taken it further. A fucking saint, James.'

He stood up at that and stalked out of the room, slamming the door behind him.

Chapter 26

James

I don't know how I felt when Bella told me about that cunt, but then there was that flash of violence, which brought me right back to the early years of our marriage, and I knew damn well how I felt then.

I was angry and I was scared.

I lay on the bed in the spare room that night, my heart pounding in my chest and every nerve jangling, and I wondered how everything that had been good in my life had suddenly turned to such a pile of ignominious shit.

Then a thought popped into my head, as if out of nowhere: had it really been good?

The question niggled at me.

Okay, there is no doubt that I love Bella, that she has been the love of my life. But we'd had our ups and downs. I try not to think about them, my natural disposition is to try and accentuate the positive, but there have been times when my lovely wife and I have really hurt one another.

And we have come close to splitting. In the first year of our marriage, it very nearly happened.

That first year was a rough one.

Bella was in the middle of her doctoral research, which means her fascination with Tristan Grosvenor was also at its height. I remember that, back in those days, I was still managing to get home for dinner most evenings, and every single meal was spent with her talking about *him*.

'*Tristan said such-and-such to me the other day.*'

'*Did I tell you the story about when Tristan did this, or that, or the other thing.*'

I'd try to tell her something about a case I was involved in or about what Ralph and I had been up to, and before I was finished, she'd cut in with:

'*Oh, something just like that happened with Tristan last week and he did this …*'

I was deeply unhappy with all of it because I knew Bella very well, and I could recognise that what I was seeing was not just intellectual infatuation.

She was falling for Grosvenor. *Had* fallen for him.

But I never raised the issue, never brought it up, not even once. I just hoped it was an obsession that remained inside her head, and that she hadn't acted on it. My dearest wish was that she'd finish her thesis and her daily interview sessions would end, and we'd be able to get on with our lives.

But then she published that fucking article, and everything went to absolute, complete shit.

The article was not a piece of academic writing. It was supposed to be satirical, I think, although if it was meant to be funny, I missed the joke.

The article was about the murder of Gerald Tamlyn, but it was about more than that, too.

In reality, it was a love letter to Grosvenor.

It makes me sick to my stomach to acknowledge it, but it's the truth.

In the article, Bella asserted that people like Tristan Grosvenor are, in many ways, more highly evolved than your average person, and therefore their actions are not so easily pigeon-holed or analysed. She pointed out that business practices perpetrated by CEOs like Grosvenor may seem harsh and even cruel, but are not meant personally. She claimed that the rights of individual workers sometimes has to take second place to the needs of the company as a whole – the needs of the many, which are always served by maintaining profit margins, must always outweigh the needs of the individual.

My wife wrote that, by killing Gerald Tamlyn, Tristan Grosvenor had taken the ultimate step to look after the wellbeing of Isotech's shareholders, and therefore, much further down the line, its employees. Tamlyn, after all, in a bid to further his own ends, was attempting to overthrow the policies and corporate structure of Isotech. He had already initiated litigation, had gone to the press on two separate occasions and had, ultimately, stepped outside the law by breaking into Isotech's offices, allegedly with the intention of assaulting the CEO.

The article concluded with Bella stating that Tristan Grosvenor had told her that the murder of Gerald Tamlyn was, in his eyes, a perfectly reasonable and appropriate action. In other words, that he was right to do it. That Tamlyn had, in a very real sense, gotten what he had asked for.

She signed off by saying that perhaps Grosvenor should be seen as a hero for doing what most of us wish we could but don't have the courage to follow through on.

When the article was published it was as if a hand grenade had been thrown into our lives. Grosvenor went ballistic. He couldn't sue for defamation, because amid the countless hours of interviews Bella had on file, were recordings of him saying precisely what she had quoted. However, Bella had agreed, as one of the conditions of her being permitted to interview Grosvenor, to give him veto of any published works. And she had sent this one in without his prior approval.

Grosvenor's machine clicked into overdrive. Bella had been doing media work for a number of different TV and radio stations, bringing her ability to apply psychological ideas to a range of news items, current affairs and human-interest stories. She was perfect for this: Bella is pretty, articulate, incredibly smart, and her soft Irish brogue didn't hurt one bit.

Grosvenor started his vendetta against her by contacting each and every station in London and making sure she was blacklisted. He had influence over a frightening number of businesses – as a corporate financier and investment broker, he was massively powerful, and he informed the station heads that all companies he had controlling shares in, or who were subsidiaries of Isotech, would withdraw their advertising revenue if Bella Fitzpatrick appeared on any of their shows in any capacity. The effect of this was immediate – my wife's phone stopped ringing.

The way the media works, most panellists and contributors do not have contracts with radio or TV stations but are called in on an appearance-by-appearance basis. At that time in our lives Bella had been getting calls several times a week and was starting to become a recognisable voice and face.

In one fell swoop, my wife torpedoed her burgeoning media career.

It ended there and then, never to resume.

I tried to make her feel better about it, told her it was a storm in a teacup, that it would all blow over, but in truth, I didn't even believe that myself. By then, I'd met enough people like Grosvenor to know he was not going to forgive and forget. Bella had made a grave error – she'd believed the feelings she had for him went both ways.

They did not.

I think Grosvenor enjoyed the adulation and the fangirling Bella lavished upon him, but as soon as she slipped up, she was cut off. She had used his name to advance her career, and misjudged the fact that her attraction to the darker side of life was one that was not shared by the board members of Isotech.

Grosvenor turned on her ferociously, and also did his level best to have her dismissed from City. Luckily, he was unsuccessful as he had already approved each chapter of her thesis, and the article was seen as wholly separate. There was an inquiry into whether or not Bella had behaved in a manner that brought the university into disrepute, but as it had already been established that all quotes were accurate, there was no suggestion she had lied.

The ethics of the article were another matter, but once one enters into a discussion about ethical considerations one is entering into a sphere of such vague greyness, almost nothing can be definitively decided.

And Bella insisted, right from the off, that the piece was meant to be tongue-in-cheek.

The university decided that Bella had acted rashly and without due consideration of the potential fallout of her actions but found no grounds to dismiss her. I always believed this was an easy call to make, as my wife's thesis research was clearly over, due to the fact that Grosvenor was refusing to take her calls and would never sign off on another word she wrote.

So finding in her favour cost City nothing.

The whole thing cost Bella, and me, dearly though.

My wife was convinced Grosvenor would back down, that he would, in fact, see the error of his ways and resume their contact. Her thinking during this time was so skewed, so twisted, she could not see her beloved Tristan in anything other than a heroic light.

This was not his fault, she insisted. He was being given poor advice by people who were jealous of the close relationship she had with him. He was always impulsive, it was a facet of his personality. In a way, she should take this as a compliment – he was treating her with respect, if you thought about it. The fact that he'd gone so hard on her meant he saw her as an equal.

She spent two weeks waiting for the turnaround she was

convinced would happen, and I remember it as the toughest time in our relationship. She didn't eat, she barely slept, she sat with her phone beside her, waiting for a call from the man she was clearly devoted to.

And it caused me some headaches too. My bosses had, of course, gotten wind of Bella's fall from grace, and I'd been hauled in to have a meeting with the partners.

'Your wife is drawing a lot of negative attention onto herself,' Kenworthy said, his face a mask of annoyance. 'So far, it hasn't found its way back to you. We've had feelers out, and there hasn't been a mention of your relationship so far, but we all believe that, if she attempts to push back against Grosvenor, there's no way you can avoid being brought into it.'

'Pull her into line, James,' Clifford demanded.

'How am I supposed to do that?' I asked, the misery plain in my voice.

'Be a fucking man and take charge of the situation,' Astley roared. 'Tell her to thank her lucky stars she didn't go the same way as Tamlyn. Everyone working in the City knows Grosvenor is a psycho. She should be grateful he didn't hire someone to shut her up permanently.'

'Are you serious?' I gasped, suddenly feeling nauseous.

'As death,' Clifford said. 'The fact your wife is still above ground suggests he must have some level of affection for her. Tell her to be content with that and move on. She's still young. She can retrain. It's clear she's a smart girl. There must be a hundred other things she can do.'

'We all have high hopes for you,' Astley said as he concluded the meeting, 'but if you bring any kind of harmful publicity down on this firm, you will be out on your arse faster than you can say *no, please don't!* And Grosvenor isn't the only one who can have someone blacklisted.'

I got home that night, and Bella wasn't there. I cooked us some dinner and waited, but there was no sign of her, and she wasn't answering her phone. I was frantic with worry – what if the partners were wrong and Grosvenor had decided he wanted to have my wife killed? Or what if she'd done something else foolish?

By ten that night I was about to call the police when I heard the key turn in the lock and Bella came in. I could see from her face she'd been crying, and there was a mark on her cheekbone that might have been the early stage of a bruise.

'Where have you been?' I asked.

'I went to see Tristan,' she said, not even trying to hide it. 'I thought I could reason with him. Make him see sense.'

I couldn't believe what I was hearing.

'What in the world made you think that was a good idea?' I asked, trying to keep the shock out of my voice.

'I thought what we had would still mean something to him,' she said, and I could see she was crying, tears streaming down her cheeks.

'What you had?' I asked. 'Bella, what the fuck was really going in with you and him? Like, seriously, I'm your husband. What am I supposed to think?'

'You're supposed to support me,' she said, looking at me with a coldness that scared me.

'Haven't I been? I was hauled in by the partners today, Bella. They're worried this will all come back on the firm unless it's contained. And then you go and poke the bear with a stick. What were you thinking? Haven't you done enough damage with this fucking ... this *obsession* of yours?'

'I don't care about the partners,' Bella said angrily. It was more than an anger. I heard rage. 'The work I was doing with Tristan was *important*, damn it! We were creating something that might have changed the way we looked at ourselves as a species. I don't give a fuck if those three awful old men are worried. I *had* to make one last effort to save things.'

'Did he see you?' I asked, incredulous.

She nodded.

'And?'

She shook her head and went to the fridge, taking out a bottle of Sauvignon Blanc and unscrewing the top, taking a deep gulp from the mouth of the bottle.

'What happened, Bella?'

'We ... we had a discussion.'

I looked at my wife, and I saw the hem of her jacket was torn. The mark on her cheek looked livid in the light of the kitchen, and I couldn't say for sure, but it looked like her hair was uncharacteristically disarrayed.

'Did he put his hands on you?' I heard myself asking. 'Did he hit you?'

She looked at me for a long moment but said nothing and took another slug of wine.

'Bella, I asked you a question!'

'I don't want to talk about it.'

'You owe me an answer, for fuck sake! After all that's happened, you owe me that much.'

'He's a passionate man,' she said, and she was almost shouting now. 'He feels things more powerfully than most people. You wouldn't understand!'

'Listen to yourself!' I said, my own voice raised. 'You sound like someone in an abusive relationship! What the fuck is going on here?'

And then she threw the bottle at me.

I saw it coming, sailing through the air in a strange, looping arc. It hit me broadside, connecting with my eye and cheekbone, crushing the left side of my face and forcing me to take a step backwards. I was stunned for a moment, completely taken by surprise.

I knew Bella had a temper, but this was the first time she'd actually hit me.

I stood there, my left eye closed, gazing at her in shock and misery with my right. She stared back for a long moment, then let out a kind of a wail, and ran into the bedroom, locking the door behind her.

I had a proper shiner in the morning, and as you can probably imagine, the partners were fucking furious – a black eye isn't a good look for a corporate lawyer. I was given a right ticking off.

Bella and I didn't speak for three days. I am not ashamed to admit that I was thinking seriously about leaving my wife. I could see no reason to stay. She had, as far as I was concerned, had an affair, and the fallout of this had destroyed her own career and had a detrimental impact on mine.

And when I asked her to explain what was going on, she had struck me in the face with a bottle.

I think most people would find this situation intolerable.

On day four, however, my wife put a letter on the table in front of me at dinner.

'I know I have no right to ask you to do anything,' she said, 'but please read this.'

It was a letter confirming that my wife had just been accepted onto the postgraduate Certificate in Education course.

'I'm retraining as a teacher,' she said. 'It's over. My doctoral work is finished. I want to move on. I want *us* to move on.'

I looked at her and handed the letter back.

'Okay,' I said. 'I'm glad to hear it.'

I know that must have been a really hard decision for Bella to make. I'm not negating that at all.

But when I look back, what happened in that first year of our marriage definitely paved the way for everything that followed.

And that black eye wasn't the last one I received because of Bella Fitzpatrick.

Chapter 27

Detective Sergeant Harvey Brennan

This morning at 8 a.m. I pulled the file on Tristan Grosvenor.

I saw it almost as soon as I looked at the first page.

And I could not understand how we missed it.

Tristan Grosvenor is married, but his wife kept her own surname. Her name is Abigail Armitage.

They have one child. A son.

His name is Philo.

I picked up my phone and called DI Bodhua, who had interviewed the boy in the presence of his mother.

'Why would this raise any flags, boss?' she wanted to know.

'You didn't think to cross-reference for any connections between the family and Ms Fitzpatrick?'

'She's the lad's teacher. His mum said they didn't know each other socially. The dad wasn't present at the interview, but once one parent is there, that's all we need.'

And of course I knew she was right. The simple fact of allowing the boy to bear his mother's name rather than taking his father's had created a veil behind which a very dangerous man could hide.

What exactly he has been doing in those shadows, I am still unsure.

But I will find out.

That, after all, is my job.

Chapter 28

James

Work has always been an anaesthetic. I threw myself back into it. I knew I needed time to work out what needed to be done about my marriage, but there was no way I was going to throw away the professional gains I had achieved through years of blood, sweat and tears. So while I wasn't as frantically busy as I had been, I knew it was just a lull and things would go absolutely mental in Astley, Clifford and Kenworthy as we got closer and closer to the completion of the merger.

For all of that, I did my best to be home for dinner most evenings, and I texted and called Bella a couple of times a day to check in. I wanted her to see I was, at least, trying.

The same cannot be said for my wife.

Bella disappeared into her room every evening after dinner to do her research. I could hear her on the phone, talking to various people about some high-minded theory or other, and her laptop keys were often clattering away as I headed to bed.

I appreciated that she was teaching full time, so needed to do her doctoral work when she could, but it seemed to me that she had completely disregarded all the concerns I'd voiced about returning to this goddamned fucking project, the thing that came closest to driving us apart.

I mean, she admitted being on a date and snogging another bloke, and at the same time charged back into a doctoral thesis that involved her having what could be best described as an emotional affair right under my nose.

I was, to put it mildly, deeply pissed off.

With my marriage in freefall, it was like being in the twilight zone. Nothing seemed particularly real. I got up in the morning. I put in an hour at the gym. I picked up my breakfast in Pret. I went to work, talked to my colleagues and cut my deals but I was distracted, making mistakes and missing important emails. Then when I got home after a tough day, I ate a mostly silent meal with a woman I thought I knew, but who now seemed like a stranger. As soon as she'd finished eating, Bella would go to her room without so much as a goodnight. With nothing to stay up for, I'd make my own way to the spare room, where I'd switch on the TV, but couldn't follow anything that was on the screen.

I expect you're wondering why we're still together. Why I stayed through all of that, through my wife to all intents and purposes cheating on me, and indeed why she stuck with me when she obviously had so little commitment to me or to the marriage.

The answer isn't a simple one.

Or is it? I don't even know any more. The truth is, I was in love with her. I am in love with her. I knew then, as I know now, that I won't find anyone better than Bella, and if she's sometimes complicated and hard work, well she's worth the stress.

There's also a more selfish reason – Astley, Clifford and K like to employ 'family men'. They want their lawyers to be good, upstanding chaps who will be seen as reliable and stalwart. Whether it makes sense or not in this day and age, married guys are perceived to represent those values.

It sounds cynical to say I stayed because of that, and it's not the whole reason, but it is a part of it. I'd be lying if I said it wasn't.

As for Bella, well my understanding of why she stayed is probably more complex, and yet simpler too. She never talked about her upbringing much, but I always got the sense it wasn't easy. She has virtually no relationship with her parents. I think the reason she's still here is because she feels it gives her some level of stability. A solid base. She knows how I feel about her, and it makes her feel safe.

Even if she doesn't love me like she used to. Or maybe she never loved me like I thought she did.

I haven't a clue.

My head is all over the place with the whole thing.

I have watched the first episode of *Hawkeye* four times, and I still haven't a notion what it's about.

Then, something happened that knocked me out of this weird holding pattern.

It occurred while I was in the office, three days after Bella and I had had our 'discussion'. A legal question had been raised by Valentine Drew, a member of Fahlberg's management team, relating to one of the warranties in the draft merger agreement. I wanted to check a point of law that I thought might be relevant, and tried to log on to Westlaw, a legal database. I quickly found that I was locked out. It wouldn't recognise my password.

I took a breath and tried a couple of my other regular passcodes, but none of them worked. This was weird. I use Westlaw almost every day and have never had any problems before. I knew what to do, and reached for the phone.

'Tech Helpdesk. How can I help you this afternoon?'

This time, to my delight, I got straight through to Charlotte.

'Hi Charlotte, it's James from Astley, Clifford and Kenworthy.'

'Oh. Hello James.'

I thought I noticed a gentle upward lilt to her voice. As if she was happy to hear from me. Maybe I imagined it. Or maybe I was hearing it because I was happy to be talking to her.

'I'm glad I got you. Do you know anything about Westlaw?'

'The legal research database? Yes, I'm familiar with it.'

'It's locked me out.'

I heard her working on the keys of her computer.

'That can happen if your company hasn't installed the latest version. Just give me a moment and I'll see what we can do.'

There was more clattering of her fingers on the keys. She could type so quickly it was almost like a drum roll, a soft rhythmic sound. Comforting. I felt a sudden, inexplicable happiness that she was on the other end of the phone. As if everything was going to be alright, now. In a moment or two she came back on the line.

'Yes, Westlaw published an update today, and I see your server hasn't initiated it yet. If you give me five minutes, I'll set that in motion and you should be able to get in.'

'Thanks a million, Charlotte.'

'My pleasure. Hold please.'

The classical guitar rendition of 'Help!' came on again, and I found myself singing along in a semi-operatic voice. It was stupid, me sitting there in my little office, warbling along to a song I don't even particularly like. But I felt good. For the first time in days and days, I thought things might actually be okay.

I was still singing when Charlotte's voice cut through my vocal stylings.

'Um … James?'

I couldn't help but laugh.

'You didn't expect to come back on to that cacophony, did you?' I spluttered and gave her one more run of the chorus line for good measure, telling her in mock operatic tones to *please, please help me!*

She giggled at that.

It was nice. She had a lovely warmth about her, and I had that feeling again, like the one I'd had when we'd talked about comic books that first night, that we had a connection that was more than just tech support agent and a technologically befuddled client.

'Try to log in again, please, James,' she said, the humour still there in her voice.

I did, and lo and behold, I was now in.

'Charlotte, you are a genius.'

She laughed again, and I felt a slight thrill. I was making her laugh. All I got at home were scowls. This was really nice. I needed it, in fact.

'I have been told that, from time to time,' she said cheekily.

'I bet you have.'

We went quiet, and I could sense she wanted to keep talking, but wasn't sure of herself. I decided to take the lead.

'How have you been, Charlotte?'

'I've been ... I've been good, James.'

'You been busy?'

'The work I do is more or less constant. I get about the same number of calls each day, and it keeps me as busy as I like to be.'

'What else do you enjoy doing?'

In that moment I consciously broke the barrier between professional and personal. It's a trick lawyers are taught to do, making a client feel you are more than just a legal resource to them. They begin to view you as a friend, a family member who just happens to require payment for solving all their problems. Charlotte could either accept or reject the overture. It was a gamble, but I really had nothing to lose.

'Well,' she said, and I could almost hear the cogs turning as she thought about whether or not she wanted to make the jump, 'I run a couple of websites about TV shows I enjoy. And I draw.'

'You're an artist?'

'Would you believe I've always wanted to create comic books?'

'That's amazing!' I said, and I meant it, too. 'What kind of stuff do you like?'

'Have you read a graphic novel called *Blankets*?'

'No. I've never heard of it.'

'Would you like me to send you a link? There's a digital version. It's probably my favourite book of all time.'

'I take from the title that it's not about superheroes.'

'No. It's actually about a young boy growing up in rural America who wants to be ... a comic book artist.'

I laughed at that.

'I'll definitely check it out.'

'I hope you like it.'

'I'm sure I will.'

'I'll send you the link right now.'

'I'd be very grateful.'

'Okay then. Well, it was nice speaking to you, James.'

'You saved my bacon yet again. I don't know what I'd do without you.'

'Oh, I think you'd have sorted something out.'

'I'd have ended up sitting in the corner weeping, more than likely.'

She laughed again.

'Is there anything else I can help you with today?'

'No. That's all I needed.'

'Well, thank you for calling Tech Helpdesk. Would you ...'

'Just send on the survey. I'll give you a glowing review.'

'Thank you, James.'

'You're so very welcome, Charlotte.'

And she was gone again.

I got up and went to the bathroom, splashing water on my face, and then sat back down and got what I needed from Westlaw. Just as I was sending my response to the client, my laptop beeped to inform me I had an email. It was from charlotteod@techhelpdesk. com, and contained no text, just a link to the survey, as well as a link to Amazon. I clicked and it brought me to the page for the ebook of the graphic novel she had mentioned.

I bought it right away and took a moment to read the first few pages. The art was beautiful, not like a standard comic book. This was different. It was like poetry in visual form.

I responded to the email:

Dear Charlotte,

Thank you for the recommendation. I've bought a copy of Blankets, and already love it. I see from the jacket quotes that Joss Whedon thinks it is one the greatest love stories ever written. That's no small praise. I can't wait to read more.

Thanks again for your incredible help, and for the quick chat.

Hope we can talk again soon,

James

She replied almost immediately:

Hi James,

I'm thrilled you like Blankets. It really is something very special. I came close to asking you something when we were on the phone earlier, but I wasn't brave enough. The veil of an email has given me courage.

My art teacher does some occasional work for Marvel Comics. The Odeon in Piccadilly is showing the first Iron Man movie tomorrow night, and there is to be a Q&A session afterwards with Jon Favreau, the director, and Kevin Feige, the president of Marvel Studios. I have been lucky enough to be gifted two tickets, and I was wondering if you'd like to go with me?

I understand completely if you're too busy or if you don't feel comfortable with my asking. I just thought you'd appreciate the opportunity. You did say you like the Marvel Universe.

Let me know what you think.

Chat soon,

Charlotte

And all of a sudden, I didn't know what to do.

Chapter 29

Charlotte

I attend art classes in the campus of City University, my alma mater, every Saturday morning. City is where I did both my undergrad and master's degrees and I have been coming here to indulge my love of art for three years now. It's the part of my week I cherish most.

I have always felt comfortable at City. Many of the staff remember me, and I'm still in contact with a few friends from my time as a student here. The place brings back a lot of good memories.

And these classes are perhaps the only thing I do that feels pure and real, and they make me believe that I can have a different kind of life to the one I have now. When I'm drawing, it is as if I can reach deep down inside myself and bring out what is essential and pure.

I have been tinkering about with an idea for a graphic novel since I was a child. I know the story I wish to tell. I just don't know *how* to tell it. I feel comfortable with the images. It's the words that fail me.

I attended a creative writing class a few years ago, to try to help me find the language my story requires. I found the experience distressing. Every session ended with the work of one of the students being critiqued by the class, and this made me deeply uncomfortable. I don't feel as if I am in a position to find fault with another creator's work, and having my own work dissected was intolerable.

That does not happen in the art classes.

We appreciate one another's pictures, but that's as far as it goes.

The studio is a safe place, and I love it for that.

The room itself is high-ceilinged, with a raised platform in the centre upon which both life and still-life models are placed for us to draw or paint. The room has beautiful light, which comes from a series of skylights, and there are two chandeliers that light up the room at night.

The classroom is full of plants, which brighten the space with their colour, but also make it cool, fragrant and oxygenated. It is, by far, my favourite place in all of London.

And my art teacher, Stanley, is my favourite person.

His Saturday classes have been going on for years, and he welcomes people of all ages and abilities. Once he knows you, he's great company. He is not a big talker, which is a quality I like. He gives a smile when you arrive, and at some point will come over with a cup of tea and a biscuit for you.

He usually passes little comments on whatever I'm drawing. He will pause, watch me work for a few moments, pat me gently on the back, and then wander back to whatever he is doing. This feels both comforting and supportive.

Before he came to the university, Stanley drew panels for both Marvel and DC comics, and he still does inking work for Marvel, primarily on their Iron Man books. I pointed out to him that this is synchronous, as his Christian name is a combination of both the Christian and surnames of the most celebrated head of Marvel Comics, Stan Lee. My art teacher gave me a wry smile when I said this and informed me that he was very aware of the coincidence.

'Whenever I'm in the Marvel UK offices someone makes the Stanley/Stan Lee joke, usually within the first five minutes,' he said. 'I see the funny side of it, but it hasn't gotten a laugh out of me for about twenty years.'

I told James that I had been gifted with tickets for the Iron Man screening. This was a lie. I asked Stanley for them. He gave me a quizzical look when I approached him last Saturday.

'I think I know who you want to bring,' he said, winking.

I baulked. How could he possibly know about my feelings for James? *James*, at that stage, did not know about my feelings for him!

'Who?' I asked.

'Well, I'm assuming it's Drake,' he said.

Drake also attends the Saturday classes. He is tall and slim and muscular, and he wears very fashionable clothes and he always smells good – a mix of leather and sandalwood. He draws competently, and when he concentrates, he pokes his tongue out between his teeth a little, which is endearing.

I haven't spoken to him very much, as when we are in the class together we are both drawing or painting or sketching, and there is not much requirement for conversation, but one afternoon we found ourselves standing side-by-side on the Tube, and he said to me:

'Your still-life was awesome today, Charlotte.'

I thought that was kind. He didn't have to say it.

I don't want to ask Drake to go out with me to the Iron Man screening, though. I think he's too good-looking for someone like me, and he's never expressed any interest in comic books, even when he has seen me drawing a character that would be easily recognisable to most people.

I wanted to ask James out. I like James, very much.

And now he has said yes.

And I'm terrified.

But I'm excited, too. And that feels good.

It feels very good indeed.

Chapter 30

James

I had never, up to this point, even entertained the idea of being unfaithful to my wife. Why would I? She's a stone-cold stunner, and she's smart and cool. I have never stopped finding her totally fucking hot from the first moment I laid eyes on her at Trinity College.

I suppose it's fair to say she is, in almost every sense of the word, my ideal woman. I love the quirkiest things about her, things I feel I only get the pleasure of knowing. She has this chameleon-like quality, and can almost look like a different person depending on how she wears her thick, long chestnut hair, or with how the light reflects off her green eyes. Sometimes I think they have purple flecks in them, other times they have shards of gold. I like to think that they change with her mood, even though I know it's only the light. And to me, her body is incredible. I remember the first time I saw her naked, with her tiny waist and voluptuous curves. I couldn't believe my luck that she had chosen to be with me.

I have never once looked at Bella, even when things are at their worst, and not felt something resonate inside me.

And it's not just about the way she looks.

Bella is brilliant. I know I'm smart, but my wife is *way* smarter than me. She leaves me way behind, and I'm not too proud to admit it. I have, at times, sat and listened to her debate an issue with a friend, and just been agog at her ability to think her way around a problem. I've always been attracted to brains, and Bella's mind is a huge turn-on for me.

And, if I'm being completely honest, her ambitious personality attracted me to her at the beginning. I recognised it as a quality we shared. Now I feel as if this ambition, her drive and determination to finish what she started, has done the most damage to our marriage.

Usually, I just have to look at Bella, and any thoughts of straying are cast aside.

But she had never snogged another bloke before – at least, not that I know of. I may have suspected things went further than I wanted to admit with Grosvenor, but there was no denying that she had strayed now.

That was a gamechanger for me.

Call me old-fashioned, but I liked the idea that Bella was only interested in kissing me. That's a big deal for me. If she's now bestowing that privilege on other guys, what exactly is special about her relationship with me? And if the marriage doesn't carry the same level of significance to her as it does to me, why should I fight to protect it?

I came to the conclusion that I might as well have a night out myself.

Hadn't she done just that?

It took me a solid two hours of agonising, but finally I replied to Charlotte's email, with a 'yes'. She responded by saying to meet her at the cinema, and advising we get there for around seven. The screening began at eight, but she wasn't sure whether or not we'd have to queue.

This struck me as a little odd, as I figured an event like this would have assigned seats, but I told her I'd be there, and that was that.

Once we'd made the arrangement, I veered between feeling like shit and being delighted for the rest of the day. Half a dozen times I came close to emailing her and cancelling.

But I didn't.

So, last night, I went out with Charlotte from the helpdesk, and I had a pretty fucking amazing time!

I had no idea what to wear. This has never been an issue for me because nights out with the firm always involve wearing exactly the same as during the day, except on the occasions where we have to don a tux. This evening was different. I tried on a few different combos, and finally settled on a casual black blazer, a pair of distressed denim jeans, red Converse All Stars, and a Marvel *Civil War* t-shirt, which has Iron Man on one side and Captain America on the other.

I looked in the mirror, and the only thing I didn't like was my hair. It was too done. Rich man's hair, as Bella jokingly calls it. I looked like a lawyer trying to dress casually, which was exactly what I was. I dampened it, and worked some mousse through, then tousled the top. It worked. I now looked artfully scruffy, what my wife might have called 'windswept and interesting'.

Not that I'd be asking for her opinion.

I got a black cab to Piccadilly. I made sure I was early, because I had no idea what this woman looked like.

She had told me she'd be wearing a black dress with purple boots, so I kept this in mind as I scanned the crowd congregating outside the Odeon. I had a feeling she would be punctual. She said she'd see me at 7 p.m., and lo and behold, at two minutes to the hour I spied a woman coming through the crowds, dressed in a black leather jacket, a short black dress, fishnets and purple Doc Marten boots.

This is going to sound desperately superficial, but I had been really nervous about what Charlotte might look like. I had been worried that she'd be a mousy, nerdy little thing, dressed in a hand-knitted cardigan and a tweed skirt, one leg of her glasses taped in place.

But she was nothing like that. As soon as I set eyes on her, I felt bad for even thinking she might be.

Charlotte was probably about five three, slim and athletic. I'd guess she either runs or works out because she's quite toned. Her brown hair was so dark it was almost black, with scarlet highlights streaked through it. And she was pretty, in a girl-next-door way, with dark-blue eyes and a kind, shy smile.

I was trying to look casual when she spotted me right away.

Her face broke out into a smile, and she gave me a quick wave and hurried over.

'James,' she said formally, offering me her hand to shake. 'It's a pleasure to finally meet you in person.'

'Charlotte,' I said, and took her hand, but then leaned in for a kind of side hug.

To my delight she accepted and gave me a tentative kiss on the cheek.

I liked that. It felt natural, as if she wasn't trying to play it cool or hold herself back. And it bode well for the evening ahead.

'I thought we'd have to wait in line,' she said, 'but my art lecturer tells me it's assigned seating, so we can go right in.'

'Lead the way,' I said.

'I was a little worried you might not be here,' she said as we walked towards the steps that run up to the double doors. 'We barely know one another, and it was a bit forward of me to ask.'

'I like to think of myself as a gentleman,' I said. 'I would never stand up a lady.'

'I'm really glad you came,' she said, and she gave me the most beautiful look – it was vulnerable and sweet and open, and it seemed to be saying: *I really like you, please don't hurt me*.

I decided then and there that I wouldn't. I'd just been hurt, and I didn't want to be the cause of anyone else feeling the same way.

'I never asked you, have you seen this film before?' Charlotte asked as we mounted the steps.

'Oh yes,' I told her. 'I've seen it a few times. I love Robert Downey Jr as Tony Stark. He gets it just right, I think.'

'I was a little disappointed they didn't explore Tony's alcoholism in the films,' she said. 'It's such an important theme in the comics, and I think it would have been interesting to see Downey Jr play that.'

'Might come off as type-casting,' I suggested.

'Maybe,' she said.

We were at the door now.

'Ladies first,' I said, standing back.

'Very courteous of you.' She smiled, stepping inside. 'You really are a gentleman.'

'Well, of course,' I said. 'But more importantly, you've got the tickets.'

'Courteous and practical,' she laughed.

The movie was as good as I remembered and the Q&A with Favreau and Feige was fascinating. Charlotte turned out to be one of the stars of the night, asking an interesting question about how the character of Tony Stark had changed since his first appearance in the comics in 1962. She proposed that he started out as a vehicle to examine America's role in the Cold War, particularly the way it used technology and weapons. However, it was now more of an exploration of liberalism and how business magnates like Elon Musk or Jeff Bezos could be a force for either good or evil in the modern world.

This sparked a lively debate, and I loved the way she sat

back and allowed people to take her idea and run with it, but occasionally stepped in to move the discussion on. Favreau was hilarious, and at one stage asked Charlotte if she wanted a job as a story advisor for the next movie.

'You couldn't afford me,' she quipped.

She was witty, self-deprecating and totally in control.

And I thought she was sexy as hell. I have always been a sucker for strong, smart and powerful women, and Charlotte is most definitely one of those.

When the Q&A was over it was almost ten o'clock.

'So what do you want to do now?' I asked, as we filed out of the cinema, our bodies pressed close together in the crush of the crowd. I felt elated after the event, and was keen for the night to continue. 'We could go and get some food, or a drink? Or, it's a bit cold but we could go for a stroll along Embankment, if you like. I always love the river and the lights of the city at night.'

Charlotte seemed happy. Maybe even a little giddy. I could tell she was pleased by how the evening had gone, and she stood close beside me, and I could feel the warmth of her body.

'I live five minutes' walk away from here,' she said, 'on Gerrard Street. If you're okay with it, we could pick up a bottle of something and go back to mine? It'd be more comfortable, and no one will call time on us.'

I shrugged, trying to look nonchalant, but I felt a thrill go right through me. As I had thought earlier, she wasn't holding back.

'That sounds like a plan,' I said.

'Good. There's an off-licence just up the road.'

'Well, great.' I was trying not to sound too pleased at this turn of events. 'Lead the way.'

She reached out and took my hand.

'Is this okay?' she asked, looking at me tentatively. 'I've wanted to do it all night. But … well, you haven't said, but you're wearing a wedding ring and I've used my tech skills to track you down on social media …'

I had no doubt she'd had a look at my social media, just as I had looked for hers. The fact that I'm married to Bella is not hidden. I had been wondering when she would bring it up.

'I am married,' I said, 'but things are complicated at the moment. I … I don't know if I'm going to be married for much longer.'

She continued to hold my hand, gazing up at me with those deep-blue eyes of hers.

'The accepted response would be that I'm sorry things are going badly for you,' she said. 'But it would be a lie if I said that.'

'I'm not asking you to say anything of the sort,' I said. 'Tonight, I'm just happy to be here with you. I would say I'm happy for the first time in a while, actually.'

'Taking your hand is okay then?'

'It is,' I said. 'It's better than okay.'

So together, hand in hand, we walked into the night.

Chapter 31

Charlotte

The evening went so much better than I expected.

It was as if, out of nowhere, I knew exactly what to say and how to act. I was me, but a better, calmer, more intelligent version. The fact I was at the screening with a man like James made me feel different, as if I could do anything. It was like I had superpowers.

When the question-and-answer session was over, it was obvious we both wanted the night to continue, and James, gentleman that he is, suggested we go to a bar, or a restaurant, or for a walk somewhere. And any of those would have been lovely. But I believed they would only delay what we both really wanted.

The screening had been an icebreaker, allowing us to relax in one another's company. Now it was time to really get acquainted, and the best place to do that was somewhere quiet and private, where we could talk without being interrupted by waitstaff or having to shout over loud music.

And I wanted to break the barrier of touch. Yes, we had hugged and kissed a hello, but I wanted more. I had been dreaming of being with James.

I knew taking his hand was a gamble, and so was coming out and asking him about his marriage. I knew he might interpret my proposal to go back to my place as simply an invitation for sex.

If I am to be wholly transparent, I did not mind if he wished to take it like that. But I hoped he would also see it as a wish to open a dialogue that might bring us to a new, better understanding. I wanted to really *know* this man, and I very much hoped he wanted to know me, too.

The walk to the off-licence only took five minutes, and during that time we did not talk. I was deeply aware of the sensation of his hand in mine, of the fact he was close. I could smell his aftershave and feel the rhythm of his steps and I liked it. I had seen him looking at me a couple of times during the evening, and I knew he fancied me.

He found me attractive.

And for a woman working in the corporate world in London in 2019 that is not an easy sentence to write. It is loaded with the weight of complication.

The simple truth is that I liked James, and wanted him to like me. I know men find me physically attractive. I have a great figure that I work hard for. I'm good-looking, but not intimidatingly so, and I know what clothes look good on me.

So of course, I had dressed and behaved in a manner I hoped he would find attractive. Is that wrong? Is it weak or antifeminist? I do not believe so, and I feel I should not have to apologise for it.

Did I want the night to end with a sexual encounter with James Fitzpatrick? Yes, I will happily admit that I did.

We got to the off-licence.

'What would you like?' he asked me, as he scanned the shelves.

'I'm not a big drinker,' I admitted. 'But when I do, I quite like bourbon.'

He grinned.

'I'm usually a Scotch man, but I will never say no to a shot of Jim Beam.'

'Jim Beam will do nicely,' I said.

He insisted on paying for the bottle, and we continued up the road towards my apartment.

'You were impressive at the Q&A,' he said to me as he took my hand again. 'I consider myself a Marvel fan, but I think you knew more than Kevin Feige did himself!'

'I'm one of those people who collects facts,' I told him. 'I did an aptitude test once in school, and the results showed I would be ideal as a librarian or a museum curator.'

'Yet you work in tech,' he said.

'It was never my plan. I wanted to be a mathematician. I studied applied maths in college, in fact.'

'How'd you end up in computers then?'

I considered fobbing him off with a story that was more pleasant than the reality. I did not want him to feel sorry for me, to think of me differently than he did just at that moment. I don't enjoy talking about myself, and experience has very often taught me that things I say will end up being thrown back at me at some point in the future. I have learned to remain circumspect. I don't want to give ammunition to someone who could potentially hurt me.

But I couldn't see James in that way. He had been honest with me about his marriage. I believed I could be honest with him, too.

'When I was in the third year of my degree I wrote a paper on the use of data analytic techniques to streamline blended teaching methodologies for students with learning difficulties. It was published in the university magazine, and I was contacted by the computer science department, who asked me if I wanted to see if my theories could be put to the test. They offered to fund a master's degree, and I thought it was too good an opportunity to pass up. My undergrad work was being paid for by a scholarship, so it was like free money.'

'Your parents must have been thrilled,' he said. 'And proud.'

'My dad died when I was in my early twenties,' I replied, surprising myself. I would *never* usually share this, but I felt so much at ease, I thought I might as well just tell him everything. 'It's funny, the things I remember most acutely: the smell of aftershave and his laugh – he had a great deep laugh. I don't believe my mother ever got over losing him. She was always emotionally delicate, and I think his death made her worse.'

James squeezed my hand.

'Nothing fosters independence like having no other choice,' he said sympathetically.

'I graduated from City University with a master's degree in Applied Mathematics and Computer Science. I thought I'd be snapped right up by Google or Facebook, but as luck would have it, I came out of college just as the world economy crashed, and no one was hiring. Plus, I had just lost my dad so I was deep in grief. I found it difficult to focus on job hunting. The university gave me some work doing tech support for students, but it just wasn't enough to sustain me. It was a scary time.'

'I remember it very well,' James said. 'I was worried I might be let go from the firm. A lot of people I knew were made redundant.'

'I didn't have a job to be made redundant from,' I said. 'I sent out my CV, complete with glowing references and a copy of my article, to every company I could think of. No one was interested. Around this time my mother was showing signs of early-onset Alzheimer's, so I needed a job and fast. It was obvious she needed full-time care, and I wasn't in a position to offer it. So when I saw the Helpdesk job advertised, I applied immediately.'

'And with your qualifications, they snapped you up right away,' James said.

'Yes. I went into it thinking it would tide me over, but as the bills mounted I saw the job was a blessing. It doesn't pay much above minimum wage, but I can work as little or as much as I need, and it gives me a lot of freedom, too. Usually I work from a desk in my flat, but I can take a call anywhere. If I need to access a company's network from my phone, I can. It's not great in terms of GDPR, but once the problem is fixed, no one asks what device was used to do it.'

'How's your mum now?'

'Sometimes she knows who I am,' I told him. 'But usually she doesn't. I don't mind, really. She wasn't very kind to me when she did know who I was, so maybe this is better.'

He stopped at that, and pulled me to him, and kissed me for the first time.

It was long and lingering and tender, and while I could feel the want in it, I understood that what James was really doing was telling me he heard me, and that he cared. It was a beautiful moment.

I cannot recall ever being so happy.

Chapter 32

James

Charlotte's apartment was small, but thoughtfully laid out, giving the impression of space despite the fact it was really three rooms crammed into one medium-sized one.

She had a cute little suite of furniture and a small dining-room table with three chairs in the main living area. The kitchen was annexed off in a corner, and was about the size of a broom cupboard, comprising of just a sink, a two-ring cooker and low-slung fridge and freezer. There was a 25-inch flat-screen TV mounted on the wall amid a lot of art, most of it comic book characters, some of whom I recognised and some I thought I knew but couldn't recall their names.

Of those I could identify were: Tintin and his dog Snowy;

Judge Dredd and Johnny Alpha, the Strontium Dog; Dennis the Menace and Gnasher, and just above them The Bash Street Kids; John Constantine sat on a rock smoking as he chatted to Swamp Thing.

'Did you paint all of these?' I asked her as I studied each picture close up.

She was taking off her leather jacket. I watched as she did. She really was beautiful.

'They're all my work, yep,' she said.

A treadmill took up a lot of the floor space, positioned by the window and overlooking the street below. In a corner of the room was a desk so small it was virtually a card table. There was a closed laptop upon it, attached to an external hard drive.

'That's where you sat the first night I called you?' I asked her.

My host had gone to the kitchen area where she took two tumblers from a cupboard above the hob.

'Yes, it is,' she said. 'Where all the magic happens.'

I wandered over to the desk. On the wall above it, so that anyone sitting there to work would just need to turn their head to see, was another picture. This one I recognised immediately.

'That's Jean Grey, from *X-Men*, isn't it?'

She was putting the bottle of bourbon, glasses and a bowl of ice on the coffee table that sat in front of the couch.

'In her *Dark Phoenix* phase, yes. Do you know the story from the comics?'

'Kind of,' I admitted.

'It's a reminder to be careful what you wish for,' Charlotte said.

I waited for her to continue, but she didn't offer any more

than that, just poured a splash of bourbon into each glass and motioned for me to sit on the couch beside her. I did.

'Will I put on some music?' she asked.

'Yeah sure, that would be nice,' I said, and she picked up the remote control for the television and put on Spotify.

It took her a couple of moments to get a playlist of Gillian Welch and Dave Rawlings playing.

'I like this,' I told her.

'Me too,' she said.

Gillian and Dave were singing about time being a revelator.

I looked at Charlotte, who was curled up against me now.

'I can't believe you're here,' she said.

'I can't either,' I said. 'The past few hours don't really seem real.'

'Are you glad you came?'

I put my glass down, and my arm around her. She nestled in as soon as I did. It felt good. Gillian was singing about how she was a pretender, not what she was supposed to be.

'I am so very, very glad I came.'

'So am I,' she said, and then we were kissing.

And we didn't say anything else for a long time.

PART II

Taken from 'Controlled Rage: Mapping the physical and psychological effects of the suppression of aggression responses in professional men and women, and an analysis of socially sanctioned dominance behaviours in the corporate world', PhD thesis by Bella Murphy Fitzpatrick, City, University of London, 2010.

Power comes in many different forms, and Tristan Grosvenor wields all of them.

He is capable, with the click of a mouse or through a rushed telephone conversation, to move millions, even billions of pounds, and affect the quality of life for vast numbers of people.

He can command fear in the people who work with him, and he demands respect in all his engagements. When he felt that I had disrespected him, by writing an article that presented him in a light he did not wish the general public to perceive, he was ruthless in his efforts to silence me and to discredit my academic and journalistic credentials.

In his social and personal relationships, he is no less aggressive. His wife and children are kept intensely private; protected from the stress and anxiety of his work, and shielded from the exposure that comes with his high profile. Yet he was open, with me, at least, about the fact that he maintains other kinds of relationships – social and sexual – that satisfy aspects of his personality he desires to keep separate from his family.

This ability to compartmentalise to such an extent shows a rigorous discipline.

Tristan Grosvenor wields power over himself, as much as he does over others.

Perhaps the way in which we see this power most acutely is where his decisions become entangled with life and death.

It would be unfair to say that Grosvenor's sacking of his employees in a bid to streamline his company was the direct cause of the deaths of two people (we must remember that as well as Tamlyn's murder, another employee took their own life), but it was certainly the indirect cause.

Obviously Grosvenor became the *actual* cause of Tamlyn's death by beating him to the extent he sustained catastrophic brain injuries, and with that the cycle of power is complete.

Tristan Grosvenor has power over the financial and economic sphere; the social and emotional; the ability to alter the structure of people's lives by hiring and firing; and he wields the power of life and death in both a physical and figurative sense.

There is no purer show of power than that.

Chapter 33

James

I woke at six the following morning and, for just a moment, I didn't know where I was. It wasn't until I looked over and realised that the woman sleeping beside me wasn't my wife that I remembered what had happened. I know this doesn't cast me in a good light, but I had a moment of unbridled panic.

What the fuck had I done? What was I thinking?

Is this what I really wanted? Yeah, I'd had fun last night. It was a fantastic event and Charlotte was cool and pretty and smart, and she obviously had a thing for me, but had I really gone along with it because my ego needed stroking? I had never been unfaithful to Bella before, and with a sickening jolt I realised that things could never be the same between us. No matter how much work we did on our relationship, even if she told me she was sorry she'd kissed that guy and wanted to make a go of things, I would always know it was *me* who had messed up *really* badly.

How could I look her in the eye again?

Charlotte stirred in her sleep and, turning, nestled into me. She smelt of soap, shampoo and some kind of perfume I didn't recognise. I liked it, even if I hated admitting I did.

Maybe the best thing I could do would be to just come clean with Bella. Tell her what had happened, throw myself on her mercy. She was the one who had strayed first, if you wanted to get technical about it, so all I was doing was responding by upping the ante.

Moving gingerly, I slid out of Charlotte's bed and grabbed my clothes.

I had my jeans on and was pulling on my t-shirt when my eyes fell on a framed photo on Charlotte's dressing table. It was of a group of ten young people, all gathered around the door of what looked to be an office block of some kind. As I looked I could make Charlotte out, on the extreme right of the bunch.

What gave me pause was the girl standing on the extreme left of the photo.

It was Bella.

I felt an uncontrollable panic surge up inside me, and I was genuinely worried I was going to have a panic attack, like I had on the night I'd first spoken to Charlotte on the phone. I took deep breaths.

How could this be happening? Was I dreaming it? I looked at the photo again, and no, I was not mistaken. My wife and my ... what should I call her? My mistress? My lover? Whatever the correct terminology was, they obviously knew one another.

And that was a whole world of pain and aggravation I did not want to even contemplate.

At that moment Charlotte sleepily opened one eye, yawned and stretched.

'Morning James,' she said, smiling as she saw me by the end of her bed.

'Hey,' I said, grabbing one of my trainers and shoving it on, my eyes frantically searching for the other one.

I know I should have at least pretended to be cool, but my mind was racing. All I wanted was to get out of there as quickly as possible.

'Are you going already?' she said, sitting up abruptly, realising that I was dressed. 'Would you like some tea before you head? Coffee? Some toast, maybe?'

I shook my head rapidly.

'I'm due in work. I need to get home to grab a shower and a suit.'

She glanced at the clock on the wall near the bedroom door.

'It's just after six,' she said. 'Surely you've got time for a quick cup of something?'

'I'm sorry, but I really don't. I'm expected in the office by eight, and I need to get across town and then back into the City.'

'Let me give you a travel mug, then. I've got two.'

'I'm fine, Charlotte. Really I am.'

I probably said that a bit too sharply, but it felt like I'd go crazy if I didn't get out of there.

'Okay,' she said. 'I'll just throw on a t-shirt and jeans and I can walk out with you.'

The look of horror that crossed my face at that suggestion stopped her in her tracks. I saw her freeze, and I did feel a little bit bad, but I'd be lying if I didn't admit the feeling passed pretty quickly.

'That really won't be necessary,' I said firmly. 'Thanks for last night, I had fun. I'll catch up with you again, yeah?'

Her face brightened at that, and I wished it hadn't. I'd only meant the words as a kind of a goodbye, not a promise we'd see each other again. Because I didn't think that would be a good idea. Not at all. She, on the other hand, grabbed it with both hands.

'Yes, great. I'll call you, shall I?'

'I'm pretty busy the next couple of weeks with this big transaction,' I said, throwing on my jacket and making for the door. How about I call you?'

'Okay ...' she said, but then I was out the door of her bedroom, through her front door and going down the stairs to the street.

Maybe this wasn't going to be as much of a problem as I'd thought; I would just keep contact minimal until Charlotte got the hint.

I just needed to put it out of my mind, and focus on getting things right with my wife.

Chapter 34

Charlotte

I am not a stupid person.

I am not unfeeling and even though I sometimes suffer from social anxiety, I am quite good at reading people.

So when I awoke and James was getting dressed and could not get out of my apartment quickly enough, I immediately knew he was regretting our night together. The fact it was a night that had meant a great deal to me didn't seem to matter to him. Not that I told him how I felt, of course. I did what I do and pretended everything was okay. It is a coping mechanism that has worked for me ever since I was a small child.

I do not always remember my father clearly, but, strangely, I do have a memory of how my mother was when he died.

That always seems odd to me, but I am aware the human mind does not always make sense in how it processes experiences, particularly traumatic ones.

I remember her lying on the floor of our living room, sobbing. I was twenty-four years old, an adult, and I should have been her equal – someone she could accept support from. I tried to comfort her, but she kept on pushing me away.

'Leave me alone,' she said. 'This is all your fault. If we didn't have your college fees to pay, he might not have taken losing his job so hard.'

I remember going to my room and sitting on my bed, crying, telling myself this was all my fault.

I now know it wasn't. That it was someone else's fault.

But it took me a while to work that out. And even longer to learn there was something I could do about it.

I also now know my mother always suffered from mental health issues. She was diagnosed as having bipolar disorder years ago, and my life for as long as I could remember had been a rollercoaster of manic highs and crushing lows. I had never been able to decide which was more tolerable. I found it exhausting when she was rushing around the house, frantically hoovering every floor and wiping down every surface, Abba's greatest hits blaring at high volume from the stereo in the living room, and I would half-pray for her to fall into a low period.

The relief was always short-lived.

There would be days of her lying in bed, refusing to get up. She constantly self-harmed – cutting herself usually, but when I hid the knives she would bite herself and pull out fistfuls of hair. When she was low she refused to eat, existing instead on the calories she absorbed from the endless bottles of wine she would send me out to buy. Very quickly, the grinding misery of it would have me wishing with all my bones for her to bounce into a manic episode again.

My life has been spent enduring. I would tell myself that this was okay, this was manageable. As long as I could get through this, the next stage would be better. Then I would get there, and realise it was just as bad, only a different kind of bad, but I had survived the last one so I will survive this, too.

Is James going to be something I have to survive?

When he bolted from my room I sat in bed, just as I had as a child, and I cried.

Was there anything to salvage from the experience?

The sex had been okay. I wouldn't call him a generous lover – the interaction was mostly about his enjoyment – but I was excited enough that, with a bit of effort at the end, I was able to achieve climax. He didn't seem to care if I did or not, so it was just as well that I have learned to care for my own needs.

But it had never been just about the sex for me. I wanted to be with him physically because I knew it would be a way to connect with him on a deeper, emotional level. I wanted the intimacy. No matter how I examine the evening I always reach the same conclusion: James and I found something in each other. Something meaningful.

He talked to me about his marriage, and I was open with him about my dad dying and my mother ending up in the nursing home. There was definitely a spark between us. I know he was attracted to me. When we were in bed, he kept telling me how beautiful I am. How he loved my body. Of course, guys say that when they're in the throes of passion, but I think he was trying to express more than that. I think he was telling me he cared for me.

That was real. I didn't dream it.

And when he was leaving, he said: '*How about I call you?*' Those exact words.

That must mean he wants to see me. There is no other possible interpretation.

He did mention that I should wait for him to call, but as I thought more about it, it occurred to me that, if he is busy, the onus should be on me to make contact. It would be wrong of me to place that responsibility on him.

And if he is having problems within his marriage, his wife is probably not looking after him very well. I know he works too hard. After all, the first time we spoke was when he called me at two o'clock in the morning. Anyone who is still at their desk at that time needs to find some perspective in their life.

Maybe, I thought, just maybe I could be the one to help him find balance again.

That gave me some hope.

I wasn't working that day, so I decided to spend it doing things for James. Show him just how important he is to me, and how I can be important to him, too.

I threw off my duvet, jumped in the shower, had a hearty breakfast, and made a plan.

Chapter 35

James

There was no sound from Bella's room – *our room* – when I got
back to the apartment.

Trying to be deathly silent in case I woke her, I removed every
item of clothing and threw the lot into the washing machine
for a long wash and spin cycle. Then I showered, keeping the
temperature as hot as I could bear and standing under the jets
for as long as I could. When this was done I brushed my teeth
thoroughly and gargled with anti-bacterial mouthwash.

Then I felt somewhat better.

I didn't do any of that because I found Charlotte disgusting;
I just wanted things to get back to normal. I wanted to get back

on track with my wife and I wanted the upheaval of the past few weeks to be behind us.

The thought that Bella and Charlotte might know one another, might even be in touch on social media, terrified me. But then it occurred to me that, if they were, surely Charlotte would have known. She'd have picked up on it and let me know.

I reckoned the best thing to do was just not to worry about it. It was too vast a problem, anyway.

I still hadn't decided if I was going to tell Bella or not. There was a large part of me that thought it was the only way to move forward. Maybe the marriage was over anyway, and there was no going back. It could well have been over way before I ever went out with Charlotte.

But I had to believe there was still a chance. I liked Charlotte, I was attracted to her, but she couldn't hold a candle to my wife. Bella was smart, beautiful and incredibly sexy, and yes, she could be difficult and intimidating too, at times.

But I'd never met anyone else like her.

I was prepared to admit I had fucked up and would fight to keep her.

I stood outside her bedroom door and thought about knocking and coming clean right away. I had my fist raised to do so when my legal training kicked in.

Never go into a negotiation without having fully prepared your argument.

I needed to think about how to approach this. Present myself as best I could.

Feeling a bit more like myself, I went into work, stopping to get my usual coffee and bagel with cream cheese at Pret along the way.

I didn't know it then, but it was going to be a long day.

Chapter 36

Bella

I heard James coming in that morning, early. For a split second, the question of where he'd spent the night passed through my mind. But where else would James have been but holed up in his office working on the deal of the century? I had more important things to think about.

I was already awake and at my desk in my study when I heard him tiptoe past our bedroom and into the bathroom. I was reading through some notes I'd made the night before, after a meeting with Professor Edgar McKinley, an eminent behavioural psychologist. He had agreed to meet me for dinner in the Savoy, and over a meal that was so packed with butter and cream I could almost feel my arteries clogging as we ate, he listened intently as I told him my theories about Grosvenor, and then about how I proposed to widen those ideas out to the wider community.

'It's not a wholly original idea,' he said, when I finished talking. 'Wasn't it Lord Acton who said that power corrupts, but absolute power corrupts absolutely?'

'You see, that's where you're not quite following me,' I said.

McKinley smiled indulgently as he took a long sip of whiskey. He was a slight man in his late sixties, his face flushed from, I suspected, a love of red wine and whiskey, and he had the bushiest eyebrows I had ever seen. He was wearing a suit that looked new but was tailored in an Edwardian style, and I liked him immediately.

He was all old-school courtesy and gentle manners.

'Well, please enlighten me,' he said, kindly.

'I do not believe aggression is a bad thing. I think it is *necessary*. But if we do not find healthy ways of expressing it, there will be more casualties like Gerald Tamlyn. And those must be avoided, if possible.'

'Did you not declare Grosvenor as something of a hero in your article in *The Grapevine*?'

'You read it?' I asked, flushing.

'That rag is a guilty pleasure. I thought your piece was very interesting, if a bit one-dimensional.'

'I wanted to give Tristan the chance to tell his side of it.'

'Then you should not have offered your opinion at the end. You could have let it just be his voice.'

'At the time ...' I said, 'at the time he and I were ... well, we were very close.'

He raised those eyebrows again.

'You were intimate with him?'

I took a deep breath and admitted to him what I had not admitted to anyone else. Sometimes not even to myself.

'Yes. I was having an affair with him. I was young and I was completely infatuated.'

'And you allowed that to compromise your research.'

I nodded, barely able to meet his gaze.

'I abandoned it, for a time,' I said.

'Which was the right thing to do,' he agreed, signalling to the waiter for another glass of whiskey.

'But I'm a different person now. He tried to destroy me, Grosvenor did, but he didn't succeed. I'm ready to finish what I started.'

'You may draw this man's ire down upon you again,' McKinley said. 'Are you prepared for that?'

'Bring it on,' I said, grinning. 'I'd welcome it, if I'm honest.'

'Might I suggest, then, that you focus not on the murder that everyone knows took place, but the widely held belief that men like Grosvenor, once they get away with murder once, are considered highly likely to kill again? Do you have any evidence something like that might be the case?'

I smiled.

'As it happens, I have a plan to find out.'

'Well then, I think your research offers a lot of promise.'

I patted the old man on the back of his hand.

'I do too.'

Taken from 'Controlled Rage: Mapping the physical and psychological effects of the suppression of aggression responses in professional men and women, and an analysis of socially sanctioned dominance behaviours in the corporate world', PhD thesis by Bella Murphy Fitzpatrick, City, University of London, 2010.

Tristan Grosvenor, despite the fact he beat a man to death in his office, is still spoken of as charming and well-mannered by those who work closely with him. It is as if the murder was committed by someone else.

In the first phase of my research for this thesis in 2010, I interviewed him over many hours. For a brief time, he took me into his world and into his bed. He told me he was as fascinated by me as I was by him, and insisted that I possessed a darker side to my personality, and it was this darkness that made us kindred spirits.

He told me that, together, we could accomplish anything.

I believed him. I had just got married to a man I thought I loved, but it seemed to me during those days that Tristan Grosvenor was the soulmate I had searched all my life for. The more time I spent with him, the more I came to think of him as the only person who truly understood me. He seemed to grasp truths about human nature, to accept the shadow that exists in the hearts of all of us with not just calm resignation, but with a sense of joy. A knowledge that by so doing, he was freeing himself from the shackles that force so many of us to live compromised and limited lives.

I was excited by his philosophies on both business and life.

I wanted to share them, not just within the hallowed halls of academia, but also on forums where non-academics might have access to them. I genuinely believed I had, through my conversations with Grosvenor, happened upon something important, something that might be an answer to the crushing mental health issues that currently beset the population of the West.

It was a concept that was beautiful and simple: aggression and, yes, even violence, are not always bad. In fact, sometimes they are necessary and even morally right. Our modern culture teaches us to suppress them, but in reality they always find a way to leak out, and when they do, they often do so in ways that end up being far more psychologically damaging than if they'd just been released up-front in their purer form, and dealt with in a considered way.

Happiness, I thought, could perhaps be achieved much more easily if we all embraced aggression more and gave it voice.

By the time I was putting together this psychological model, which I was going to call Extroverted Shadow Expression, I thought I was in love with Tristan Grosvenor. He had become my muse, my inspiration, the guru for my intellectual development, and the example upon which I thought I could model my life.

The mistake I made was thinking a man who so comfortably fit the criteria of a sociopath would ever be able to love me back.

When I published my article about him in *The City Grapevine* (see Appendix 1 of this thesis) I was trying to explain to the world at large that what Grosvenor had done was not only understandable, but a completely natural human response for someone who had adopted a 'tribal chief'-like role within his family and his business.

I attempted to suggest that, while the death of another human being was far from desirable, it was an indirect cause of the kind of problem-solving strategies someone in Tristan Grosvenor's position would apply to a physically violent situation.

And that if Gerald Tamlyn had not died, Grosvenor may well have been hailed as a hero.

When I shared these insights in a widely read, populist publication, Grosvenor cast me aside and tried to ruin me.

And in many ways, he succeeded. I abandoned my research, I was forced out of a promising career in the media, and I had no option but to retrain as a secondary school teacher.

I had to rebuild my life.

Yet, despite the undisputed fact that Tristan Grosvenor was a killer, he remained unscathed. The world very quickly forgot about that night of blood and violence. It was as if Grosvenor was absolved of any stain upon his character, continuing to be heralded as a captain of industry, despite his proclivities.

I hope this thesis can be added to the weight of evidence that this man should not be walking free.

Because I believe he is dangerous.

Tristan Grosvenor is a killer, hiding in plain sight.

Unless someone stops him, he will kill again.

Of that, there can be no doubt.

Chapter 37

James

The morning started out as an ordinary morning at the office.

It was finally signing and completion day on the Fahlberg/Copping merger. Our team had spent hours meticulously preparing all the documentation, and now, after weeks of blood, sweat and tears, we were nearly at the finish line. Luckily, the final stage was done online, with the signature pages sent to the directors of both companies to sign. I always feel like it's a complete anti-climax after the pre-signing drama of intense document reviews, negotiation, drafting and tight deadlines.

At one thirty I got a call from Maisie on the front desk. I

clicked off the timer application on my laptop that was recording my billable time.

'James, there's a young lady here for you.'

I wasn't expecting anyone, but maybe it was someone delivering the new Bose speakers I had ordered the week before. The front desk crew hate personal deliveries coming in for the lawyers, so I was expecting a bit of hostility from Maisie.

'Who's she from?' I asked.

'She says she's got lunch for you.'

That stumped me.

'I didn't order anything, Maisie. She's probably looking for John Fenton or Jason Farrier. Maybe she got the names mixed up. Try them.'

'Okay. Sorry to disturb you, James.'

I hung up and went back to my emails. Two minutes later, my phone rang again.

'There's no mistake,' Maisie said. 'She says it's definitely you she wants to see. James Fitzpatrick. She says you and her are … friends.'

'She said that?'

'Well … she says her name is Charlotte Odette, and she's your girlfriend. But obviously, I know that's not true—'

I cut in before she said another word.

'Tell her I'm not here.'

'Um … well …'

Her voice dropped to hushed tones.

'James, she's sitting five feet away from me, and knows I'm talking to you.'

'I don't care. *Tell her I am not here*. That I've had to pop out and had my calls forwarded to my mobile.'

'Right you be.' Then in a louder voice: 'Thank you, James. Yes, of course I'll pass that on.'

I sat there, sweat starting to prickle at my forehead, wondering what the fuck I had unleashed.

I had messed up royally. This whole sorry business needed to be shut down, and fast. I could only hope that this would send a message that I was, as I had indicated when I left Charlotte's apartment just a few hours previously, very busy, and therefore unavailable.

I expected the phone to ring again within a few minutes, Maisie informing me that my 'girlfriend' had refused to leave and was staging a sit-in in the reception area. But no call came and, after waiting five nervous minutes, I relaxed a bit and continued to work.

Ten minutes later there was a knock on my door.

My heart sinking, I called out:

'Come in.'

It was Maisie, carrying – I shit you not – an old-fashioned wicker picnic basket.

'Your friend insisted I deliver this to you personally. She says I am to tell you to not work so hard, and that she'll see you soon.'

'This is crazy, she just helped me out a few times with IT issues and now she's stalking me,' I told Maisie, really hoping she was buying my story.

'I'm sure,' Maisie smirked. 'She left you a note, by the way.'

I could tell Maisie was revelling in my discomfort. And that made me very nervous. Because Maisie is a mouthpiece, and her knowing anything … actually, scratch that, her not knowing but just vaguely suspecting is the equivalent of the entire office being involved in the discussion.

She plonked the basket on my table, gave me a knowing look, and sashayed out.

As soon as the door was closed, I got up, walked around the desk and peered out into the hallway to make sure Maisie had really gone. Once I knew the coast was clear, I undid the straps and opened the packed lunch Charlotte had sent.

She had gone all out. There was a very good Sauvignon Blanc and a large bottle of San Pellegrino sparkling water, as well as two wine glasses and two water glasses. The drinks were accompanied by a wheel of creamy Camembert, a small loaf of sourdough, grapes, Parma ham, a jar of olives, another of sundried tomatoes and a little pot with mixed nuts. To finish, she had placed two chocolate bombs, and a small tub of Chantilly cream. Knives, forks and spoons were tied in a bundle with a purple ribbon.

Stuck to the underside of the lid was a note:

Dear James,
As you're so busy, I thought I'd bring you some lunch. It's really important, even when we're in the throes of a crazy schedule, to make the time to eat and take stock. I'm sorry I can't share lunch with you, but I'll be happy knowing you're enjoying it at some stage today.

James, last night was lovely. You were so kind to join me at the screening and you listened to me when we talked. Spending the night together was just so special. I hated that you had to run this morning, but I understand you are rushed off your feet at the moment, so I'm not going to put a lot of pressure on you.

When you are free, I'd love to see you again.

Enjoy the food.

Love,

Charlotte x

The note made me think two things.

Firstly, maybe Charlotte wasn't the crazy bitch I'd been painting her for the last fifteen minutes. Okay, so she was trying a bit hard, but once you got over that, all I really got from the note was kindness.

And secondly, between the time I spoke to her and she arrived into my office, there was no way Maisie had not read the note.

Which meant I was fucked.

Chapter 38

Charlotte

I spent the morning putting together a lovely lunch hamper for me and James, picking out all the things I thought I would like to have delivered to my place of work if someone cared about me enough to do such a thing. I stopped by Delicario, a luxurious gourmet food shop a short stroll from James's office. I bought everything I needed, even the glassware and the knives and forks. It cost a fortune, but it was worth it. I thought it would be no harm to have them as part of the picnic basket going forward. I hoped we would get to use it a lot more.

Once I had everything purchased and packed safely into the basket, I strolled to Temple and to the impressive offices of Astley, Clifford and Kenworthy. The girl at reception was called Maisie, according to the sign on her desk. She was a slim, tanned-skinned woman, her shiny black hair pulled back into a sleek ponytail. She was wearing a tailored black jacket and her whole look was immaculately put together. I told that I'd like to see James.

This seemed to cause some consternation.

At first, she informed me he was in his office and she would let him know I was there. Then she appeared to be under the impression there was some mistake and a few more phone calls were made before I grasped that she believed I was a delivery person for a catering company.

Clearing my throat, I got up and went back over to her desk.

'Maisie,' I said sharply.

'Yes?'

'My name is Charlotte Odette. I am here to see James Fitzpatrick. He and I are friends. Close friends. I've come to take him out for a picnic lunch, so would you mind calling James again and let him know I'm waiting?'

She looked at me with an expression that suggested she would like to vault the desk and throttle me. But she smiled like she was enjoying this charade, and said:

'Of course, Ms Odette, please take a seat. I'll call Mr Fitzpatrick one more time and see if we can sort this out.'

I did as she asked, and waited some more.

The conversation this time was hushed. There was a lot of whispering. Several furtive glances were thrown my way. Then she hung up and, standing, came out from behind her desk and over to the seating area where I was waiting.

'I'm afraid Mr Fitzpatrick is out of the office at a client

meeting. I'm very sorry, but I didn't realise that his calls were forwarded to his mobile.'

'Okay,' I said. 'That's fine. Can I ask you to give him the basket so he can eat when he comes in?'

'Of course. I'd be happy to.'

'And do you have some paper that I might scribble a message on?'

'I'll get one for you right way.'

I wrote a few lines on the headed notepaper that she had handed me, then stuck it to the inside of the basket's lid, buckled it and gave it to Maisie.

'There you go. Thanks so much for your help.'

'Of course,' the receptionist said. 'Can I let you in on something, though? You know he's married, right?'

'I don't think that's any of your business.'

She looked at me with something approximating pity.

'Of course it's not,' she said quietly. 'It's just, well, us girls have to stick together, don't we? I just don't want to see you getting hurt. He'll use you for what he can get and then move on. I've seen it before. But look, you do you. If you're getting something out of the relationship, well good for you.'

'I think I'm going to go now,' I said, turning to leave.

'I'll pass on your message and the basket,' Maisie said in hissed tones, 'but I wouldn't hold my breath waiting for a big thank you, if I were you. I'd be surprised if you hear anything back at all.'

I tried to blot out the words and fled from the building, running up the street towards the nearest Tube station. I had to get as far away from that awful law firm as quickly as I could.

Was that horrendous woman telling me that I was not the first of James's conquests? That this was a pattern of behaviour? Meet a girl, make her believe he's sincere and sweet, bed her and then ghost her? If I hadn't woken this morning before he left, would he have even said goodbye?

I reached the station, found a bench and sat, feeling hollow. Empty.

Was I so pathetic and naïve? Had I allowed myself to be played so easily?

I must have been the easiest notch James Fitzpatrick had ever put in his bedpost.

I told myself I would not cry. I was better than that. Stronger. By the time I was on the Tube bound for home, I was angry.

And that was when I decided I might try to get even.

It was time James Fitzpatrick knew what it felt like to lose a little of his dignity.

Chapter 39

James

By 3 p.m. I had put the Charlotte incident to the back of my mind. I was drafting one tiny amendment to a vital share purchase agreement and attempted to log into my email in order to send it to a client.

I couldn't get in. I tried using the 'forgot your password' protocols, but they wouldn't recognise any password I entered; each time I did I was told there was a problem, so I finally gave up.

I realised, at that point, that I had access to the email account of Mark Johnson, a junior associate on my team. I rang him quickly, and asked if I could send the agreement from his account, as I'd been locked out of mine, and that it was urgent.

Like a good junior, he didn't question me.

I uploaded the file, wrote a brief cover-email, and clicked 'send'.

It seemed to send, but then a second later a message popped into Johnson's inbox, informing him (and me) that there had been a problem sending the email. I scanned down through it, but none of it made sense to me.

You do not have the authority to send this message. Please try again when you have made better life choices.

What? Surely that had to be a joke!

I tried again and got the same message.

Sighing, I grabbed my phone. I remember Charlotte mentioning she wasn't working today, which would make the call an easier experience.

'Hi James.' The voice that answered was immediately familiar. My heart sank.

'Charlotte,' I said. 'I thought you had the day off today.'

I know I did not sound happy, but she didn't let on she noticed.

'I got drafted in after all,' she said. 'Luckily, I didn't have any plans. So how can I help you?'

I told her, and read out the failed email message, wondering as I did so if this was all quite the coincidence it seemed.

'That's an odd one, isn't it?' she asked brightly.

'Very strange,' I agreed.

'Let's see if we can get things moving for you again, shall we?'

'I'd appreciate that.'

Keys clattered. She was humming. For a moment I couldn't place it, but then I did. It was a Gillian Welch song: 'The Way It Will Be'.

'Mark Johnson's email account is fine and shouldn't

encounter any more error messages, but you'll need to reset your password,' she said after a minute or two. 'I've given you a new one for the moment. Would you like to write it down?'

'Yes. I have a pen here. What is it?'

'It's fuckboy1.'

I froze, pen still hovering over the page.

'Excuse me?'

'Would you like me to spell it for you?'

'No, thank you. I think I've got it.'

'Is there anything else Tech Helpdesk can do for you this afternoon, James?'

'No thanks.'

'Would you be open to taking a brief survey for us about your experience?'

'You know,' I said, 'I don't think I would today.'

'That's quite alright. Thanks for calling us.'

'Okay. Goodbye, Charlotte.'

'Bye for now. I'll catch up with you again, yeah?'

'Charlotte …'

But she was gone.

I went into my work account and put my email password back to what it usually is, but then thought better of it and changed it for a random selection of letters and numbers, which I scribbled on a bit of paper and put in my desk drawer for easy access.

I was pretty sure it wouldn't keep Charlotte out – she could probably reset it with very little effort. But as far as I knew, to do that she'd need to at least enter the current password, and I wasn't going to make it unnecessarily easy for her.

I sent the document, and this time it went without any problems or weird error messages.

When it was gone I sat looking at the picnic basket. I was hungry, but all the drama had also soured me to the idea of eating.

Picking up the basket, I brought it downstairs to the bin and chucked the whole lot in.

I know it was a waste, but I was starting to worry the food in it might be poisoned.

I left the office early that evening, arriving home just after 5 p.m. The emotional stress of the day had taken its toll on me. But I soon discovered that it wasn't going to be a relaxing evening in front of the TV.

I made a sandwich and opened a bottle of Heineken and plonked down in front of the TV to try and watch *Hawkeye* for the umpteenth time. I was no more successful now than I had been before. Except now my mind was whirring. I hadn't seen hide not hair of Bella that morning, and now she wasn't home at her usual time either.

Even if she was going back out again, this was odd.

I tried calling her, but got no response. After two unanswered calls, I tried to text her, both from our network and by WhatsApp. The message was delivered but not read.

I messaged her through Instagram, but the message wasn't looked at either.

I couldn't rest.

My mind told me she'd either gone out with the bloke she'd

snogged again or – probably more likely – was out pursuing her research. But would that prevent her from answering a text message? The radio silence had been going on for two hours at this stage, and I was getting extremely anxious.

Finally I got up and went into what used to be our bedroom, but which I now thought of as hers.

The one thing about Bella is that she's usually meticulous.

The room, however, was a mess. Clothes were everywhere, drawers left hanging open, wardrobe doors still flung wide, as if someone had been searching frantically for something and had been unable to find it. A shoe rack that stood by the wall had been upended and Bella's shoes were scattered around the floor.

I was taking all this in when I saw the bed was still unmade and there was a stain in the middle of the sheet. I went to the bed and knelt down to take a closer look. The stain was about the size of a saucer, irregularly shaped, and a brownish red in colour.

I'm not a detective, but I knew this was blood.

Several thoughts went through my head, but I have to admit up front that my heart was beating fast.

Could Bella be having her period? I suppose there are blokes who would never know their wife's or girlfriend's cycle, but I usually did. If we'd been sleeping together I would have known, and the fact I didn't felt like a slap in the face.

There was a second thought that came rapidly after this one.

Bella has a history of self-harming. When I first met her, she would cut occasionally when she was stressed. The behaviour resurfaced after the publication of the Grosvenor article and its terrible fallout, but she got help for it, and to the best of my knowledge, hadn't cut for years. But that didn't mean she hadn't now. It was well dried in. I'm not a forensic scientist or a blood-spatter expert, so I couldn't say how old it was. I figured either last night or early this morning.

Which didn't help me at all.

The third thing that passed through my mind, and it was something I fought hard to dismiss, was that something dangerous had happened to Bella. I didn't have a clue what this might be, but what I did know what that my wife seemed to be missing, she was not responding to my calls or messages, there were signs of disturbance in our room, and there was a bloodstain on our bed. And everything I knew about her told me that if Bella had created the stain herself in some way, she would not have left it for me to find.

I tried calling her again, but the call rang out each time.

The thought that kept nagging at me was that Bella might have left me.

Or she might have been taken.

But that was completely off the wall.

Wasn't it?

Chapter 40

Bella

I had to run.

There was nothing else I could do.

The wheels I had set in motion were turning faster than I had expected they would, and when I realised that, the only thing I could do was dive for cover.

Despite my anger, I wanted to send James a message to let him know everything was not as it appeared, and by trashing my bedroom, I thought he would know I was telling him I had a plan and that I was in control of things.

I accept that I have not always been in control. That when things got bad before, I allowed myself to become compromised.

But that is not going to happen now. Because this time, I am not alone.

This time, I have help from someone who is just as invested as I am in seeing that justice is served.

Together, we will make sure that it is.

Chapter 41

James

I was intensely worried about Bella.

And I was very uncertain as to what to do about it. Should I call the police? Had she been taken or had she just run off? Left me?

The cold, hard reality was that I didn't have a clue. All these possibilities seemed plausible.

She'd been basically having an affair, and when I confronted her on it she expressed no remorse, and in fact became violently angry when I expressed my unhappiness at the situation. So, thinking she might have decided to throw her lot in with this bloke was not in any way unreasonable.

Then there was the Grosvenor angle.

Which scared me. I hated to think Bella might have walked out on me, run to the arms of another man, but the idea she might have been abducted because of some crazy risk she'd taken to get close to that fucking murderer terrified me.

I knew Grosvenor was dangerous. I always believed he let Bella go the last time because he thought she was psychologically fragile enough to buckle under the pressure he had so effectively put her under. Grosvenor was, and indeed still is, as good a psychologist as Bella is. He knew she was head over heels for him, and he thought his rejection of her would be enough to crush her.

It nearly was.

Now she's back, though, and he will see she's not as broken as he believed … what will he be compelled to do?

And what might she have done to force his hand?

The whole thing made me think of the one and only time I met Bella's parents, something her father said to me on the day we got married.

While we were dating she told me she was 'estranged' from them, that she'd had some kind of row with her dad, who had, in her words, 'anger management issues', and 'was never present', and her mother was, again these are her words, 'weak-minded and a moral coward'.

I had no idea what those terms really meant until I met them.

Our wedding was a … a weird day, really.

I remember during the reception one of her 'friends' (a guy named Randy, funnily enough) got drunk and, in what I took to be a rush of jealous vitriol, informed me Bella had been fucking several of her lecturers, sometimes two or even three at a time. I had Ralph and another mate, Nicholas, throw good old Randy out on his arse, and I never saw him again.

It's only lately that conversation has come back to me. Events have caused it to resurface, I suppose.

I lost sight of Bella's parents, Neil and Thomasina, for most of the night, but as I was returning from having ejected the drunken Randy, I spied Neil standing beside his wife at the bar. I noted he had his coat on, and reasoned he was probably about to leave.

'Can I get you and Mrs Murphy a drink before you hit the road?' I asked.

They both looked deeply uncomfortable. Despite it being his daughter's wedding day, Neil Murphy hadn't shaved, and his wife looked tired and haggard.

My father-in-law looked at me through rheumy eyes, and said:

'Thommy don't drink. But I'll take a whiskey.'

I ordered two and handed him one.

'I can see you love my daughter,' the old man said.

'I do.'

'She can be a hard girl to love, at times,' he continued, taking a large swallow of his drink.

'That's good, because I can be pretty hard to love too,' I laughed.

'Maybe,' he said. 'Maybe. But mark my words, Mr Fitzpatrick, you will have your hands full with my girl. She don't talk to me no more, I don't even know why she asked us to come – my best guess is to show us she's made something of herself. But a day will come when she will test your love. I am telling you that as a courtesy.'

'I think you should leave now,' I said.

'We're going,' Murphy said, and slammed his empty glass on the bar, grasped Thomasina firmly by the elbow and shuffled out. We haven't seen them since.

As it happened, our marriage started out very solid.

But it didn't take long before we were confronted with the first of many tests.

Chapter 42

Charlotte

James was a crushing disappointment.

I had never intended to like him as much as I did, and when I discovered he was as weak and as simple-minded as most of the other men I have encountered, I won't pretend that wasn't a blow to me. I had started to think he might be different. That he and I could build something.

By then, I knew his relationship with Bella was over. Of that I was certain, and I knew she thought it was over, too.

I had watched her, the beautiful Bella Murphy, as she was then, when we were both students at City University. She was doing her MA, I was doing my BSc in Computer Science, but we had some classes on the same campus a couple of times a week, and I would see her in the canteen, or in the library.

She fascinated me. There was something about her – a self-assured confidence, tempered with a hint of darkness that made me want to know more about her. She had a couple of social media pages, but she barely ever posted on them. Clearly she was someone who preferred to lurk and view other people's behaviour online. I took to watching her when I could, positioning myself near her when she ate her lunch and while she studied.

One evening, when she walked home, I followed at a discreet distance.

She was living in a small bedsit near Notting Hill.

I sat on a bench adjacent to her doorway for three nights and saw many different male callers coming and going.

I now know that one of them was James. They were living together, but he was working such long hours, you'd barely have known that it was his place too. I probably should have recognised him when I met him through my job, but in truth, I didn't.

It almost made me feel sorry for him. He didn't know he was being cuckolded.

Bella and I had been good friends back then. And in the intervening years we kept in touch. When she came back to City to complete her thesis, we had picked up right where we left off.

And of course, Bella was able to view it all philosophically when I told her that I'd slept with James. At least, that's how I chose to interpret her silence.

Bella is a remarkable person. She loved her husband, but was under no illusions about him, either.

And when he needed to be taught a lesson, well, she was okay with that, too.

Of course, as it turned out, James was going to be collateral damage in a way none of us could have foreseen.

Not that we minded.

As I said, James was a big disappointment.

Chapter 43

James

I called Bea, Bella's friend and colleague.

'I thought she was at home sick,' Bea informed me. 'She wasn't at school yesterday or today.'

Now I felt real panic rising.

'Do you have any idea where she might be?'

Bea seemed to think for a moment, before saying:

'Caleb wasn't in school today, either. Have you tried calling him?'

I felt the bottom drop out of my stomach.

'I don't have his number,' I said, trying to keep a tremble from my voice.

'Pity. I don't either. He was always much more interested in Bella than me.'

I felt like telling Bea to fuck right off, but right then didn't seem the time.

'Do you honestly believe she'd just run off with this guy without telling anyone?'

'I don't know what your wife would do. After all the shit that's gone down in the school over the past couple of weeks or so, I'd guess she's skating on very thin ice.'

'What shit?'

Bea gave a cynical little laugh.

'The police have been in and interviewed everyone, James. It's pretty serious.'

What the fuck was going on? What was Bella involved in?

'The police were in?'

'Oh yeah. In force. Uniforms, detectives, the lot.'

'Why?'

'Bella was attacked by some of the students. Probably would have been raped if Caleb hadn't stepped in.'

I wanted to scream. Why was I the last one to hear about this? How had things gotten so bad between us that she didn't tell me about this?

'Do you have the name of any of the police officers?'

'The guy who interviewed me was an Irish guy, said he was from the Violent Crimes Task Force at the Met. DS Harvey Brennan.'

'Thanks, Bea.'

'Don't mention it.'

I hung up and dialled the London Metropolitan Police.

DS Harvey Brennan did not look like a cop, or at least not how I would have expected one to look. He seemed much more like a down-at-heel used-car salesman. His partner, on the other hand, DI Carol Bodhua, looked exactly how modern policing should be, and that gave me some confidence.

'And how long has it been since you've heard from Ms Fitzpatrick?' Brennan asked.

He and Bodhua were seated on our living-room couch, sipping coffees I had made them and nibbling on M&S Chocolate Shortbreads.

'I'd say about thirty-six hours,' I said.

'You'd say? Are you uncertain of the precise moment, Mr Fitzpatrick?'

'Yes. I would say that I am a bit hazy. It could have been an hour before or two hours after. I didn't know I should have kept a close and accurate record of the hours I spend with my wife.'

Brennan dunked his biscuit delicately into his mug before consuming half of it.

'As a lawyer I would have thought you would keep very accurate records of everything you do.'

'Who told you that?'

'I've been working on the force, and alongside members of the legal profession, for a long time now, Mr Fitzpatrick. I have become accustomed to solicitors and their ways.'

'Well, my ways are different.'

'Would you err on the side of thirty-six hours or thirty-eight?' Bodhua cut in, giving her partner a hard look which he completely ignored.

'Thirty-six,' I said. 'About a day and a half.'

'Is it true you and Ms Fitzpatrick were estranged?' Brennan

asked in tones that suggested the import of such a question meant little to him.

'Where in the hell did you hear that?' I seethed.

'One of your wife's friends hinted at it,' Brennan said happily.

'Bea,' I said, ruefully.

'Is it true?'

'We'd been having some problems, yes. But nothing extreme.'

'Have these problems been linked to your wife's relationship with a Mr Caleb Westlake, a substitute physical education teacher at her school?'

I wanted to throw up. I guess I must have turned a shade of green because Bodhua leaned forward and said:

'Are you alright, Mr Fitzpatrick? Would you like me to fetch you some water?'

I shook my head.

'I'm okay, thank you. Yes, I'd say that was where some of our problems began.'

'And did these problems have anything to do with the alleged sexual assault your wife experienced at the school?'

I almost choked.

'I wasn't aware of any sexual assault, Bella never told me. The first I heard of it was this evening when Bea told me. That's why I contacted you straightaway.'

'You were aware of the affair with Mr Westlake.'

'I wouldn't call it an affair. They went out for a meal and she told me they kissed.'

'Are you sure you haven't hurt your wife, Mr Fitzpatrick?'

'Of course I'm sure I haven't hurt her! Why would I call you if I had done? Wouldn't that be a bit stupid?'

'You'd be surprised, sir,' Brennan said. 'Some people seem to think it will throw us off the scent. Which is very silly, if you don't mind my saying so.'

'That's not what happened here,' I said. 'I am genuinely worried for Bella's safety and welfare.'

'Can you think of anyone who might want to harm her?'

'What about this Caleb bloke? I'm told he wasn't in school today either. Have you looked into him?'

'We don't usually discuss our methods with members of the public, Mr Fitzpatrick. Even those of them who are … ahem … members of the legal profession.'

'I'd start there.'

'Are you in contact with her parents?' Bodhua asked.

'Not very much, no.'

'Can you furnish us with an address for them?'

'I'm sure they're in a notebook that Bella kept in a drawer in the kitchen. I can get it for you.'

'I do like that,' Brennan said. 'I enjoy a nice notebook myself.'

'What about your own family?' Bodhua asked. 'Did they get on with your wife?'

'They don't really talk much. But they like her well enough.'

'Seems an odd way to show how much they liked her if they didn't talk,' Brennan said. 'But I'm sure you're right, of course.'

I was about to bring up Bella's resumed PhD research on Tristan Grosvenor when, at that precise moment, a text message came through on my phone. I knew from the ringtone that it was work, and for a message to come in from work at this time of evening meant only one thing: an emergency.

'I need to look at this, I'm dreadfully sorry,' I said, as I glanced at my phone, and swiped to unlock the screen so I could read the message.

'Urgent, is it?' Brennan asked, his expression all innocent interest.

'Yes. It's work.'

'Then you'd better peruse it post-haste.'

'Thank you.'

I did. And felt my stomach lurch all over again.

'I need to go,' I said. 'Right now.'

'Don't let us stop you,' Brennan said. 'By which I mean, don't let us prevent you from going into the office this evening. I am going to be forced to ask you not to leave town, however, until we've looked into what has become of your good lady wife.'

'I'm not going anywhere until I know she's safe,' I said. 'I'm really sorry, but I'm going to have to ask you to excuse me.'

'You don't require such a pardon in your own home,' Brennan said, smiling winsomely and standing. Bodhua, towering over him, did the same. 'We'll chat again very soon.'

I just nodded and ran for my coat.

Chapter 44

Detective Sergeant Harvey Brennan

Now Bella Fitzpatrick has disappeared.

I am puzzled.

There was no sign of a break-in at the apartment. In fact, breaking in would have posed a supreme challenge to even the most talented of thieves. The gate mechanism requires both a key card and a code before it will open, and each apartment has a heavy-duty security door with a triple-locking mechanism.

DI Bodhua checked the logs for the gate, and no one other than residents had come in or out, and it was clear to see the doors had not been interfered with.

The Fitzpatricks also have an alarm that's fitted with a panic button, situated in the living room. This triggers a response from a security guard situated in the grounds, and also rings in the local station so a uniformed officer can be sent forthwith.

The alarm had not been triggered and no panic had been reported.

Mr and Ms Fitzpatrick's room was in disarray, and her husband insists this is out of character. However, the mess does not look to me like the result of a struggle. It looks … purposeful.

It's as if someone scattered items here and there, thither and yon, in an attempt to suggest a struggle may have taken place.

The blood on the sheets is just as enigmatic.

In my experience of visiting crime scenes, blood stains are irregular. They are smears and spatters and pools and streaks. They mirror the desperate moments that caused them to be created. I have never encountered a circular, regular stain before.

I cannot imagine the circumstances that left such a mark.

Except for someone depositing a sample of blood with the express purpose of it being found, and its discoverer to exclaim: 'Look, a bloodstain.'

I have taken a sample, but I am prepared to hazard a guess that it is Ms Fitzpatrick's.

Chapter 45

James

There has been a security breach that has been tracked to your account. Come in immediately.

The text message was from Kenworthy.

Receiving a text message from Kenworthy is never a good thing.

When I got to the offices, the three partners were sitting in the main conference room with a man called Gifford, who heads up the team of private investigators they keep on the payroll. I'd never had any personal dealings with him before, but I've heard he used to be a Royal Marine before being dishonourably discharged. Whether this is true or not is anyone's guess, but I can tell you, he is scary looking. At least six foot four, with a head that looks like it was made from a mis-shaped turnip, arms like tree trunks and legs like pillars of stone, all of it squeezed into a black suit with an open-necked white shirt, from which sprouted a single white chest hair that I couldn't help but find distracting. I wonder why he didn't trim it.

Maybe he wants people distracted.

Whatever the reason, he eyed me when I came in as if I was something that had crawled out from under a stone and he was trying to work out what to do with me. No one asked me to sit.

'What's going on?' I asked anxiously, doing my best to pay him no heed. 'You said my account has been breached?'

I thought I was going mad.

Gifford sat in a chair near me, scrolling on his phone. Clifford was beside him, glowering at me.

'What happened?' I asked, trying to keep the panic that was threatening to overwhelm me out of my voice.

'Where's the money?' the investigator asked.

'What money?'

'You can stop bullshitting,' he said. 'We know everything.'

'I have no clue what you're talking about.'

Clifford sighed and leaned over to me.

'You're a smart guy, Fitzpatrick. I always knew you were. Too smart for your own good, at the end of the day.'

'I'm completely lost,' I said.

'Okay, I'll play along,' Clifford said. 'You know the Fahlberg/Copping merger completed today.'

'Of course I do,' I said.

The papers had been signed and money transferred today. As

far as I was aware, the rest of the team were downing bottles of Taittinger in Soho House as I stood looking at the furious faces in front of me.

'So you know that, in advance of that, a very sizeable amount of money had been transferred by Fahlberg's accountants into the client account here at the firm to be held in escrow until it could be transferred to Copping's bank account as soon as all the paperwork was signed this morning.'

'Yes, I'm aware of the process, but I don't understand why you are telling me all of this and what it has to do with me.'

'Because Philip Kemp, one of our junior accountants, received an email from you this afternoon giving him the authority to transfer the funds to Copping's bank account. You said in your email that the bank account details had changed, and you were providing the new account information.'

'I didn't send that email,' I said, my voice barely audible.

'You didn't?'

'No. I didn't.'

'The bank account that the money was transferred to belonged to a shell company based in the Cayman Islands,' Clifford said. 'We've checked them out. They started trading a week ago, and blinked out of existence as soon as the money was transferred to them.'

'They're gone,' Gifford said bleakly. 'And so is the money. Two billion, James. Just like that.'

'Transfer it back,' Clifford demanded.

'If I could, I'd be happy to,' I said.

'Wrong answer.'

He covered the space shockingly quickly for a man of his

size. Before I could do anything about it he punched me in the balls. The pain was immediate and all-consuming and I thought I'd pass out.

'We can do that all night,' Gifford said in that lilting voice. 'But I doubt your *cajones* would stand it.'

I put my head down and threw up all over the big man's shoes.

'*You fucking bastard!*' he swore, and looked about for something to clean them before taking a handkerchief from his pocket.

And that was when, in spite of the pain, I grabbed the conference table and overturned it, spilling papers and water glasses all over the partners, and ran for it.

It's amazing what adrenaline can make you do.

Chapter 46

Charlotte

I volunteer once a week at the nursing home where my mother resides.

I usually begin the evening by sitting with her for an hour, which I feel is more to benefit me than her. She doesn't know who I am, and most of the time in her room involves her either staring into space, talking about people who are either dead or might as well be, or asking me who I am and why have I taken something from her.

My mother, in her confusion, is convinced the staff of the home – of which she seems to think I am one – is stealing from her.

When I can bear to be with her no longer, I go to a room up the corridor and read books to an old man called Arthur.

Arthur is eighty-three years old, and thinks I am his wife. And it seems he absolutely hated his wife with a vengeance. The two hours I spend trudging through a Robert Ludlum or a Lee Child are usually interspersed with comments about how Arthur would like to punch me in the face or throw me against the wall and screw me.

I know this is not really Arthur talking, that the dementia has taken the filter that prevents us from speaking like that to one another, but it still feels awful. It still makes me angry. I try to tell myself not to take it personally, but it's difficult not to when someone is shouting that they would like to bend you over and do whatever they want to you.

But it is good experience for my job. If I can cope with Arthur's constant verbal assaults, I can cope with anything.

After my stint at the nursing home, I got the bus back to Piccadilly. I was thinking a lot about what I had done to James. I couldn't decide if I felt bad about it or not. I thought I probably felt a tiny amount of guilt, but at the same time I also believed he had it coming. He had treated me in a very cavalier manner, and I felt a little payback was certainly due.

It had just been a bit of harmless fun, and I thought it might do him good to teach him some humility. That I could reach out and deliver a blow that hurt him, just as he had hurt me.

I was almost at my flat when I spotted two large men standing outside, waiting around at the door. Something made me hang back, I don't know what, just a general feeling of unease. I waited, watched, and as I did, I saw one of them, the taller one who looked as if he had been constructed from spare parts, reach out and push the buzzer. He waited, and his friend, the shorter, squarer one, stepped up and banged on the door with his closed fist.

I didn't know if I should go over or not. They had to be looking for me, but something about them told me whatever purpose they had was not good. I stepped back a little until I was in the shadows of a shop doorway and watched.

They lingered, buzzing and banging, for another six minutes before finally deciding I was not at home, and walking away towards the parking complex for the station.

I waited a further fifteen minutes in my hiding place to be sure they were gone before going into my apartment.

While I waited, I made a phone call.

It looked to me as if things were beginning to escalate.

And to be honest, I couldn't have been happier.

'Psycho or Hero' by Bella Fitzpatrick, published in *The City Grapevine* magazine, 20 August 2010

Tristan Grosvenor, the well-known fifty-six-year-old business tycoon, killed a man.

Not many CEOs have that on their CVs.

On December 6th, 2008, as the UK was on the brink of recession, amidst an endemic of bankruptcies, job cuts, and financial uncertainty, Gerald Tamlyn, a former employee of Isotech, the company Grosvenor built from the ground up, and of which he was still the Chief Executive Officer, gained access to Isotech's London offices using an old security card, and made his way to Mr Grosvenor's office on the fifteenth floor.

There is disagreement as to the purpose of Tamlyn's visit to his former boss. His wife asserts he wanted to clear the air and make peace – Tamlyn had been very vocal about what he viewed as ill-treatment at the hands of his employer. He had gone to the media and had also initiated an unfair dismissal claim against Isotech.

Grosvenor, on the other hand, insists Tamlyn was only after one thing: a violent confrontation.

Whatever the truth, the end result is undisputed. Tristan Grosvenor beat Gerald Tamlyn about the head with a solid granite paperweight, fracturing his skull and causing catastrophic brain injury. Tamlyn was dead when paramedics arrived on the scene.

The trial that followed is well documented, as is the fact that the charges against Mr Grosvenor were dismissed due to breaches in the chain of custody relating to certain items of evidence. There has been widespread conjecture as to what exactly happened that night in 2008, and Tristan Grosvenor, outside of his trial, has refused to speak to anyone about it.

Until now, that is.

Because I can reveal that, in a series of tell-all interviews, the man whose killer instinct extends beyond the field of finance has finally shared his side of the story.

'It was a very simple decision to make,' Grosvenor told me. 'It became clear to me shortly after Tamlyn arrived to my office unannounced and uninvited that it was going to be a case of him or me surviving the encounter, and I am here to tell you, the loser in that exchange was not going to be me.'

Grosvenor is known in true crime circles as the *CEO Killer*, but in reality, he made a name for himself long before his deadly encounter with Tamlyn by creating one of the largest finance and investment companies in the world, earning his first million before he was twenty-one and announcing his first billion on the day of his thirtieth birthday.

He is listed currently as having a net worth of £34 billion, and is numbered among the ten richest industrialists in the world.

In person, he is a fascinating, compelling and charming man.

The first thing you notice about him is his eyes. They are an impossibly pale blue, and seem to look right into your soul, immediately knowing what makes you tick.

'The ability to read people is an essential skill for anyone in business,' he agreed when I put it to him that he seemed to have an innate understanding of what motivates individuals. 'I always knew Tamlyn was psychologically delicate – he was a numbers man, not a people person, and when he was on my team, I was happy enough to let him fiddle away at his spreadsheets and manipulate his statistics, but when the financial world went belly-up, I could no longer afford to keep someone whose job could just as easily be done by some of the new software packages one of my tech companies had developed. He had to go. I knew he'd be upset, but this wasn't a matter of choice. To keep Isotech operating, we had to streamline.'

If Grosvenor knew Tamlyn would be upset, did he foresee how that unhappiness would manifest itself?

'I'm not psychic,' he said, dismissing my suggestion. 'I thought he might need some therapy or just go away and lick his wounds, maybe spend some time travelling. Of course I didn't expect he'd break in and try to kill me.'

Wouldn't it be difficult for Tamlyn to go on a Mediterranean cruise, considering he had not been granted severance pay, which was one of the main issues that Tamlyn and his associates were so activated about?

'Not my problem,' Grosvenor said, waving the suggestion off with one of his slender hands (he has the fingers of a musician or a surgeon). 'All of those staff whose contracts I terminated were fully cognisant of the conditions of their employment, and would have known that, in 2008, we were trading below average. There were emails being sent to every single employee on a weekly basis, informing them of our profit margin. I refuse to take responsibility for the fact some people's feelings were hurt. If I could have given them a good redundancy package, I would have. But those were the times we were living in. Everyone had to cut their cloth accordingly.'

I put it to Grosvenor that this casts him in quite an unsympathetic light.

'Maybe it does.' He shrugged. 'But you should remember, these people were all on very large salaries. If they'd had any common sense they'd have seen the writing on the wall and made sure they'd tucked a few quid away for a rainy day. Cast me as a cold-hearted Scrooge if you wish, but I stand over my decisions. No one was singled out for callous treatment. I hadn't taken a salary myself for more than ten months. That's the way these things go.'

Was he hurt by the response of Tamlyn and his recently unemployed associates? By the hounding he received in the press and left-leaning media?

'Are you asking me if I had an axe to grind against the man I subsequently killed?' Grosvenor asked me, mildly.

I told him I was.

'I did not. I bore Gerald no animosity. I understood his actions were a foolhardy attempt to get me to either change my mind and re-employ him or offer him some sort of pay-out. He'd known me for fifteen years and should have realised that was never going to happen. But this was business. He had to try.'

Surely being presented as a callous, unfeeling monster must have rankled, though.

'I am neither callous nor unfeeling. The people who know me are aware of that. If the rest of the world thinks I'm a cold-hearted bastard, and that makes my competitors a bit less inclined to take me on, then that's all to the good. I can live with it.'

Did he regret how that night had played out? The loss of a life at his hands?

'That's a complicated question,' Grosvenor said. 'If I could go back in time to try and prevent it from happening, would I? Well, I'm not sure I could, you see. I believe our operating policy was, and is, a sound one. It incentivises performance. My employees protect their own working conditions by ensuring we experience a healthy profit margin, and I think that is not only defensible, but a highly commendable way to run a company. In light of what happened would I go back and flout that policy and give Tamlyn and his cronies a big redundancy payment? No, I would not.'

A lot of readers will probably find that shocking, I told him.

'Well, prepare to be shocked even more,' he said ominously. 'If I had that *evening* to play over, would I do it differently? Once again, I'd have to say I would not. Tamlyn threatened me. He was behaving violently and was a clear and present danger. I made a decision, and I eradicated that threat in the only way I could think of. Could I have physically restrained him and waited for someone to come to help? Perhaps, but it seemed to me Tamlyn was extremely agitated, and I would be hard-pressed to hold him for very long. I absolutely believed my life was under threat, and, as I said earlier, if it came down to him or me, I was not going to let it be me. So I did what needed to be done to ensure I walked out of that room alive.'

I asked him if he slept soundly at night with the fallout of that decision.

'I have no guilt,' Grosvenor said. 'Do I feel bad for his family and the people who loved him? Of course I do, but then I thought Tamlyn was my friend, too. I'd employed him for more than a decade. If anyone is entitled to sympathy, surely it's me!'

Did he feel the decision to dismiss the crown case against him for manslaughter was fair?

'I did nothing wrong,' he said. 'I did not commit a crime. I defended myself against an intruder. Has our society become so wishy-washy and pathetic that we are now suggesting a man should lie down and await his fate if a thug breaks into his home or place of work? If that is the case, might I suggest we need to seriously examine the trajectory of our culture.'

To some, Tristan Grosvenor is the epitome of the entitled rich – someone who clearly believes he can do whatever he wishes – and the legal response or lack thereof would seem to back that position up.

Might I suggest that this is an opinion based on error.

Modern life has made us impotent. If the Tristan Grosvenor story teaches us anything, it is to be active agents in our own lives. And if that means standing up and facing the consequences, then so be it.

The fact Grosvenor sleeps soundly, unaffected by guilt, should not be seen as an indictment of his character, but rather a sign that his personality is in a state of balance. Through my research I have come to believe that the aggressive drive and the violence it sometimes entails might in fact offer the pathway to a healthy mind. Grosvenor's actions and his seemingly cold analysis of them may be the key to a new, happier, more content society.

No one can deny we are in the grip of a mental health crisis – our young people, and indeed many of our older citizens, seem to be in the clutches of self-loathing and personal doubt.

Tristan Grosvenor's willingness to accept the implications of his decisions, and his refusal to condemn himself, stands in marked contrast.

And if we take a step back from the court case and the publicity it received, maybe we can look at what happened with a more objective eye.

Might I offer the view that, if Gerald Tamlyn had not died, Grosvenor would be heralded as a hero, someone who struck a blow for his business, his personal space, and his right to run both as he saw fit.

The only reason people are so appalled is because his actions proved fatal.

Had Grosvenor's hand not grasped that paperweight, had his blows fallen at a slightly different angle, had Tamlyn had a thicker skull, we would be having a very different conversation.

Aggression and – it's not a popular thing to say, but I am going to walk out onto the precipice and say it – aggression and *violence* are not always bad, and are sometimes (admittedly on rare occasions, but that doesn't make this statement less true) morally and ethically justified.

Maybe we could all learn something important from a man like Tristan Grosvenor.

Chapter 47

Charlotte

I got ready for bed as usual, but when I climbed in between the covers, I found it impossible to sleep. I was not surprised to hear the noises when they came. I had expected them.

I heard a scraping sound and knew someone was trying to pick the lock on my apartment door. I lay there in the dark and listened to the methodical scratching, the sound of a metal implement teasing its way around the component parts of the mechanism that was the main safeguard between my home and the outside world.

I remained on my back on my bed for a while, straining my ears. Scrape. Scrape. Scrape.

I heard a kind of dragging noise, and then the click, click

of the tumblers falling, and I knew they were in. Or would be within seconds.

As silently as I could I stood up and walked into the living room. In the corner of the room, between the big window where I keep my treadmill there is a patch where the light from the streetlamps never reaches, so at night it is always wreathed in shadow. I pressed myself in close to the place where the walls met, and waited.

The door was pushed open, and two figures stepped inside.

It's funny, because I knew they were coming and I was as prepared as it is possible to be for someone to break into your home with a view to abducting you, but still my mind seemed to freeze, and for a long moment I could see myself being dragged towards the door to the steps that led to the street.

I imagined them pushing me into a car and saw myself watching the door to my apartment get further and further away through the rear window of the vehicle as I was driven away, making for an unknown destination, to be subjected to God knows what.

In the space of seconds I saw this, and it was enough to shake me from my reverie.

The first figure, the taller of the two, took a step into my living room, and I didn't let him take a second one. I took the taser I had hanging from my belt, pointed it at the central mass of the lead man, and fired, sending two barbs across the short distance and into his chest. I kept my finger on the trigger, activating the electric charge.

The taser is a wonderful device.

The one I own is called the TASER 7, and is generally used by the police or professional security operatives, and is not legally available to civilians. However, most things can be purchased online if you know where to look, and I did not have much difficulty getting my hands on this particular model.

Some TV shows present these non-lethal weapons very inaccurately. They do not, as is so often depicted, shoot crackling lightning bolts, nor do they make a buzzing sound as they shock their victims. The only noise that could be heard in my silent apartment was a soft *click* as I pressed the trigger, followed by a gulp from the man I'd just electrocuted.

Another inaccuracy TV shows perpetuate about tasers is that you can get second-hand shocked by them. The reality is, you can grab someone who is being shocked by a taser and not receive any of the current yourself. The weapon is, in fact, designed for this, as police officers can get a tased person cuffed and safe before switching off the charge and releasing them from its grip.

The only way another person can be harmed when someone nearby is being tasered is if they touch the barbs themselves.

Most people don't know this.

But once again, the internet is a wonderful source of information if you just take the time to seek it out.

The taller of the intruders went rigid with the shock and began to fall over. People who have been tasered report it is like being repeatedly punched in the solar plexus by the biggest man you've ever seen. I timed my move perfectly and covered the distance between me and the prone man with two steps. Grabbing him by the shoulders I spun him fully around and shoved him into the man behind him, putting my hands into the small of his back so he fell onto his associate chest first, thereby ensuring the barbs connected.

Which locked the two of them together in mutual agony.

The TASER 7 will pulse for five seconds before switching itself off, but this is enough to render even the biggest and fittest person unconscious. It's why our American friends call it 'the stun gun'.

The two intruders jerked and spasmed for a couple of seconds before collapsing in a tangle of limbs on my carpet. I quickly removed the barbs, and abandoned them where they were.

I had somewhere else to be.

Chapter 48

James

In hindsight, it was probably stupid to go back to my apartment, but I couldn't think of anywhere else to go.

I locked and double-locked the front door as soon as I was inside.

What the fuck was going on? I was terrified and confused, and I didn't know what to do. I was sitting in the hallway, my hands wrapped around my knees, when I heard a voice I hadn't expected to hear.

'James?'

I looked up and there, standing at the end of the hallway, looking exactly as she had the last time I had seen her, was my wife. My missing/presumed abducted/possibly dead wife.

'Bella …' I said, and then no more words would come.

'James, what the fuck are you doing here?' she asked.

'I fucking live here!' I said, angry as well as scared now.

I stood up to go to her when, from out of the living room, stepped someone else I wasn't expecting to see. Charlotte, my one-night stand, was standing in my hallway. With my wife. My brain just locked. I thought that maybe I was going insane.

'How …?' I said. 'What …?'

'James, you're messing about with something you cannot possibly understand,' Bella said, and at that moment the door of our apartment was blown inwards. I threw myself sideways, but I still felt splinters and shards of metal slicing my face and arms. The sound was deafening, and I lay for a moment with my ears ringing. Not for long, though. Someone delivered a sharp kick to my kidneys, and I moaned in pain.

'Get up, get up,' said a male voice I didn't recognise.

Groaning, I did as I was instructed. The man who had blasted his way into my home was wearing an expensive suit. He was tall, slender and had blond hair, worn long and brushed back on his head. And he was carrying a large gun which looked like it should be in the possession of Tony Montana. I noticed his eyes were moving in a strange herky-jerky motion that was disconcerting.

I immediately knew who he was. I hadn't had a lot of dealings with him, but I knew his company, Isotech, was the primary shareholders of Fahlberg Financials, and while he did not sit on the board of that company, several of his representatives did.

And of course, my wife knew him very well, even if they were, as far as I knew, currently estranged.

But she's been poking the bear with a stick, I thought. *And now he's come for her, and we're all in trouble.*

I tried to stall for time.

'What do you want?' I asked, probably sounding utterly bewildered and scared half to death. Which is exactly how I felt. 'What the fuck is going on?'

'He came here looking to bring our relationship to its conclusion,' Bella said. 'He's here for me, not you.'

'I'll take you both,' Grosvenor said. 'All the more fun.'

He peered at Charlotte, seemingly as puzzled about her presence as I was.

'Who's this?'

'Oh, we haven't met. But I know you.'

Tristan Grosvenor shook his head in irritation.

'What's your name, darling?'

Charlotte smiled. It was the last expression I expected to see on her face. I'd seen her smile before, and then it had been warm and pleasant, and it lit up her features. This smile was different.

This smile was scary.

'I'm Charlotte,' she said. 'Charlotte Odette *Tamlyn*.'

I saw puzzlement make its way across Grosvenor's face.

'Tamlyn?'

'Yes.'

'Seriously?'

'Oh yes. I've been waiting a long time to meet you.'

'Charmed I'm sure,' the man with the gun said. 'I'm glad I could make your wish come true, just before you shuffle off this mortal coil. Now get into the living room. In my enthusiasm

I've been a bit noisier than I intended to be, so we don't have as much time as I'd like.'

I swayed slightly on my feet. The left side of my face, which had been nearest the blast, felt wet and was beginning to sting quite badly.

'Hey, hubby boy, stay with us,' Grosvenor said, grabbing me by my hair and shaking my head back and forth so it pounded. 'Now move!'

And with the barrel of the gun pressed into my back, I followed my recently resurrected wife, and the woman with whom I had cheated on her, into our living area.

'Bella, what's going on?' I asked. 'Please tell me what's happening.'

'You're going to die is what's happening,' the blond man cackled. 'I wasn't planning on killing you, too, James, my boy. I was only going to ruin you and leave you to grieve a missing wife for the rest of your days. But seeing as you're here ...'

'I don't know why *you're* here!' I said, sitting down heavily on the couch.

Bella sat beside me, and Charlotte beside her.

'I'm here because your missus there called me,' Grosvenor said, standing in front of us, the gun held in the crook of his arm. 'When she went missing, I was quite ... disturbed. She had begun involving herself in my life again in quite intrusive ways, and the material I'd been receiving from her recently refreshed thesis was rather distressing in nature. I had all but decided it was time she and I became personally reacquainted.'

'My disappearing was meant to draw you out,' Bella said. 'It was Charlotte's idea.'

'I still have no idea what's happening!' I said.

'Enough,' Grosvenor said. 'I've waited a long time for the pleasure of shutting Bella Fitzpatrick up. I'm not going to wait a moment longer. And to my delight, I also get the added bonus of taking out Gerald Tamlyn's progeny while I'm about. Wipe his name from the face of the earth.'

He raised the gun and I took Bella's hand in mine.

Grosvenor cocked the weapon. I saw his finger tighten.

And then Detective Sergeant Harvey Brennan stepped into the room, casually, as if he was wandering into a supermarket. The rumpled detective sergeant was holding a snub-nosed revolver.

'Mr Grosvenor, I'm going to ask you to place your weapon on the ground, please, and to then put your hands behind your head.'

The blond man spluttered once but didn't move.

'I think you know me better than that, you miserable Irish *peasant*. I'll have these three dead before you can move.'

'Then you will go to prison for the rest of your natural life.'

'Will I? I got away with a very public murder once before. And you have *no idea* of what I've been doing in the shadows. I'm prepared to take my chances again.'

'I had no choice but to let you walk once before,' Brennan said. 'I won't let you hurt these people.'

'You don't have it in you to stop me,' Grosvenor said. 'Shall we both make our best moves and see who wins?'

Then three things happened all at once.

Grosvenor brought the rifle to his shoulder.

Brennan raised his revolver.

And Charlotte, with a motion that was so fast it was almost a blur, whipped something that looked like a toy gun from out of nowhere and shot Grosvenor with it. He tensed for a moment and I thought he would go down, but for some reason, he didn't. His face contorted and he spasmed, his finger tightening involuntarily on the trigger of his weapon, sending a burst of automatic fire into the wall over our heads.

Brennan, shaking his head sadly, discharged his own weapon, and a red hole appeared in Tristan Grosvenor's forehead. The industrialist remained suspended upright for a moment, and then collapsed as if he was folding in on himself.

I think I screamed. The air seemed to be full of roaring noise and the coppery smell of blood. The everything fell silent, and I thought I might have gone deaf.

'What …' I remember gasping. 'What the fuck is happening? Won't someone please tell me what the fuck is going on?'

'I think the only person who can help us with that,' Brennan offered, 'is your recently resurrected wife.'

'Yes, it's quite a long story,' Bella said.

Brennan called the station, and when this was done we all gathered in the kitchen.

'Ms Fitzpatrick, you have been playing a dangerous game,' DS Brennan said to Bella.

'I took some risks, I'll agree,' she said. 'But it was worth it. That man was a predator of the worst kind.'

'You should have brought whatever evidence you had to me

and let the police do their jobs. Of course, that wouldn't have satiated your desire for revenge, would it?'

He cast his doleful gaze at Charlotte.

'You, I did not expect, Ms Tamlyn. How exactly did you two come to be sisters-in-arms?'

'We met while we were both students at City in two thousand and nine,' Bella said.

'She was my stalker,' Bella said. 'Developed quite the fixation on me, didn't you, Charlie?'

'We were *friends*,' Charlotte said, looking irritated.

'Yeah, the kind that follow one another home and hang around outside spying for hours at a time. I realised Charlie was following me and turned the tables on her. I took to watching her while she was watching me. I played a game where I'd pick routes where I'd be able to turn a corner and then just stop, and be waiting for her when she took the turning. Finally, I put her out of her misery and confronted her, let her know I was on to her. And yes, we became friends. Very good friends.'

I looked at the two of them, agog.

'So you two knew one another from the start?'

'Oh yes,' Bella said.

'I don't believe it,' I said.

'It was Charlie who told me all about Tristan Grosvenor, and by so doing gave me the idea for my thesis. And well ... that's what set all of this in motion.'

'They told me at the university that there were rumours you and Grosvenor were intimately acquainted,' Brennan said, gazing intently at Bella.

'Yes,' my wife said, giving me a glance. 'He and I had a brief but very intense relationship.'

'Which destroyed our friendship for quite a few years,' Charlotte said.

'And didn't do our marriage much good either,' I said, feeling sick to my stomach. 'Thank you for finally admitting it, though.'

'What have I got left to lose?' Bella asked, looking at me with tired eyes.

'This affair occurred while you were interviewing Grosvenor for your research?' Brennan asked.

'Yes. He was ... I was appalled by him and attracted to him all at the same time,' Bella said. 'There was something about him that was so ... well, he was like no one I'd ever met before. He was a man who truly did whatever moved him at any given moment. He was supremely confident and utterly charming and, as I was to finally learn, completely without a conscience.

'I was drawn to him and repelled in equal measure,' Bella went on. 'He could make me feel as if I was the only person in the world he cared about one moment, and then he would dismiss me like I was nothing. One moment I was his queen, the next I was lower than the lowest member of his staff. Yet I was hopelessly in love with him. Or maybe it was a powerful infatuation. Either way, I was locked into a compulsion I could not rid myself of.'

I felt tears spring to my eyes unbidden, and wiped them aside. I'd always known, I suppose, but hearing it was horrendous.

Even with the girl with whom I had cheated on my wife seated opposite me.

Charlotte snorted.

'I know it was a mistake,' Bella said, patting the other woman's hand. 'He groomed me and I fell for it hook, line and sinker.'

'When you published that article on him in the magazine, he had you blacklisted in all media outlets in London,' Brennan said. 'That must have hurt.'

'You have no idea. I was tipped to do well. I had degrees in psychology and I was young, pretty ... I was meant to be the next big thing. That article was supposed to be my big break.'

'And it ended up finishing you before you'd even started,' Brennan said.

'Not only that, Tristan shut me out. There was no conversation, I was given no chance to explain myself; I was simply dead to him.'

'In the article you portrayed him as utterly without remorse,' Brennan said. 'You even quoted him as saying he was deserving of sympathy. What did you expect him to do?'

'I was simply repeating what he'd told me,' Bella said. 'He was *proud* of what he'd done. I thought he'd be happy I was acknowledging what he spoke of as his God-given right as a gentleman to defend his honour and his property from scoundrels and vagabonds.'

'He said that?'

'All the time. He hinted at other murders. Didn't quite come out and say it, but it was an unspoken thing. Tristan Grosvenor was a murderer. A serial killer. And he was unashamed of the fact. He loved that he was, in fact.'

'He might have loved to crow about such things in private,' Brennan said, 'but he was smart enough not to want to push his luck with law enforcement. He'd dodged a prison cell once. I don't think he wanted to be put in that position again.'

'When he had me black-balled and my work discredited, I abandoned my thesis and tried to build another life. I got into teaching, tried to live a different kind of life.'

'I spent the intervening years doing the same thing,' Charlotte said. 'I'd tried to put Tristan Grosvenor, and the fact he had killed my father and tipped my mother into early-onset Alzheimer's, behind me and get on with my own life. I missed Bella and I disliked my job, but I had a life and I was retraining as an artist, in the hope I could forge another career.'

'So what happened?' Brennan asked.

'Bella and I ran into one another again when she went back to her thesis in January,' Charlotte said. 'I was working as tech support in the university, and she needed help with her laptop, and purely by coincidence, I ended up taking the call. We got to talking about old times, and about Grosvenor, and she told me she had a plan. And I knew I wanted to be a part of it. I wanted in very much indeed.'

'You went back to your thesis to get revenge,' Brennan said, looking directly at Bella. 'Was this your plan all along?'

'Not at all,' Bella said. 'I wanted no part of Grosvenor or his poison.'

'What happened then?'

'Quite by accident, I found myself working with his son,' Bella said. 'And when I saw what a deranged and unpleasant teenager Grosvenor had produced, when I saw that he was replicating himself, breeding another toxic little sociopath, I knew I couldn't just let things slide.'

'What did you decide to do?' Brennan wanted to know.

'I made it my mission to draw him out,' Bella said. 'The world needed to see who he really was, and I was determined to make that happen.'

'And I agreed to help,' Charlotte said.

'The attack at the school,' Brennan said, 'were you actually behind that?'

Bella sighed and looked troubled for a moment.

'I will admit to setting the wheels in motion,' she said. 'I wanted to get the little shit in trouble, cause his parents some stress. I never expected it to go as far as it did. If Caleb hadn't been there, things could have gone very badly for me indeed.'

'It did give us the added bonus of the police being involved though,' Charlotte said. 'We were looking for a way to do that, something that might cause you to investigate Grosvenor again. So this saved us the bother.'

'What was your part in all of this?' Brennan asked.

'Yes, I'd like to know that, too,' I said.

'Have you ever looked into who exactly the Fahlberg end of your wonderful merger actually are?' Charlotte asked, looking at me with thinly veiled contempt.

'I'm good at my job,' I said. 'Yes, I know who they are.'

'You know then that the Fahlberg board,' Charlotte said, 'are basically puppets.'

'I know they are all in thrall to Tristan Grosvenor,' I said. 'I tried to keep that fact from Bella because I needed this deal to make partner. I hated working for the man I suspected she'd been in love with, but as a lawyer you often need to do things you aren't very happy with. I sucked it up and just got on with it.'

'I thought you were just blind to it,' Bella said. 'Or that you didn't care.'

'Of course I fucking cared,' I snapped. Then I looked at Charlotte. 'When I lost the files that night, that was you all along?'

'Yes. When I retrieved them for you, I added in some malware and some trojans, which allowed me to keep an eye on the comings and goings in Fahlberg. And it afforded me an introduction to you.'

'Why did you want to meet me?'

'Bella, when she was supposed to be exposing Tristan Grosvenor, ended up fucking him. I thought it was long overdue time I returned the favour.'

'So you and me …' I said, feeling like a complete fool.

'You were a chance to get some payback,' Charlotte said. 'And I have to say, you were easy.'

'I had reason to be,' I said.

'Oh poor you,' Bella said, sounding tired and annoyed. 'You're not a saint, I'm not a saint; it looks like we both know who we're married to now.'

'Can we get back to the matter at hand, please?' Brennan asked. 'So while all of this was going on, you were continuing with your thesis and making sure chapters were being sent to

Grosvenor on a regular basis. So he was receiving missives in which you were alleging he was a dangerous sociopath, while I was investigating his son for a sexual assault on the author of those missives.'

'That about sums it up, yes,' Bella said.

'Meanwhile, I had sent an anonymous email to his office,' Charlotte said, 'letting him know that the lawyer who was managing the merger of one of his largest companies was, in fact, the husband of that same woman. I kept an eye on communications coming to and from his office, and I could sense him getting more and more agitated.'

'We were turning the screws pretty tightly,' Bella agreed. 'When I went missing, I wanted it to look like I'd been assaulted. His son had brought in some of his mates to help in the attack, and any of them might have decided to take another shot at me. We knew he was having me watched, and that he'd be worried this would all come back on him.'

'We decided it was time to strike,' Charlotte said. 'So we arranged for James to be out of the apartment, and I called Tristan and told him I wanted to meet him in here.'

'And you called me,' Brennan said, looking at Bella.

'Yes. I knew he'd come here with the intention of killing me. I wanted you here to witness it for yourself.'

'What about me?' I asked. 'Your funny little attempt to get me into work nearly ended up getting me killed!'

'All I did was send an email,' Charlotte said. 'I don't know about anything else.'

'Money was stolen,' I said. 'Seemingly by me.'

'I didn't do that,' Charlotte said. 'My guess is that Grosvenor had it done.'

'I agree,' Brennan said. 'I think he wanted you here. He was going to kill you both.'

At that moment the doorbell rang.

'That'll be the uniform guys and forensics,' Brennan said. 'I'm going to need to take an official statement from all of you.'

Chapter 49

Bella

Police and forensics and more men in suits whom I was told were homicide detectives from Scotland Yard came, and it was mid-afternoon before the apartment was clear and James and I were alone – someone drove Charlotte back to her place.

I was still reeling after everything that had happened, and I didn't have the energy for hostilities.

James went to the fridge and opened a bottle of white for me, taking down a glass and pouring for me, before getting a Scotch for himself.

'Do you think we should talk?' he asked when he was seated at the counter.

I accepted the glass he offered.

'Thanks. We probably should, but where should we begin?'

He shook his head.

'I have no fucking clue.'

Then he said: 'Are you going to stay on in the school?'

'I think dear old Joel is trying to have me run out.'

'Are you going to allow him to?'

I smiled sadly.

'Doing my best not to.'

'That's my girl,' he said, and I saw something pass across his face. 'I probably don't have the right to call you that any more,' he said.

'You probably haven't for quite a while now,' I agreed.

He took a long drink.

'I fucked up, Bella,' he said suddenly.

I didn't look at him. I just sipped my wine and gazed out the window.

He didn't need to say any more.

'It's alright, James,' I heard myself saying.

'What?'

'It's okay. You don't need to say anything else. I messed up, you messed up. Let's leave it at that for now and just try to keep moving forward as best we can.'

'Are you serious?'

'I really am. Looking back on everything, I realise I've been wrong about a lot of things. Maybe it's because I don't want to deal with this right now, or maybe it's because I've felt rotten about some things that I've done, and maybe it's because I've had a few days that have been like stepping into my own personal horror movie. Whatever the reason, it doesn't matter. I am saying to you, James Arthur Fitzpatrick, that I am drawing a line under all of this. Whatever you did or didn't do, I don't want to know. Let's just agree we aren't going to talk about it ever again.'

'Deal,' he said. 'I'm just going to pop to the loo. Back in a tick.'

When he was gone, I leaned against the countertop and let the tears come. I cried hard but silently.

The choking sobs were finished by the time he came back.

I didn't know what life would hold going forward.

But I knew I had no choice but to find out.

Chapter 50

James

Neither Bella nor Charlotte had committed any serious crimes. Bella had manipulated some students, but ultimately the choice to assault her was theirs, though the school still refused to discipline them. Charlotte had sailed closer to the wind when she hacked into the Astley, Clifford and Kenworthy computer system, but the firm decided not to press any charges for fear of any negative publicity. I'm not sure how happy Detective Brennan was about that. But he's not the kind of man you'd ask.

Of course, my staying on at Astley, Clifford and Kenworthy was completely untenable, but I negotiated a substantial settlement. I had been physically assaulted, after all, as well as being falsely accused of embezzlement, and I left to set up my own firm.

I work from an office in our apartment for the moment.

I do human rights work, mostly pro bono. It's not like I need the money.

I've never been happier in my work.

My wife left Ashton Wood. Her thesis is almost finished, and she's published a few articles, to widespread acclaim. With Grosvenor dead, there's no barrier to her doing media work, and one or two offers are coming in. Between those, some lecturing at City and a few research projects on the horizon, I think she might have quite a good future ahead.

And as for our relationship … well.

We're trying.

Some days we succeed. Others we fail.

Mostly, we just plug along.

And I suppose that's okay.

Chapter 51

Charlotte

I met James Fitzpatrick outside City University one Saturday morning as I was coming out of art class.

He was waiting for me, leaning against a very modest-looking saloon car.

'Hey Charlotte,' he said.

'Hello James,' I said, and kept walking.

'Charlotte … I just wanted to say sorry,' he called after me.

I stopped. I turned to face him

'I used you,' I said, 'and you used me. Let's just leave it at that.'

'When you hacked my email,' he said, 'I got the impression you were hurt. That it wasn't just a game to you.'

I blushed a little at that.

'Maybe I did it to make a point.'

'I know,' he said. 'And I probably deserved it.'

'You did.'

I paused for a moment.

'I actually did like you.'

'I liked you too,' he said. 'I just wasn't in the place where I could give you anything more than that one night, and I probably shouldn't have given you that.'

'You're still with Bella?'

'Yes. I wanted to tell you in person. I was a coward that morning, running away from you. I should have stayed and talked. Let you know what was going on in my head.'

'Your receptionist made me feel like a harlot,' I said.

'I am very sorry about that. She's not my receptionist any more.'

'You fired her? That seems a bit over the top.'

'No. I resigned. I don't work for the firm any more.'

I looked at him.

He seemed somehow less anxious. More open. Genuinely apologetic.

'Thank you for coming to see me,' I said. 'Good luck in whatever you're doing now.'

'Thanks, Charlotte,' he said.

I had taken a few steps when he said:

'It wasn't Grosvenor who stole the funds, was it?'

I froze.

'The email that was sent to the accounts guy,' James continued, 'I had a look at it. The shell company was named

Coppinng Insurances. Just one extra letter, easily missed. Very clever indeed. And we both know it's impossible to find out who set up a shell company like that. I followed it up, though. The company was registered in the Caymans, and whoever set it up doesn't have to provide any identifying information. But do you want to know what gave you away?'

I didn't say a word. I had been wondering when he'd work it out.

'It was the name of the sole director of the company. Edwin Jarvis. I remembered that first conversation we had, about you being Tony Stark and me being Pepper Potts. Jarvis is Tony Stark's AI. The ghost in the machine.'

I turned.

'It doesn't prove anything,' I said.

'No, it doesn't,' he said. 'But I want you to know, I think it was a stroke of genius. In one fell swoop, you destroyed the reputation of Isotech and made sure they'd be fully audited and pored over by forensic accountants for the next God knows how many years, looking for money that's not even there. You also inflicted a wound on Astley, Clifford and Kenworthy that they'll probably never recover from: a corporate law firm that loses twelve billion pounds? Who'd want to employ them? You got your revenge on Bella for her emotional betrayal of you, and through your machinations, I was run out of my job and punched in the nuts to boot, which I probably deserved – the punch, not losing my job, but actually, it's worked out quite well.'

Hearing everything listed like that, I had to admit, I was proud.

'And then there's the fact that the man who murdered your father is dead. And to top it all off, the icing on the cake, you're rich.'

I shrugged at that.

'You will have to be very careful how you spend it,' he said. 'Detective Brennan is going to be watching you, I'd say.'

'Goodbye, James,' I said.

'If I … if I ever need tech support, can I call you?'

I looked into his eyes. Those grey eyes I had dreamed about. That I had, that night we'd spent together, gazed into with such longing. I looked at this man I had adored and said:

'No. I don't think that would be a good idea at all.'

And I walked away from James Fitzpatrick, and towards the rest of my life.

Afterword & Acknowledgements

The Helpdesk is a book that took a long time to struggle into the light of day.

Maybe its murky subject matter and the questionable motivations of almost all of its characters (excepting the stoic Detective Brennan) had something to do with it, but it certainly took its time getting written.

The first conversation that was had about it occurred back in 2019, after I had completed the Dunnigan series and was discussing what the next project might be with my editor and friend, Ciara Doorley. Over coffee, Ciara and I discussed an idea I'd had for a stand-alone novel, and as luck would have it, Ciara had been thinking along similar lines. This led to a conversation about perhaps doing a series of stand-alone novels, each dealing with a different, relatively mundane aspect of our day-to-day lives, but taking a slightly skewed look, and finding the inherent threat many of us choose to ignore.

I mean, we're all carrying around surveillance devices these days, and they do say that our computers know more about who we truly are as individuals than any human being in our immediate circle. If that's not scary, I don't know what is.

Ciara and I batted the idea around a bit, and finally settled on two ideas we both liked. I can state without hesitation that *The Helpdesk* was Ciara's concept: what if an ordinary guy, working late in the office one night on the deal of his life, has a major emergency and has to ring tech support, and the woman at the other end helps him out, and a relationship blossoms, but then, suddenly, things start to go wrong.

She's gotten into his computer, and now she has control of his life.

Kind of *Fatal Attraction* but for the twenty-first century.

I thought it was a great idea and wrote a lengthy outline. The characters immediately came alive in my head. My oldest friend, Ronan Lowney, is a corporate lawyer in the UK, and while Ciara had originally suggested our bumbling hero might be a criminal lawyer, I'd heard lots of stories set in the world of tax law, and I knew it was a ground fertile for ploughing.

James Fitzpatrick became a tax lawyer, and the seedy world of Astley, Clifford and Kenworthy took shape. So far so good.

It was Bella who threw a spanner in the works.

From the moment I started writing her, I found her voice utterly compelling, and I knew she had a story to tell, one we probably hadn't originally envisioned for this book! As the novel took shape, it was clear to me that it was going to be a very different story to the one Ciara and I had initially intended to recount. I sat down and tried to work out what to do about this. I wrote two drafts of the book, moving plot points around, trying to get the focus back on our deranged tech support worker.

But by then, I knew Charlotte wasn't deranged at all.

In fact, Charlotte wasn't the criminal of this story.

And James wasn't really the hero, either.

It became clear to me, Bella was the anti-hero of the book, and there wasn't much I could do about it. She just wasn't going to be quiet.

All credit here to Ciara, who was extremely patient with me. We had a few lengthy discussions about the structure and plot, and there were things I wanted to hold on to and things Ciara wanted to hold on to, and we finally, as people who know one another well often do, decided to bring in an outside eye.

Claire Pelly's contribution was wonderful. As an editor she was able to take a step back and tease out the various plot threads, and pinpoint where things needed to be fine-tuned. It made the process of removing the weeds and saving the crop we'd planted much easier than it could have been.

I am deeply grateful to both Ciara and Claire for going on this journey with me.

A word of thanks as always to my agent, Ivan Mulcahy, of MMB Creative. Ivan manages to combine being supportive and kind with a complete intolerance for bullshit. He is always at the end of the phone to offer a word of advice or to listen to me vent, or to give me a kick up the arse and tell me to cop on, whichever I need on any given day.

Ivan, I could not do what I do without you.

A word of thanks to my family and close friends, who have to put up with me disappearing for weeks on end when I'm in the critical stages of a book. I can only promise that I am doing my level best not to do that any more and to take a more sensible approach to the writing process.

Maybe this time, I'll actually do it!

This book is dedicated to Kristina, who was an inspiration during its writing and remains so now it's complete.

Finally, thanks to you, dear reader, for continuously coming back for these strange stories I write and these worlds I create. If you didn't, there would hardly be any point in writing them.

It means the world to me that you remain constant.

Shane Dunphy
Wexford and Waterford (Ireland)
Lipany (Slovakia)
2022

'Cracking'
IRISH INDEPENDENT

AFTER
SHE
VANISHED

Is it possible to disappear without a trace?

S. A. DUNPHY

'A cracking debut thriller packed with great characters that leaves
the reader wanting more'
Irish Independent

Five people living on Dublin's streets have gone missing and
criminologist David Dunnigan has been tasked with finding them.

His search leads him to ten-year-old Harry, living alone in an
abandoned warehouse, who has been waiting days for his parents'
return ...

Dunnigan knows more than he would wish to about unexplained
disappearances. Almost twenty years ago, his young niece Beth
vanished during their annual Christmas shopping trip. No trace of
her was ever discovered. And the tragic mystery has loomed over
Dunnigan's life ever since.

As his current investigation draws him deeper into the city's
dark underbelly, Dunnigan's resolve to help Harry and unravel this
mystery grows stronger.

And could it lead him one step closer to finding out what became
of Beth?

Criminologist David Dunnigan's niece has been missing for eighteen years without a trace – until now.

A HEART-STOPPING CLUE

Someone has sent Dunnigan a shoe – one Beth was wearing the day she disappeared – and the investigation is swiftly reignited, along with her uncle's hopes of finding her alive. But is he ready for what else he might find?

A DANGEROUS JOURNEY

As new evidence starts to link Beth's abduction to a series of apparent suicides and a horrifying people-trafficking network, Dunnigan furiously chases down leads before the trail goes cold once more and Beth is lost forever. And when the search brings Dunnigan, accompanied by his loyal friend Miley and ex-soldier partner-in-crime Diane, to the frozen north of Greenland, the hunt starts to become more and more dangerous.

BUT WHERE WILL IT END?

Will it lead him to Beth, after all this time?

'Taut, compelling and authentic ... an edge-of-your-seat thriller'
Andrea Carter

David Dunnigan just received the phone call he has spent eighteen years waiting for.

A young woman has been found – and she's claiming to be his niece Beth, who disappeared as a child. Is she telling the truth? And, if she is, will Dunnigan finally rid himself of his demons, and help her to rebuild her life?

Meanwhile, an investigation into a gruesome murder leads the criminologist to five prominent men, seemingly unlinked, who say they are being stalked by a shadowy figure. But 'Mother Joan' seems to merely be an urban legend, a ghostly avenger who punishes the wicked. So, if these men fear her wrath, what sins have they committed?

As Dunnigan pursues this strange mystery, enemies from his past are closing in. And when the case leads him to the crowded streets of London and then to the dark forest of Kielder, myth and reality become terrifyingly linked.

But is Dunnigan prepared for what, and who, he will face?

'A dark, chilling and fantastic read'
Patricia Gibney

Criminologist David Dunnigan and his troubled niece Beth are on the run.

Beth has been accused of killing a high-profile detective and everyone thinks she's guilty. Even Beth, who has no memory of what happened, wonders if she is capable of murder.

As Dunnigan and Beth set out to prove her innocence, they are hunted by the same forces responsible for Beth's abduction nearly twenty years ago.

In a chase that takes them from Hamburg to Prague, to a compound in the bleak expanse of the Nevada desert, Dunnigan eventually comes face-to-face with their enemies.

But did Beth really kill the man she had come to think of as a friend, and what secret will Dunnigan discover that could end Frobisher's After Dark Campaign once and for all?

The time has come for Dunnigan to make a decision: will he be brave enough to make it, knowing that everyone he loves can't possibly make it out of this alive?